THE
Caged Graves

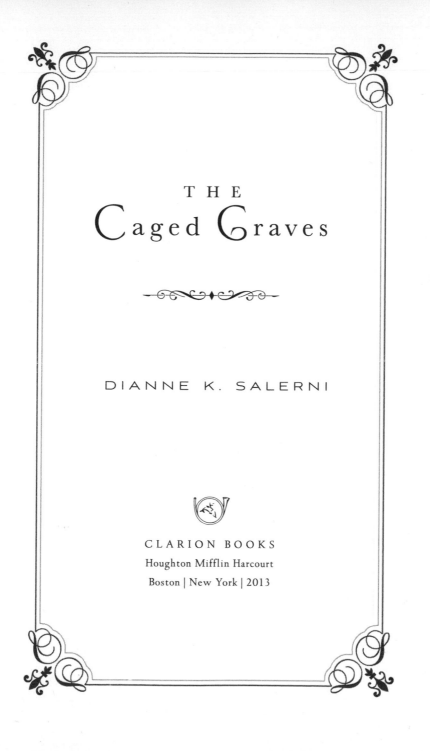

THE
Caged Graves

DIANNE K. SALERNI

CLARION BOOKS
Houghton Mifflin Harcourt
Boston | New York | 2013

CLARION BOOKS
215 Park Avenue South
New York, New York 10003

Copyright © 2013 by Dianne K. Salerni

Clarion Books is an imprint of
Houghton Mifflin Harcourt Publishing Company.

www.hmhbooks.com

The text was set in LTC Deepdene.

Library of Congress Cataloging-in-Publication Data
Salerni, Dianne K.
The caged graves / by Dianne K. Salerni.
p. cm.
Summary: Returning to her hometown of Catawissa, Pennsylvania,
in 1867 to marry a man she has never met, seventeen-year-old Verity
Boone gets caught up in a mystery surrounding the graves of her
mother and aunt and a dangerous hunt for Revolutionary-era gold.
ISBN 978-0-547-86853-0 (hardcover)
[1. Arranged marriage--Fiction. 2. Love--Fiction. 3. Buried treasure--
Fiction. 4. Murder--Fiction. 5. Community life--Pennsylvania--
Fiction. 6. Pennsylvania--History--1865---Fiction.] I. Title.
PZ7.S152114Cag 2013
[Fic]--dc23   2012021008

Manufactured in the United States of America
DOC 10 9 8 7 6 5 4 3 2 1
4500406807

To my parents,

Fred and Rosemarie,

and my mother-in-law,

Madeline,

for all their support, encouragement,

and occasional shameless promotion

Wyoming Valley, Pennsylvania

VEN FACING probable death, Private Silas Clayton couldn't stop thinking about that leather satchel.

Screams and gunfire echoed off the mountain walls in the distance. Light from burning homesteads flickered through the trees, and smoke hung over the valley, obscuring the stars. Silas knelt in the dirt, his hands bound behind his back and all his thoughts bent toward that bag, which fellow captive Sergeant Anders wore slung across his chest.

Across the clearing, British officers consulted, occasionally passing cold eyes over their prisoners as they considered what to do with two dozen stray Continentals.

Silas hadn't known much luck in his eighteen years. The sixth child of nine on a failing farm never had much to look forward to growing up, except hunger and the sure fact that there wasn't enough of anything to go around. Joining the militia hadn't improved his lot in life, only reinforced his conviction that luck was something he'd have to make for himself.

Tonight, his luck—and his life—hung in the balance. If his regiment had waited for reinforcements inside Forty Fort as originally planned, he'd have been sleeping safe inside the stronghold tonight, but then he would never have come within reach of that satchel. As it was, goaded by Captain Stewart's brashness, Colonel Butler had led them out against the enemy, and the whole damn militia was routed in less than an hour.

Stewart was dead now, and God knew where the colonel was. Silas had fled the battlefield during the confusion, doggedly following Sergeant Anders through the mountain forest. With his usual luck, he'd run right into the hands of the blasted Indians.

Mohawks, he'd been told, with some French blood thrown in. They had hidden in the shadows between trees and rocks, rising up out of the ground like ghosts to corner him just when he had freedom in sight. Now they stood patiently behind the British soldiers, waiting for orders.

Somewhere out in the darkness a woman screamed —a harrowing cry cut unnaturally short—and the British officers lifted their heads only briefly before returning to their conversation, unmoved. Judging by the ominous glow over the treetops, it seemed the Redcoats and their Indian allies were burning every homestead in the valley.

Meanwhile, this small regiment of British soldiers had just been saddled with a score of prisoners they didn't want. They *might* march Silas and the others back to their encampment and from there to imprisonment, or they might do something a lot less honorable. Silas had seen their treatment of his fellow soldiers on the battlefield, even ones who'd surrendered, and had no intention of waiting around for the inevitable decision.

For the last several minutes, he'd been sawing at his bonds with the knife that had been concealed in his boot. It was slow work, holding the knife upside down in sweat-slicked hands to reach the rope around his own wrists, and every time one of the soldiers looked his way, he had to stop, lest he draw their attention. Anders knew what Silas was doing; the big blond sergeant glanced sideways at him every now and then, and Silas could swear Captain Striker—also bound and kneeling across the clearing—was watching him too.

Captain Striker. How he hated that puffed-up old rooster! In the last fifteen months the captain had whipped Silas more than his father ever had—for insubordination, for disobedience, for gambling, and for everything else he could think of. "You'll never amount to anything, Clayton!" Striker had shouted just two days ago, after he'd caught Silas carving dice out of musket balls. "You'll end up in a pauper's grave, boy, mark my words!"

Silas didn't plan on going to the grave anytime soon, and he wasn't going to be a pauper when he did.

The ropes around his wrists gave way suddenly, and he lurched forward as his arms swung free. Regaining his balance, he jerked himself back to his previous position and looked around to see if anyone had noticed.

Anders had. His blue eyes were wide and worried. "C'mere," Silas whispered, and the sergeant scuttled nearer on his knees. Reaching behind Anders's back, Silas pressed the blade of his knife against the rope and sawed as hard as he could. This was harder to conceal, two prisoners leaning together like a pair of fainting women. He'd have to be fast.

"You there!" an officer called. "Move apart!" Silas didn't even look up, redoubling his efforts. The British captain strode across the clearing, his hand reaching for his sword as his eyes raked over the two of them. "What do you have there, Sergeant?" Now he'd spotted the leather bag Anders wore, and the officer looked back at his own men in disgust. "Didn't anyone search these prisoners? Someone get that satchel off him."

No time for subtlety left. Silas wrenched his blade up through the rope, hoping it would be enough, and surged to his feet with a roar. He took the officer by surprise, grabbing the man's sword hand before the weapon had cleared the scabbard and thrusting forward with the knife. The captain howled as the knife grazed his ribs but caught Silas's wrist before he could strike again. For a moment they grappled like a pair of wrestlers, while the British enlisted men shouted and brought their muskets to their shoulders. Silas raised himself up on the balls of his feet and smashed the taller man in the nose with his forehead.

Blood spurted; the officer roared, and Silas shoved him backwards toward his men and bolted for the woods.

Anders had thrown off his bonds and was already yards ahead of Silas, his long limbs churning up the dirt. Not a coward normally, nor one to spurn a fight, he didn't stop to help Silas or look back to see if he was following. He had his orders regarding that satchel, and Silas knew the sergeant would follow them, loyal to the cause until the last.

Musket fire erupted just as Silas reached the line of trees, chewing up bark on either side of him. The Indians who'd been standing behind the British melted away from the clearing as though they'd never been there. Silas plunged headlong into the forest, hunkering low and straining to spot the sergeant's blond head dodging between the trees.

There was hardly a point to escaping if he didn't keep up with Anders.

The Redcoats gave pursuit, cursing and crashing

through the underbrush. Between their noise and their bright uniforms, Silas had no fear they'd catch him unawares. The Indians would be the far deadlier foe. Somehow, he'd retained a grip on his knife. It wouldn't make much of a defense against a musket ball or a tomahawk, but he clenched his fingers around it anyway. Leaping over fallen trees and dodging low branches, he sprinted through the thick forest growth and came upon Anders sooner than he'd expected.

The big sergeant had stopped, lost and disoriented. He flinched when Silas appeared but didn't argue when the younger man grabbed him by the sleeve and pulled him onward, hissing, "This way!" The ground sloped steadily downward, into the valley of the Susquehanna River. The sound of pursuit diminished to shouts in the distance, but Silas pushed onward without stopping. The more dangerous enemy would come upon them silently, and he was certain they were still on the hunt.

Soon their feet sank into moist earth, and water welled up around their ankles. They staggered to a halt, up to their knees in water. This wasn't the river. This was the foul bog that filled up the lowland in the valley along the river's edge.

Silas tried to glide through the marsh without splashing, and Anders followed. The stink of decaying plants and animals filled the air. Silas kept to the edge, avoiding the open areas where moonlight illuminated masses of floating weeds. Sounds echoed on the water, and he heard distant splashing . . . voices . . . sobs.

They weren't alone in the swamp. There were others fleeing through the water: burned-out settlers, maybe even fellow soldiers who'd escaped the battlefield that day. In fact, as Silas stood still to listen and watch, he realized the swamp was filled with refugees—and slinking behind them, shadows.

The sobbing grew louder. In the middle of the water, which lay like a putrid lake beneath the stars, a woman was crossing with two children slung across her shoulders. Silas saw her struggle to drag her sodden skirts through the mire, but with both arms burdened, she was making little headway. He didn't know why she was trying to cross the open water, except that she must have feared what she couldn't see more than what could see her.

The sergeant had been resting, crouched over with his hands on his knees, trying to catch his breath. Strong as he was, the day had taken its toll: the battle; their first flight, which had ended in capture; and now this dash for freedom—all while carrying that heavy satchel. Nevertheless, at the sight of the woman and her children, he straightened with a sigh. "We have to help them."

Silas shook his head. "Carrying that bag?" He glanced up at the trees. "'Twould be better to hide it and come back when the Redcoats are gone. Why don't you hang it on one of those limbs?"

A flicker of suspicion crossed the young sergeant's eyes. "You know I can't do that. Captain Stewart charged me with its safety. With his *dying breath*, Clayton! I got to get this bag to Colonel Dennison. But first, these people need our help. It's our duty." Anders turned away, toward the black waters of the bog, the woman and her children . . . and the waiting Indians.

Silas nodded grimly. It was time for him and Anders to part company. "Wait, Sergeant. I'll come with you." He caught hold of the other man's arm and moved quickly to his side.

Anders grunted and groaned — then swayed like a tree that didn't know which way to fall. He stared at Silas in confusion, one hand shaking as he felt his way down his own chest and encountered the hilt of a knife. His knees gave out, and the big man folded, sinking into the filthy water. "Why?" he gasped.

"You know why." Silas grabbed hold of the leather straps with both hands and shook the satchel free of the other man. Slipping it over his own head, he felt its weight with satisfaction.

"Oh please, dear Lord, help me," the sergeant moaned as he collapsed into the water.

Silas turned away. Without so much as a glance back at his fallen comrade, he pushed aside the marsh grass and disappeared into the dark.

ONE

N COMPLETE disregard of the conductor's instructions, Verity Boone sprang from her seat before the train came to a full stop. The other passengers glanced at her with disapproval, but she paid no heed. As the locomotive slowed, Verity fluffed out her curls beneath her bonnet and smoothed her dress. If *he* was waiting on the platform, she wanted to make a perfect first impression. Then, satisfied she'd done her best after two days of travel across three states, she gazed out at the town of her birth — a place she hadn't seen in fifteen years. She'd known she was leaving city life behind when she'd departed from Worcester, Massachusetts, but she hoped Catawissa wouldn't be as rural as she feared.

The conductor opened the door, scowling at the young miss standing so boldly where she shouldn't be. When her traveling companions, two widowed sisters from Worcester, had disembarked at the previous stop, they'd asked the conductor to watch over her until she reached her destination. Verity wasn't sure whether she herself or the conductor was more relieved to see his responsibility for her come to an end.

She stepped onto wooden planks speckled with raindrops. The darkening sky suggested that more rain could be expected, and she glanced up and down the platform anxiously. In a matter of minutes the clouds would open and a deluge would fall, but with any luck she'd be under the roof of a carriage by then. Surely he would already be here to greet her. Verity hoped she'd recognize him, for it would be humiliating to bumble around from stranger to stranger.

Then she spied a figure at the end of the platform and sighed. She did recognize the man who'd come for her, although he wasn't the one she'd been hoping for. She'd seen this man only twice in the last five years, but she knew him at once.

Ransloe Boone. Her father.

Of course her father had come to meet her train. Verity chastised herself for a moment's disappointment. Their eyes met, and he looked startled. Verity knew she had changed more than he had in the years since their last meeting. A young woman of seventeen was quite different from a girl of . . . what had she been? . . . fourteen at his last visit?

Verity forced down any feeling of discontent. She should be *happy* her father had come for her. It was just that she'd thought *Nate* might be waiting at the station.

"Verity?" her father asked when he reached her side, as if he still weren't sure.

"Hello, Father." She offered a smile in greeting, but he seemed too dumbfounded to return it, sweeping his gaze over her from bonnet to boot. She surveyed him more discreetly, noting his overlong hair, his patched coat, and the dingy shirt he wore open at the collar without a tie or cravat.

"Your trunks?" he inquired after an awkward moment of silence. Verity produced a ticket, and her father accepted it with relief, as if claiming the baggage were a more comfortable task than greeting a grown daughter he barely knew.

To Verity's distress, her father had brought a farm wagon to fetch her from the station. She had a feeling it was all he owned, but—glancing apprehensively at the sky—she wished he had borrowed a covered conveyance.

He supervised the loading of her trunks, then climbed up onto the driver's seat and took the reins. Only when the porter handed Verity up beside him did her father seem to realize he should have done that himself. He half rose from his seat, looking embarrassed, but Aunt Mary-ett had warned Verity not to mind his brusqueness. "He's been alone too long," she'd said. "You'll probably have to reteach him his manners. Go gently with him!" Verity smiled at her father and settled her skirts around her.

Ransloe Boone drove the wagon down the main street of town, away from the Susquehanna River, past square lots filled with businesses and houses. Verity was relieved to spot at least one store and a lovely town common, as well as a telegraph office, a hotel, and the business sign of a photographer hanging outside a well-kept home. Perhaps she hadn't consigned herself to the wilderness after all, although she would miss Worcester's sidewalks and gas streetlamps—and the only home she could remember.

Yesterday morning she'd awakened for the very last time in the bed she'd shared for years with her Gaines cousins. Polly had cried until her nose turned red. "Write us every week," her cousin and closest friend had implored her. "Tell me all about *him*, and whatever you do, try to make a good impression and show some tact!"

Mindful of this, Verity bottled up her thoughts for almost a quarter of a mile, but eventually she could not resist turning to her father and blurting out, "I thought Nate might come to the station."

Ransloe Boone looked at her with a furrowed brow. "Nate?"

"Nathaniel McClure," she said pointedly. Her father ought to know whom she meant; he'd agreed to their engagement.

"Why would he come?" her father grunted. He turned

back to face the road and clucked at the horse. "You've never met him."

"Precisely why I thought he might come."

"It wouldn't have been suitable for him to fetch you from the station," her father went on. "Besides, you'll meet him on Friday."

Not until Friday? That was four days away! She managed to bite back her first thought and shared only her second. "Why on Friday?"

"The McClures expect us to attend a party." Her father said the word *party* as if it meant having a tooth pulled. "Fanny McClure wants to welcome you home. That's Nathaniel's mother," he added.

"Yes, I know," Verity replied. "He's written me about his family." Over the course of the last five months, they'd exchanged letters regularly. There'd been gifts as well: hair ribbons, and then kid gloves, and most recently a book of poems by Elizabeth Barrett Browning.

"You'll meet him then." Ransloe Boone glanced at her. "That's soon enough, isn't it?"

Verity smiled prettily, and her father took that as agreement.

The rain started falling before they'd left the town. Verity glared at the sky, offended that it should rain on her homecoming. Ransloe Boone reached under the seat and hauled out an umbrella, which he handed to his daughter.

She made an attempt to cover both of them, but he waved it off and settled his hat more firmly on his head.

The country road passed verdant fields and hills, dairy farms, and orchards, interrupted by wooded areas of shrubs with long, folded leaves and bunches of white and pink flowers. She caught a hint of their sweet fragrance in the rain as they passed by. When the horse turned onto a narrow dirt road without a signal, Verity knew they must be nearly home.

The first dwelling on the road was a green farmhouse with white shutters, immaculately tended. Rosebushes flanked the porch, and an arbor led to a garden in the back.

"That's the Thomas house," her father said.

Verity nodded. Her mother had grown up in this house, and her mother's brother, John Thomas, now lived here with his family. Verity had no memory of the house or her uncle; she knew the Thomases only from their mention in letters. They were her father's closest neighbors, although she saw this meant something different in the country than it did in the city.

The Boone house was entirely hidden from view until they had gone nearly a mile down the mountain road and around a wide turn. The sight of it did not particularly cheer her. Small and plain, it had been painted a stark and serviceable white. She could see no speck of color anywhere, and overall the property seemed as unprepossessing as her stiff and distant father.

A longing for Worcester and the family she'd left behind gripped her heart with startling intensity. She'd envisioned a happy — even romantic — arrival in Catawissa. Instead she was wet, bedraggled, and a stranger here.

After hauling his daughter's trunks upstairs, Ransloe Boone vanished, claiming an urgent need to store his farm equipment out of the rain. Verity surveyed the room she'd been given with dismay. She hadn't expected anything like the bedchamber she'd shared with Polly and little Susan, adorned with personal mementos and steeped in laughter and shared confidences. But Aunt Maryett would have put out fresh flowers for a visitor, and no one had done that here. There was a bed with a plain counterpane, a wardrobe, a dressing table with a chair, a small washstand, and that was all.

It was too quiet. She'd grown up in a house where the floorboards always shook with the vibration of running feet and the walls weren't thick enough to muffle the mayhem caused by four boys. The Boone house, by contrast, was as lively as a tomb. Verity wandered downstairs to explore, hoping to find *something* that pleased her.

The front parlor was clean and neat, but the curtains and furnishings were outdated. She doubted anything had been changed in the years since she'd left, yet not a single thing was familiar. *I learned to walk here*, she thought, looking around. *I was an infant, and my mother rocked me — probably in that very chair.* She touched the old wooden rocker with wonder. It was as if time had stopped in this house when Verity's mother had died and Ransloe Boone had sent his only child away to be raised by distant relatives.

In the old-fashioned dining room a framed photograph on the wall drew her eye. A dark-haired, dark-eyed woman with a luminous complexion and a knowing smile gazed out of the portrait — Sarah Ann Boone, her mother and the mistress of this house, dead these past fifteen years. Verity turned to look at her own reflection in the glass doors of the china cabinet. She took after her father, with light hair and green eyes.

Returning her wistful gaze to the face of the mother she didn't remember, she recalled Aunt Maryett's strange farewell at the station the day before. The woman who'd raised her since the age of two had embraced her tearfully. Aunt Maryett had been opposed to this betrothal, arranged solely through letters. But Verity had been determined, and when her father sent money for the train tickets, Aunt Maryett gave in. At the last possible moment, she clasped Verity's face between her hands and whispered, "Don't mind anything you hear about your mother, dear. Sarah Ann was a generous and warm-hearted soul, but people can be spiteful, even after all these years. If it's too terrible, you can always come home to us."

Verity had pulled back with a puzzled expression. But the train whistle was screaming, her chaperones eager to board lest they not find seats to their liking, and there'd been no time to ask questions.

Now, after one last curious glance at the portrait, Verity left the dining room, heading for the kitchen, where she heard signs of life. When she entered, a tiny, white-haired woman turned to look at her with pursed lips and a wrinkled brow. Verity paused. She knew her father had a housekeeper — even knew her name — but hadn't expected to be greeted with a scowl. "Hello. You must be Beulah Poole. I'm Verity."

"I know who you are." The woman hefted a cast-iron pot onto the stove and returned to her work. She was dark skinned, perhaps part Indian, and her expression seemed no more welcoming than anything else in this house.

"Can I help you with supper?" Verity peered over the woman's shoulder. "I like to cook."

"I do the cooking." The housekeeper scuttled sideways and looked at Verity in offense. "That's my job."

"But —"

"You're probably tired from your trip. Why don't you lie down, and I'll call you when supper's ready." Beulah Poole dismissed her with a wave. Verity backed away, unhappy to be rebuffed but not prepared to quarrel with her father's housekeeper in her first hour here.

Retreating to her room, she started unpacking her trunks. When she came to a bundle of Nate's letters, she sighed in relief. These, at least, were a comfort in this unfriendly place. Smiling, she opened the first one she'd ever received from him:

> *My mother and your father would like to see us matched, and so I thought we should correspond and see if we might find each other agreeable. Your father has given me permission to write, but I will not presume beyond this one letter unless you write back and tell me I am welcome to send more.*

And, of course, there was the one in which he'd proposed.

> *I am not often inclined to impulsive acts, but my instincts tell me we are of one mind on this matter. If I dare express myself boldly — I wish you would come home to Catawissa. And I will further expose myself to your mercy by venturing to offer you my heart, my home, and my hand in marriage.*

He'd included a formal portrait in one of his early letters. Nathaniel McClure was a solidly built young man with dark eyes and a stern gaze. His dark hair had been severely parted and combed down for the photograph. Verity thought he was nearly handsome and might be more so when he smiled. Surely a young man who read Elizabeth Barrett Browning would have a handsome smile.

Friday, she thought with a little flutter of the heart. *On Friday I will meet my future husband.*

TWO

HEN VERITY'S first callers appeared shortly after noon the next day, she went out on the front porch to meet them. Several of them broke into a run at the sight of her, and she braced herself for the assault of a throng of small boys. "Cousin Verity! Cousin Verity!" they cried, elbowing one another out of the way in their eagerness to shove grubby handfuls of wilted flowers into her face.

"Easy there, boys!" The man she guessed must be her uncle climbed up the stairs to the porch, holding a pie safely over his head. "You'll knock her over! She might not be used to wrangling rascals like you."

"Oh, I'm accustomed to it well enough," Verity assured him. The Gaines boys had been a rambunctious lot, too.

"Welcome, Verity! I'm your uncle John." He offered

his free hand as soon as she was able to take it. John Thomas was a well-built, handsome man with dark hair and a bright, amiable smile. She saw the resemblance to her mother's photograph at once.

Verity glanced at the road, but no one else was in sight. Her uncle seemed to guess her thoughts. "My wife and my daughter couldn't come this afternoon," he explained. "They're up to their elbows in blueberry pies. But I couldn't hold back the boys any longer—they wanted to come up here last night, and I had to restrain them. So I availed myself of a pie and brought them for a visit, not knowing what mischief they might cause if I didn't."

The boys rampaged past Verity, heading straight for the kitchen. Beulah took the pie from John Thomas's hands, sliced it, and served it. As the children devoured the warm pastry, their father introduced them.

The oldest and quietest of the lot was John Jr., who alone among the boys had not thrown himself into Verity's arms upon arrival. At twelve Johnny seemed awkward and tongue-tied, although he held the promise of one day being as handsome as his father. By contrast the middle child, Piper, didn't stop talking for a second. His face aglow with excitement, he bombarded Verity with questions about the trains she'd ridden from Massachusetts—what types of engines, how many cars, what speed, how much coal, and other queries she was ill-equipped to answer.

The six-year-old twins, Samuel and Stephen, were

indistinguishable even before they smeared blueberry all over themselves. "How will I tell them apart?" Verity exclaimed.

"I can't tell them apart," her uncle admitted. He put a hand on the top of one twin's head and turned it to face him. "Which one are you?" The child just grinned at his father with blue teeth.

While the boys begged second slices from Beulah, John Thomas turned to Verity and raised the subject everyone was still talking about—the War Between the States. "Is Worcester recovering from the war? Did the city lose many men?"

"There wasn't any family unaffected," she said. "Everybody lost a husband, a son, or a brother, or had someone return gravely injured." Her uncle Benjamin Gaines had left for war in 1863 a strong and confident man and returned in 1865 with a permanent limp and a tendency to cringe at loud noises.

Uncle John nodded his understanding. "The same can be said here. I'm just grateful the war ended before Johnny came of age. It would have cost us a fortune to keep him out."

Verity knew some men hired a substitute or paid a commutation fee to avoid conscription. Looking at the dapper and cheery man seated across from her, Verity wondered if he had done so. Her uncle didn't look as if he'd ever seen a battlefield. The Gaines family hadn't been able to afford such a luxury. Neither had her father, who'd served briefly at the end of the war.

Mindful of Polly's advice on tact, Verity kept back her opinion of men who paid their way out of service and agreed it was a very good thing her cousins would not have to go to war.

Uncle John looked around. "Where's Ransloe? Out in the fields working?" He turned and spoke to Beulah Poole. "Even with his daughter just come home after fifteen years away?"

"He works hard," Verity said in her father's defense. John Thomas had his own farmland to tend but somehow found time to make social calls in the middle of the day. "I understand it's a big property," she continued. "He has only two men to help him. Beulah's grandsons, I think."

"Grandsons, nephews, cousins," her uncle said glibly. "They switch off periodically, don't they, Beulah?" The woman nodded without even looking up from the sink. "We've got passels of Pooles around here; it's one thing we're never short of."

He spoke as if Beulah's relations were weeds choking out the better crops. Verity frowned. She'd grown up among people committed to social reform and the rights of all men and women. She understood that country townsfolk might not be as enlightened, but her uncle's comment had been downright rude. Verity glanced at Beulah, but the woman never turned around.

"It'll do Ransloe good to have Nathaniel here to help run things," John Thomas went on, apparently unaware that he'd offended his niece and possibly his brother-in-law's housekeeper.

Verity nodded. She knew that her return and her proposed marriage were primarily a business arrangement between Ransloe Boone and the McClure family. The Mc-Clures wanted to acquire the land; her father didn't want to let it go, but he was willing to pass it on to a son-in-law. It had been a frightening idea to Verity at first, but Nate had put her at ease with his letters and the book he'd sent as a gift. The volume of love poems, written by Eliza-beth Barrett during her courtship with Robert Browning, had completely won her over.

"Nathaniel's a sensible boy," her uncle said. "He'll be an asset here, and it'll be good to see life in this old house again." A thought seemed to strike him. "Will you live here? Or with the McClures?"

"We haven't decided that yet," Verity said. The sub-ject had not come up in their letters.

"You should live with Ransloe. Trust me, Verity; you don't want to throw yourself into the stewpot at the Mc-Clure house." Nathaniel had three older sisters, all mar-ried and living at the McClure house with their husbands and children. "You'd be better off establishing yourself here — wouldn't she, Beulah?"

"I couldn't say, Mr. Thomas," the housekeeper responded without looking up.

Verity thought her uncle was probably correct, but she didn't wish to speak for her intended—or her father.

Beulah handed John Thomas the pie plate, now washed clean. The children had eaten every bite. "Not much of a gift, boys," he remarked. "We bring it over and devour it ourselves. Verity will bar the door next time she sees us coming." The proud expression on his face belied his words. "Clara and Liza will come calling in their own time."

"How old is your daughter?" Verity asked.

"She'll be fourteen this fall." Then her uncle added in a thoughtless manner that Verity was beginning to suspect was typical of him, "Come to think of it, for a long time Liza had her cap set at your Nathaniel. I expect she's shifted her affections to someone else now, since your engagement was announced."

Grand, thought Verity as she watched them all leave. *A jealous cousin. That's just grand.*

Perhaps Aunt Clara and Cousin Liza would come calling later, and there might be other visitors as well. She decided to bake a cake. Beulah put her hands on her bony hips and protested, "I'm expecting a delivery from the butcher. You'll be in the way."

"I won't take up much space," Verity said, then promptly spilled flour all over herself, the table, and the floor. Beulah's expression soured even more. "I'm not a very tidy cook," Verity admitted, "but I clean up after myself when I'm done. I won't leave it for you."

"I'll get the broom" was Beulah's only response. She left by the back kitchen door and let it slam shut behind her.

Verity returned to her work, wiping flour off her nose with her sleeve and humming happily. She liked to bake. Once the war shortages had let up, she and Polly had spent hours cooking for the pure joy of it. There wasn't a charity bake sale in Worcester that hadn't held a table full of cakes and sweets prepared by Verity Boone and Polly Gaines.

She heard the back door open again but didn't bother to turn around until Beulah called her name. "Miss Verity!"

Glancing over her shoulder, she saw Beulah standing in the doorway with a broom in her hand and, behind her, a young man lingering on the threshold. "Are you from the butcher?" Verity asked. "You can just put everything in the springhouse." She used her sleeve again to wipe her face and went on beating the batter.

Nobody moved. The fellow cleared his throat uncomfortably. "He's not from the butcher, Miss Verity," said Beulah.

Her tone gave Verity pause. Very carefully, she laid

down the spoon and turned around again, wiping her hands across her apron. The housekeeper smiled smugly.

Verity took another look at the young man in the doorway.

"Hello, Verity," he said.

"Oh," she replied. "Hello, Nate."

THREE

ELATEDLY SHE recognized his face—those dark brows and that stern gaze. His eyes were a surprise. They had appeared dark in the photograph, but they were blue—the deep indigo of a stormy sky. He looked quite different dressed in the casual attire of a gentleman farmer, a shirt open at the throat and a coat that had been patched several times. His dark hair was tousled, as if he'd been riding or walking without a hat, and he had a rugged look, quite unlike the stiff young man in the photograph.

At the moment Verity didn't much resemble the formal portrait she'd sent him either. She forced herself to untie her apron slowly, with dignity, rather than ripping it off. Removing the apron wouldn't help much. She was wearing her oldest dress, her hair was messily tied up out of the way, and her face was smudged with flour.

"I'm sorry I came unannounced," he said.

She summoned a brave smile. "I didn't expect to see you until Friday."

That seemed to puzzle him for a moment, but then he nodded. "Oh, the party. My mother wanted to welcome you home with a celebration. She also thought," he added slowly, "that if you and I met for the first time in front of my family and yours and everybody in town, it would be highly *amusing*. For her and everybody else." Nathaniel Mc-Clure watched her intently; Verity found herself unable to look away. "I decided I'd come meet you on my own terms."

An admirable plan, Verity thought, but he still could have sent a calling card. He could have arrived by the front door and allowed her to meet him in the parlor, dressed to receive company.

"I thought we might go for a walk down the lane, if you like," he said.

He'd already seen her looking like a kitchen drudge; it was too late to cater to her vanity. Verity would have to make the best of it. "Very well."

When he backed out of the doorway, she followed. He waited while she shook out her skirts and then started down the road, away from the Thomas house and town. He didn't offer his arm to her, and she was relieved. This was just too strange — and he was too much a stranger.

They walked side by side in silence, not strolling so much as trudging. Verity glanced up at him curiously and caught him looking down at her. "How do you like Cata-wissa?" he blurted out.

"It's very pretty, although I haven't seen much of it yet. My father brought me straight home from the station, and he's been in the fields ever since." Immediately, she wished she could take that back. It sounded like a complaint.

Nate defended her father with almost the same words she'd spoken to her uncle earlier. "He works hard. It's a big property. And this is a busy time of year for a farm."

"I know that, and he doesn't have a lot of help." That sounded like another complaint, she realized.

"My family has always lent him a hand when he needed it." Nate glanced at her again, looking pained. "He and my father were friends—"

"Yes, I know," Verity hurriedly assured him. "He wrote about your father many times and was grieved by his passing. And, of course, I'm grateful for the help you gave my father during the war."

When Verity's father had been called up by the army three years ago, Nate had taken over the running of the Boone farm. He'd been only fifteen at the time, and he'd had guidance from his family, but according to what her father had written in his letters, it was primarily due to Nate that the property hadn't fallen into wrack and ruin while Ransloe Boone was absent.

Ahead of them the road split in two, one branch

continuing uphill and the other turning sharply left and winding down a steep incline. "Where do these lead?" she asked.

He nodded uphill. "That road takes you to my family's land. The other heads down to the church."

"Can we go this way?" Verity indicated the path toward the church. She was already embarrassed that Nate had seen her in her current state of dress; she didn't want to encounter any of his relatives. "It's downhill."

He shrugged. "If you like. We'll have to walk back up again, though."

So far, this had been a very awkward meeting, entirely lacking the ease of their correspondence. Verity collected her thoughts, determined to change the course of the conversation.

"I want to thank you again for the book of poems. I cannot tell you how much I've enjoyed them."

That provoked a small smile — his first. "I'm glad you liked it."

"I think she was a very talented poetess," Verity went on.

They walked on in silence for a few moments. Then Nate shoved his hands into the pockets of his coat and frowned. "You're referring to the Portuguese poems?" he asked.

She looked up at him. "They're not *really* Portuguese poems. She wrote them all herself."

"Who did?"

"Elizabeth Barrett." Now Verity was pointing out his mistake, and that was even worse than complaining. She wanted to return to the top of the hill and start over — possibly take the other path — but it was too late. They were both breathing heavily as they descended a steep section of the road. Below them a building had just become visible, and beyond it a graveyard.

"*Sonnets from the Portuguese?*" Nate asked. It sounded as if he wasn't sure they were talking about the same book.

She wanted to change the subject, but if she dropped it now, she might offend him more. "She only pretended she was translating poems from another language," Verity explained, "because they were her love poems to Robert Browning and highly personal. I thought you knew."

Nate's blue eyes seemed a bit hunted now; he looked everywhere except at her face. "No, I don't read poetry. I asked my sisters to pick out gifts you might like."

Verity caught her breath at the word *gifts*. Not just the one, but all of them.

He hadn't known he was sending her love poems. He'd let his sisters pick out the book — and the gloves, and even the hair ribbons. Her temper flared. "Did your sisters write your letters as well as choose your gifts?"

They were now walking five or six feet apart, separated only by the breadth of the road, but it might as well have been a canyon. Nate's silence for the span of several paces was answer enough. Then he said: "No, I wrote my own letters. That is, they gave me advice about what I should say . . ."

Verity could picture it in her mind now: this awkward young farmer bent over a desk, writing under his sisters' instruction, while *they* composed the words that would win her heart. No doubt they'd stuffed him into formal clothes and combed down his hair for the photograph, too.

She was walking—no, running!—down this horribly steep lane with a complete stranger. And here, to make matters worse, was the church in which she was expected to marry him! The Mount Zion Methodist Church was nothing more than a plain log building on a country road. Verity had left a home with a beloved family in worldly Worcester to live in a backwoods mountain town with a father she didn't know and to marry a man who'd let *his sisters* court her.

As the road leveled out, her steps slowed, and she put both hands to her face, trying to catch her breath and calm her thoughts.

"I warned you it was steep," Nate said behind her. She shot him a glance of irritation. He had *not* warned her it was steep; he'd merely reminded her they'd have to walk back up—something she didn't think she could do just then. They'd have to poke around the cemetery until she recovered her breath.

Verity had no idea what to talk about now. Every conversational topic she'd chosen had led to disaster, and he didn't seem capable of helping. He was looking around as if he might find something worthwhile by the side of the road, scowling as if he regretted meeting her at all.

She too looked around, hoping to find a neutral subject for discourse, and her eyes alighted on an interesting sight outside the graveyard. "What are those?" she asked, and strode across the grass to get a closer look.

Outside the cemetery wall stood two odd metal frameworks that looked like tiny conservatories without the glass. Verity had never seen anything like them.

Behind her she heard Nate's voice. "Oh . . . no — wait a minute."

They weren't conservatories — how could they be? Now they looked like overlarge birdcages.

"Verity!"

Strangely large iron-filigree cages, each one about as high as her shoulder and — she felt a shiver run through her — not much longer and wider than a casket.

"Miss Boone!" Nate exclaimed.

Hearing him return to a formality they had left behind in their letters made her turn around. His sisters had decided when he should ask permission to use her given name. They had read *her* responses, Verity suddenly realized, and possibly decided as a group how Nate would answer each one. He *should* go back to calling her Miss

Boone, she thought indignantly. He should start from the beginning and introduce himself all over again.

"Please," he said urgently, still standing on the road and holding out his hand to her. "I think we should go back." He looked so wretched that she felt sympathy for him in spite of her disappointment.

She would have done what he asked without another word if he'd stopped talking then, but he didn't. "I'm sorry I brought you here," he said. "I should have realized you hadn't seen them yet."

Verity felt as if her heart had dropped straight through her body. He wasn't apologizing for being a buffoon; he was apologizing for something else entirely. Ignoring his hand, she turned back toward the cemetery.

Outside each cage there was a headstone.

She broke into a run, holding up her skirt in both hands, her feet pounding across the grass.

Iron cages surrounded two graves outside the cemetery wall. With a growing dread she approached the nearest one, and her eyes made out the lettering on the marker.

SARAH ANN
Wife of Ransloe Boone

FOUR

HE WORLD tipped sideways.

Her mother's grave, confined within an iron cage, seemed to swing around to stand on its side, the blue sky pitching over the grass in a sickening, topsy-turvy wave.

Two hands gripped her shoulders, and then she found herself wrapped around by arms strong enough to support her even if her legs gave way. Verity raised a hand, slipped her arm free of the protective embrace, and punched Nate in the chest.

"Ow!"

"Let me go!"

She staggered backward as he released her. He stared at her, looking tousled and confused. "I thought you were going to faint!"

"I never faint!"

Her fists clenched at her sides, she turned around to look again at the marker on her mother's tomb.

SARAH ANN
Wife of Ransloe Boone
Entered into Rest
November 15, 1852
Aged 22 Years
Beloved Wife and Mother

It was all very ordinary information, nothing Verity had not known before. Except that the marker stood beside an iron cage that completely enclosed the grave, and the grave was *outside* the cemetery.

She wrapped her fingers around the heavy wire that crisscrossed the structure in a diamond pattern. Her hands were slender, but she would have been hard-pressed to reach through the latticework. There was a small stone marker inside the cage, engraved simply with initials: S.A.B. A hinged door at the far end of the cage was padlocked shut.

"Why?" Her voice was raw and hoarse. "Why is my mother's grave inside a cage?"

Nate was watching her worriedly. "I'm not sure."

"What do you mean, you're not sure?" She looked up. "You must know."

"I don't know the whole story."

"What did she do? Why is she buried outside the churchyard?" Verity drew in a horrified breath. "This is unhallowed ground!"

He looked uncomfortable. "I think you should talk to your father."

Rather unsteadily, she walked over to the other caged grave and read the tombstone.

ASENATH
Wife of John Thomas
Entered into Rest
November 15, 1852
Aged 17 Years

A second round of chills ran up and down her body. "Who was this?"

"John Thomas's first wife," said Nate. "Your aunt by marriage, I suppose."

Her mother and her aunt, both confined in iron bars outside the cemetery after death, as if they were . . . what? Witches?

"They died the same day," she said. "Was it a sickness?"

He shook his head again helplessly. "I really don't know."

Verity looked at her mother's grave again, a terrible pain in her heart.

"Well, I know two men who *must* know," she said.

Ransloe Boone was not happy with Nathaniel McClure. "You took her to the cemetery?"

"Yes, sir."

"Of all the darned fool things to do!"

"Yes, sir."

Verity lifted her head. As angry as she was, she noticed that Nate did not make excuses or try to divert the blame but honestly acknowledged his mistake. It was a point in his favor, and heaven knew he needed one.

"It was my idea to walk down that road," she said. "I don't think he thought about what I would see there until it was too late." Then, having accepted the responsibility that was hers, she turned on her father. "It was *your* place to tell me. He should not have needed to worry about it."

Her father ran a hand through his unkempt hair and paced the length of the parlor. "I would have taken you there," he said finally. "I just didn't have the chance."

"Why?" Verity demanded. "Why is she buried outside the churchyard in a *cage?*"

Her father leaned against the back of the sofa, staring down at the floor.

"It was protection for her," he said finally. "To protect her remains from . . . from grave robbers."

"Grave robbers?" Verity repeated in disbelief. "What was she buried with that anyone would want to steal?"

"Nothing," Ransloe Boone said sharply. "Why would you ask that? Who's been talking to you?"

Startled, Verity held her hands out. "No one! You said grave robbers!"

Nate cleared his throat. "In Ohio last year, bodies were stolen from graves and sold to medical students for study. Is that what you mean, sir?"

Ransloe Boone cast a grateful look in Nate's direction. "Yes . . . something like that."

"Sold to medical students?" Verity repeated, horrified. "For *study*?"

"There was some reason for concern," her father explained. "There'd been an . . . incident at our cemetery. We were worried, and your grandmother was nearly mad with grief. To lose her daughter and daughter-in-law so suddenly, not to mention the babes they were carrying—"

Verity's fingers curled around the fabric of the settee. "They were expecting? My mother was carrying a child?"

Ransloe Boone's face, when he looked at his daughter, was drawn and gray with old sorrow. "No one ever told you?"

She turned away, stricken by grief for a mother she didn't remember and a sibling who'd never been born. She herself had been sent away at the age of two to be raised by her father's relatives. Who would have told her?

She wiped at her eyes before tears could fall. "Why

aren't they in the cemetery? Why did you bury them in *unblessed* ground?"

Her father rubbed his brow as if in pain. "That's more difficult to explain. It was just easier that way, Verity. It was the quickest way to get them a decent burial."

"I don't understand. Had they done something wrong?"

He looked up, his eyes ablaze. "Your mother never did anything wrong. Neither did John's wife, for that matter. Asenath was hardly more than a girl—no older than you."

"Then why—"

"Because people are spiteful." Verity blinked to hear him echo Aunt Maryett's words. "I gave in because it was simpler that way. I regretted it afterward . . . but there are plenty of things I regret that I can't do anything about now."

Abruptly, he turned on his heel and left the room. Verity bit her lip and dug her fingers into the upholstery again.

Nate stood up. "I should go. I've caused enough trouble for one day."

Verity rose, too, and faced him with embarrassment. This had been far from the meeting she'd hoped for. "It wasn't your fault," she said. "I'm sorry that my family" —*shame* was the word that came to mind, but she corrected herself—"circumstances led to our outing ending so badly." It had begun badly, too, but she didn't want to remind him. "If you come again, I promise I'll be better prepared to receive you." *Especially if you don't appear at the back door without warning.*

He glanced away, shuffling his feet, and Verity suddenly realized she'd said *if* instead of *when*. "I'm taking the spring crops to Wilkes-Barre in the morning. I won't return until Friday." When he raised his eyes to her again, Verity could see that he was just as discomfited and uncertain as she was. "I suppose I'll see you then . . . at my mother's party?"

Did he think she would revoke her word? End the engagement because of one ill-planned encounter? Did he *want* her to?

"I'll be there," she promised. He nodded and bowed politely, but she couldn't tell what he was thinking.

That night, she brushed out her hair in front of her open window.

The night was very dark, the moon only a sliver in the sky. Worcester was hardly ever dark—there were streetlights, and some of the better houses were lit by gas. It was noisy, too, with carriages passing at all hours and the sounds of people talking and laughing in neighboring homes. Here, the nearest houses were out of sight.

She'd gone to bed the previous night tired and a little homesick but hopeful for the future. A mere day later her heart felt like a stone in her chest. She'd upset her father, insulted and *punched* her intended husband, and as for her mother . . .

This is why Aunt Maryett didn't want me to come back here, Verity thought. In spite of her father's denial, her mother must have done something that made her an outcast, she and her brother's wife between them — something that resulted in their burial outside a Christian cemetery.

Turning from the window and laying down her hairbrush, she tried not to think that returning to Catawissa had been a mistake.

FIVE

N WAKING the next day, Verity was seized with a need to do something about those graves. She didn't know why her father and uncle had allowed them to be erected in that manner, barren and isolated and shameful — but Verity Boone was not going to tolerate it. Her father claimed that his wife had done no wrong, and Aunt Maryett said she'd been generous and warm-hearted. Sarah Ann Boone had been a midwife, a daughter and a sister, a farmer's wife and a young mother. She deserved a better memorial.

Verity marched into the kitchen that morning and caught her father at his breakfast. "I want to go into town," she said without preamble. "Can you take me?"

He chewed a mouthful of bread before replying. "I need the wagon in the fields today. But John usually goes to town every morning. Perhaps you can ride with him."

Verity snatched a slice of bread from the table and ran upstairs to fetch a bonnet and her coin purse.

She returned to the kitchen to borrow a shopping basket from Beulah, and her father surprised her by pressing a half dollar into her hand. "Buy yourself something pretty," he mumbled without meeting her eyes. She understood that this was his way of apologizing for not taking her himself and for allowing her to discover the state of her mother's grave without warning. After a moment of awkward silence, Verity left by the back door, unhappy that she and her father had so little to say to each other.

She felt guilty about Nate, too. As she walked down the road toward the Thomas house, she acknowledged that she'd behaved rather shrewishly in his company. There was nothing she could do about it until Friday, but she pledged to make a better impression when next she met him.

The welcoming attractiveness of the Thomas house made a sharp contrast with the Boone residence. Verity decided she would have to remedy that situation. No matter where she and Nate decided to live, it was not acceptable for her father's house to present such a sad face to the world.

John Thomas was hitching a horse to his trap just as Verity arrived. He was willing to take his niece to town with him, but her unexpected appearance presented a problem. No sooner had Verity been handed up into the trap than her three youngest cousins spilled out of the house, demanding that they, too, ride to town with Cousin Verity.

The older Thomas children trailed behind their brothers. Johnny gave Verity a shy smile, then concentrated on kicking rocks down the lane. The girl, Liza, cast an appraising glance at her cousin but looked away when Verity smiled in return. Tall and plain, Liza had a round face and a high forehead. Her hair was dark like her father's, bound in braids and pinned to the back of her head.

"Come with us, Liza," Uncle John urged. "You can get acquainted with Verity. What luck for you to finally have another young lady nearby!"

Liza shook her head. "I can't. Mama needs me this morning."

"I can't take the boys if you don't come," her father said. "I have business in town." When Liza shook her head again, he shrugged and glanced at the children, who were clambering into the trap behind him. "Out, fellows! You'll have to stay home."

Verity couldn't bear the wailing produced by this command, nor could she resist the chubby arms Stephen and Samuel threw around her neck. The twins reminded her of the Gaines boys, whom she suddenly missed very much. "I'll watch them, Uncle John," she volunteered.

"Liza!" he exclaimed. "Look what you've done—

condemned your cousin to trial by fire!" Verity wished he wouldn't press his daughter to come against her will. The girl looked sour enough already.

"I'll help," Johnny said with feigned lack of interest, as if he hadn't been looking for the opportunity to join them all along.

Liza turned and strode back up the walkway to the house. She hadn't said a single word, greeting or otherwise, to her cousin. Verity assumed that the "cap" Liza had set at Nathaniel McClure was still set firmly upon her head.

While they rode into town, Verity told her uncle the reason for her trip.

"Asenath's grave." His eyes took on a distant, dreamy look. "That's very thoughtful of you. A kind gesture." She was glad he thought so, for it had been her intention to treat his wife's grave the same as her mother's, whether he approved or not.

Sunlight flattered Catawissa more than rain clouds had, and Verity was cheered by the sight of people on the streets going about their business. The town seemed to be prosperous and growing: there were new homes with stylish gables and turrets, as well as log and stone houses that probably dated back eighty years. Leafy trees shaded the streets, and flowers bloomed in carefully tended beds.

Uncle John tied up his horse near the common and vanished, saying he had appointments to keep. Before he'd been gone ten minutes, Verity had saved either Samuel or Stephen from being trampled by a horse and pulled Piper down off a telegraph pole. When she turned around, the other twin had run off in the direction of the river, where he no doubt planned to fall in and die a horrible death under the water wheels of the Catawissa Paper Mill. She chased after him for two blocks, caught him, and carried him back on her hip, while Johnny trailed behind, dragging his feet in the dirt and being no help whatsoever.

"Listen to me!" Verity finally said in exasperation, setting the child down on the footboard of his father's trap. "You stay here, all four of you, or I'll never let you come to town with me again! I'm going into the store, and don't you dare move!"

Dyers General Goods turned out to be a sizable establishment, offering canned food and other groceries, hardware and bolts of fabric, and even a small apothecary's corner in the back. Verity was relieved to see the place so well supplied. She'd been afraid she might have to order most of her goods from Reading or Philadelphia.

Verity looked over the groceries, noting what the store had in stock, and when she spotted jam preserves, she put a jar in her basket. Jam tarts were a specialty of hers, and the party on Friday would be an occasion to bake some. Then she went to the ribbons. She planned on making wreaths to decorate the iron structures over the graves so they would look less like cages. She was examining several spools at the back of the store when a familiar name caught her attention.

"Will you attend Fanny McClure's party on Friday?" It was a woman's voice.

"Certainly," another replied. "I want to see the girl who snatched up the most eligible bachelor in town without even meeting him first!"

"Shocking, isn't it? My Amelie cried for days."

"It's because of the land, of course. Why else would Nathaniel McClure marry a girl whose mother was — well, everyone knows what she was."

Verity flinched and lost her grip on a spool of ribbon. It clattered to the floor, drawing the attention of everyone in the store. Stiffening her spine and lifting her chin, she turned around to face the women and watch their reactions. They'd never seen her before, and yet they had to know who she was.

One of them looked away, her cheeks flaming red. The other, however, smirked, completely unrepentant. Verity picked up her basket, paid for her purchases, and swept out of the store.

On the street she paused to expel the breath she'd been holding, outraged. How dare those women speak about her betrothal that way? And what they said about her *mother* . . . Looking down at the basket full of ribbon, she realized that wreaths would not be nearly enough to redeem any kind of dignity for those two graves. She closed her eyes a moment, in grief and shame, and opened them just in time to observe the disaster happening down the street.

One of the twins was standing on the seat of the trap, striking a defiant pose with his fists on his hips and shouting, "You'll never take me alive!"

Piper clambered up the back wheel of the trap. "I don't aim to!" he hollered, balancing on the wheel and hanging on to the back of the trap with one hand. "Surrender or die, Silas Clayton! You cowardly deserter!"

"Piper, get down!" Verity cried as the boy let go of his handhold to cock and aim an imaginary gun.

"I'll see you in hell first!" the standing twin shouted. Before Verity could take breath to scold him for swearing, he smacked the horse on the rump and yelled, "Git up there, Lightning!" The patient but sorely tried Thomas horse, whose name was Bill, started in alarm. The trap rolled forward, and Piper pitched face first into the dirt between the wheels.

Verity plunged down the street before he'd even commenced screaming. She shoved her basket into Johnny's arms and helped Piper sit up. His face was covered in blood. She whipped out a handkerchief and tried to wipe away the gore to discover the extent of the damage, but Piper fought her, blood mixing with snot and tears to form a horrible mess.

"Dr. Robbins lives a block down the street," Johnny said.

Verity scooped the struggling child up into her arms. "Show me."

The doctor lived in a two-story clapboard house with professional rooms in the back. They burst in through the patients' entrance like a summer storm, all thunder and lightning and commotion. Piper screamed and flailed, the twins wailed, Verity was covered in blood, and Johnny skulked in the rear.

A young man came out of the doctor's examining room wiping his hands on a towel. He took one look at them, then rushed forward and blotted Piper's face with the towel. "That's going to need stitching," he stated.

Piper howled. Verity passed him into the doctor's arms, but the boy clung to her with both hands, pulling her along with them into the examining room. "Find your father!" she shouted over her shoulder to Johnny, who bolted from the office.

"You're not their sister," the young man declared as he carried Piper to a chair.

Verity sat down first and took the boy on her lap. "No," she agreed. "Are you Dr. Robbins?"

"No." Catching Piper's wrists in one hand, he wiped away enough blood to expose a wide gash crossing the child's eyebrow. "I notice you don't faint at the sight of blood," he said.

"I never faint," she told him proudly.

His eyes were blue, but not dark like Nate's. They were pale and seemed to twinkle with good humor. Ginger haired, fair skinned, and not much older than Verity herself, he displayed a confident demeanor that calmed her racing heart. If he was not the doctor, he was giving a fair impression of one. "How are you with a needle?" he asked, letting go of Piper's hands and crossing the room to rummage in a drawer.

Verity answered him bravely. "My embroidery is excellent."

The young man laughed. "I'll handle the needle; I just want you to hold him down." He returned with a handful of peppermint candies, which he waved in the air to catch the attention of Stephen and Samuel. The twins stopped crying. Then he strode to the waiting room door and whistled as though they were a pair of dogs. They scampered after him and dove for the candy when he tossed it across the room.

He shut the adjoining door and turned back to his patient. "Now to business." Piper began to wail again as the young doctor threaded silk through a needle. "How did he hurt himself?"

Verity paused, then said, "He was trying to capture a deserter, I think."

"Really?"

Piper looked back and forth between them. "And save General Washington's payroll!"

"Oh, *that* deserter!" The young doctor turned to Verity. "Please hold his arms and his legs. Leave his head to me."

Verity settled herself in the chair. She grabbed one of Piper's hands in each of hers and crossed them over his chest, but his legs presented more difficulty. Piper raised his legs up and kicked wildly at the doctor. After a moment's consideration, Verity threw one of her own legs over both of the boy's, locking his body against her own. This position presented a wide swath of petticoats for public display, but after one brief, appreciative glance, the young man directed his attention solely to his patient.

With his free hand he grabbed a fistful of Piper's hair just above the cut and pressed the boy's head back against Verity's shoulder. "Did you get him?" he asked mildly. "The deserter, that is." He cleansed the wound with a cloth.

"I did," grunted Piper, a bit hoarse from screaming.

The doctor made quick, decisive passes with the needle, his head bent close to his patient. Feeling Piper's little body shudder with each stitch, Verity could see nothing but clean curls of ginger hair. In spite of her claims, she was finding the smell of blood pungent and unsettling. She leaned back in the chair.

"Brought him to justice, did you?" the young man murmured, snipping off the end of the thread.

"And found the gold." Piper's body sagged against Verity's.

"I'll bet you did," he said softly to Piper. "I'll bet you did." Then he raised his eyes to Verity. "Well done, Miss Not-Thomas."

Verity smiled up at him. "Thank you, Dr. Not-Robbins. That was very well done yourself."

He laughed again, a pleasant laugh filled with good humor. He wiped off his hands with a towel and held one out to her. "I'm Hadley Jones, apprentice to Dr. Robbins."

Verity set Piper on his feet and took Jones's hand, allowing him to help her stand. "I'm Verity Boone." When she tried to release his hand, hers stuck to his, and she realized her hand was covered with blood, as was much of the rest of her.

He passed her the towel. "Let me get you a washbasin."

Piper was feeling his forehead with probing fingers. "How's it look?" he asked Verity. "I hope it leaves a big scar!"

At that moment the door burst open and John Thomas appeared. "Piper!"

"Oh, Uncle John," said Verity. "I'm so sorry!"

"It's not your fault, Verity. The boy is a menace." Her uncle took his son by the chin and lifted his face. "What's the damage?"

"Keep it clean, Mr. Thomas," the apprentice said, "and it should heal easily."

While her uncle paid the doctor's fee, Verity washed her hands. "I ought to keep you on retainer, Jones," Uncle John grunted.

"It might save time, at that." The young man grinned and winked at Verity.

She stiffened and looked away. Perhaps he wasn't aware that she was an engaged woman. Heaven knew what he thought of her, showing all those petticoats. But she'd held the child still and hadn't fainted, and wasn't that what mattered?

Uncle John left the office, herding the boys before him. Verity followed but found herself glancing back, almost against her will.

Hadley Jones was leaning against the doorway, arms crossed against his chest, smiling and watching her go.

SIX

IDN'T YOU look after him at all?" Liza exclaimed at the sight of her brother.

"I did look after him!" Verity retorted. How dare this country mouse snap at her? After listening to those horrible women revile her mother and then holding Piper down for his stitches, Verity was in no mood to restrain her temper. She looked around, wanting her uncle to defend her, but John Thomas had already disappeared. She'd never met a man with such a talent for being absent when he was needed.

"You're useless," Liza said to Verity. She put both arms around Piper and drew him in through the front door of the Thomas house.

"I warrant you could have done no better!" Verity followed them over the threshold, not because she'd been invited in but because she didn't care to be dismissed in such a fashion.

The other girl's pale moon face was taut with dislike. "I don't know what passes for watching children in Worcester, but—"

"That's enough, Liza."

The words, softly spoken, stopped the girl in midrampage.

A woman strode toward them down the central hall of the house. Slender, with deep brown hair set in corkscrew ringlets, Clara Thomas was surprisingly plain, Verity thought, to be married to such a handsome man. Yet, as the woman calmly surveyed her injured son and then smacked his bottom with one efficient hand, she seemed the perfect match for Verity's flighty uncle.

"Was he patched up by Dr. Robbins or the apprentice?" she asked, turning to Verity.

"It was the apprentice."

"Good. He's stitched up my sons before, and he does neat work. It should heal cleanly." She looked her niece over from head to toe, then turned toward the back of the house. "Come with me, Verity, and I'll tend to those stains."

"Oh, that's not necessary."

"Don't be foolish," her aunt replied. "They've already set longer than they should, but I have a trick or two that might work. Come along. You too, Liza." Glaring at each other, the girls followed her.

In a washroom off the kitchen, Clara Thomas unceremoniously stripped her niece to her undergarments. To Verity it seemed overly familiar for somebody who'd never formally introduced herself, but family was family. Verity's dress went into a basin of cold water, and since she couldn't go home in her chemise and petticoats, nor in a soaking wet dress, her aunt ordered, "Liza, bring your cousin something that will fit her." Liza opened her mouth to protest but thought better of it and flounced off.

Aunt Clara fetched a jar of salt from a shelf, then cast her eyes over Verity's hair and face. "You're all Ransloe," she commented, as emotionless as if she were remarking on the weather. "I don't see much of Sarah Ann in you."

"Did you know my mother?" Verity watched her aunt take a handful of salt and scrub it into the bloodstains.

"Of course."

"Nathaniel McClure took me to the cemetery yesterday." Verity didn't mention that the visit was accidental—or that she'd punched him. "It was the first time I'd seen her grave."

Aunt Clara raised an eyebrow. "I suppose that was a startling sight. We're so accustomed to those things by now, we hardly notice them."

"I think they look too bare. I'm going to make grave wreaths for them."

Liza returned, holding a dun-colored dress Verity suspected was the ugliest she could find. She thanked the girl for lending her something to wear home — which was as truthful a statement as she could make — and turned back to her aunt. "I want to decorate *both* graves," she said. "It seems wrong to do only one. Uncle John said I could tend to Aunt Asenath's grave too."

Liza drew in her breath sharply, but Aunt Clara only nodded. "Her grave has gone neglected far too long. It should have been John's responsibility, but he was never one for unpleasant tasks."

Verity glanced out the washroom window, toward the arbor and the garden beyond it. "I'd also like to plant flowers around the graves. In Worcester we make the cemeteries look like gardens, pretty enough to walk through."

Her aunt took the hint quickly enough. "I'll give you cuttings. I'm sure I have some plants hardy enough for that rocky soil." Aunt Clara eyed her niece with speculation. "You don't remember your mother and Asenath, do you? No, of course not. You were too young."

"I don't remember them," Verity agreed sadly.

"Pity," said Aunt Clara. "I always liked Sarah Ann. Her passing caused me great sorrow. If you need help with the wreaths, Liza will assist you. She has a knack for such things."

A lifetime of practice enabled Verity to speak the complete truth without a moment's hesitation. "If I need

Liza's help, I shall definitely ask for it." She stepped into her cousin's dress and pulled it up. Liza was so tall that the skirt dragged on the ground. "I'm very sorry about Piper getting hurt this morning, Aunt Clara."

"A small army couldn't keep that boy out of trouble," her aunt replied, unconcerned. "We're lucky the war ended before he became old enough to run off and join."

"Did Uncle John serve?" Verity asked.

"No, he paid a Poole to go in his place, same as Michael McClure did." Aunt Clara helped Verity button up the back of the dress. "Nathaniel's father was too sick to serve; anyone could see that. He should never have been called up."

"I agree." Verity had seen the army take men and boys who ought to have been unfit for service. She had never met Nathaniel's father, but she knew he'd been ill even before the war started and had spent his final year of life bedridden.

Her aunt shook her head disapprovingly. "The Poole man whom John paid was killed at Gettysburg. But Michael's substitute used his fee for college after the war, if you can believe it."

Verity glanced at her aunt with surprise. It sounded as if Aunt Clara would rather the paid substitute had done his duty and died, rather than have the audacity to survive and attend college. "What about Nathaniel?" She hoped her intended husband had not paid another man to fight in his place. Not that she would have wanted him injured or killed, but . . .

"Nathaniel was eager to go, but his mother made him promise to wait until he was sixteen, and by that time the war was over." Aunt Clara eyed Verity sternly. "Life's a battle — in peacetime and in wartime. People do whatever they have to. Best you learn that while you're young."

It was a strange sentiment, and rather disturbing. Before Verity could wonder too much about it, her aunt smiled and said, "I'll let your dress soak overnight. Send Beulah for it in the morning."

Verity didn't want to ask any special favors of Beulah. "I can come back for it."

Aunt Clara smiled knowingly. "Send Beulah," she repeated. "Don't let that woman intimidate you. She's had the run of your father's house for too many years. I'm sure she hasn't taken to the idea of a new mistress, but you need to put her in her place."

Verity retrieved her basket of ribbon and said her goodbyes. Liza followed Verity through the house and onto the front porch. "I know you're not going to ask me to help with those wreaths," Liza said, "but I wouldn't have done it anyway."

"Then we are in agreement that you won't be helping," Verity responded with icy politeness.

"If you know what's good for you, you won't disturb that grave," Liza went on.

Verity narrowed her eyes. "Do you have something to say about my mother?"

She was ready to pick a quarrel, but Liza just smiled nastily. "Not your mother — *her*." The girl glanced back at the house, then leaned forward and whispered, "Asenath was a witch, you know."

"How would you know?" Verity asked. "She was dead before you were born."

"Her family's chock-full of witches. People say there's a blood curse on the lot of them."

"People are ignorant," Verity retorted, eyeing Liza up and down so the girl would know exactly which people she meant.

Liza persisted. "Why do you think they put that cage on her grave?"

Verity knew she ought not to respond, but she couldn't help herself. "Why do *you* think?"

"To make sure she didn't get out. In your mother's case, it was only a precaution, but with Asenath . . . there was reason for concern." Liza's smile was sinister now. "In Catawissa sometimes the dead don't stay where you put them."

Verity went home heartsick.

Her father clearly hadn't told her the whole story. There was some stain on her mother's reputation, something to do with the girl buried next to her. The two cages served as a reminder, making sure no one in town ever forgot.

If the two women had done nothing wrong, as her father claimed, why had he needed to bury them in such a fashion? Why hadn't her father and her uncle stood up for their wives?

If Verity was going to marry Nathaniel McClure and make a decent life for herself in this town, she was going to have to find out, and then find a remedy.

As for her cousin Liza — for all Verity cared, the girl could pine away from jealousy.

SEVEN

URING VERITY'S absence, calling cards had been left at the Boone house on behalf of Mrs. James Campbell, Mrs. Timothy Abbet, and Mrs. William McKelvy.

Nate's sisters.

Verity bolted upstairs to rip off Liza's horrible dress and put on one of her own. Mindful of Aunt Clara's advice, she next cornered Beulah in the kitchen and persuaded her to return one of her own calling cards to the McClure house, along with a note stating she would be home to visitors that afternoon.

Then she set about preparing her father's neglected parlor for callers. Stealing a cornflower-blue sash from one of her old dresses, Verity tied back the curtains to let in the sunlight. She found two matching vases in the dining room china cabinet and filled them with boughs from a flowering tree across the road. She removed an ugly tarnished mirror from the wall and replaced it with her mother's portrait. By the time the three women arrived to pay their social call, Verity was dressed, primped, and seated in an improved parlor, determined to make a better impression on the sisters than she had on the brother.

All three of the McClure ladies were dark haired, blue eyed, and rosy cheeked. The younger two, Harriet and Caroline, were twenty and twenty-two, respectively, and the eldest, Anne, almost thirty. Within ten minutes of their arrival, they'd convinced Verity to call them by their pet names—Annie, Carrie, and Hattie. They inquired about her health, they asked about her family in Worcester, they wanted to know her favorite color and whether she preferred needlepoint or embroidery.

But mostly they talked about Nate.

They adored their younger brother and were eager to regale Verity with all his positive traits: he was hard working and loyal and earnest and kind. Verity had to smile and couldn't help but warm toward their description of him. Oh, he had his faults, too. The sisters agreed that he could sometimes be *too* hard working—and probably too earnest—and kind to a fault. In fact, his virtues were his biggest faults. When Annie confessed that no one had ever been able to get Nate to eat carrots, as if this were the most terrible thing she could say about him, Verity laughed.

At first Verity thought they were trying to repair yesterday's disaster, but the more they talked, the more clear it became that they knew nothing about it; they thought Nate had left for Wilkes-Barre without meeting her. Verity felt relieved that he'd kept their ill-fated excursion to himself, another point in his favor. However, his sisters seemed to be the only ones to call him Nate instead of Nathaniel. This reinforced her conviction that their hands had guided all the letters he'd written, including the one in which he invited her to use that name.

"Have you been busy since your arrival?" Carrie asked. "I wouldn't be surprised if the whole town were trying to get a look at Ransloe Boone's daughter! Whom have you met?"

"I haven't had many callers yet," Verity admitted, carefully not mentioning Nate's visit. "Today I spent the entire morning failing to mind the Thomas boys carefully enough and then helping to stitch one up." She described her attempts to prevent her cousins from being trampled, run over, crushed, or maimed. "Luckily for me," she said, "Piper's telling everyone his injury came from fighting a deserter over General Washington's payroll."

"Oh, is he, now?" Carrie leaned forward, her eyes twinkling. "He hasn't said where the payroll's hidden, has he?"

"Carrie!" Annie gasped, tapping her sister with her fan. "For shame!"

"Well, if anyone knows, it's those boys!"

"I'm afraid I don't know what you're talking about," said Verity.

The sisters seemed caught between laughter and embarrassment.

"It's the old story about the Battle of Wyoming and the lost treasure," Hattie said. "Carrie, you silly thing! All the boys play that game; it doesn't mean anything! Nate used to act it out when he was little. He made me play old Silas all the time, running through the swamp and knifing people —"

Annie exclaimed, "Hattie!"

Verity laughed. "I don't know the story, but that does sound like what they were playing."

"It was part of the Battle of Wyoming, in the War for Independence," Carrie said.

"I learned about it at school." Verity cast her mind back. "As I recall, we lost."

"The Americans were ambushed and routed," Hattie confirmed. "Afterward the British ordered the Indians to burn all the homesteads in the area."

"The Indians were working with the British?"

"Indeed. Mohawks, mostly," said Carrie. "With French blood. They had a score to settle with the Americans."

"Dutch blood, too," put in Hattie.

"Not Dutch," Annie corrected.

Hattie pursed her lips. "Yes, Dutch. I know there's Vanderpooles in that line."

"Very true! The name was shortened to Poole somewhere along the way." Carrie raised her eyebrows at Verity. "Your Beulah Poole's ancestors were on the wrong side of that war, and most people around here never forgot it."

"The British captured or killed most of the patriot soldiers," Hattie continued, "but according to legend, some of the men got away with a whole packet of gold coins, a payroll for the Continental army. They disappeared into a swamp—"

"Along with all the settlers who were trying to escape the Indian raiders," added Annie.

"And none of them ever came out again." Hattie lowered her voice to a sepulchral tone. "We call that place the Shades of Death now." Verity shuddered obligingly, and Hattie appeared gratified.

"Well," Carrie said, "one man came out—with the gold. Silas Clayton."

"I don't believe it," Annie replied. "His descendants live here still, and they're as poor as dirt."

"Because the army caught up with him a few years later and shot him for desertion," Harriet retorted. "And no one ever found where he hid the gold."

Carrie turned to Verity again. "Over the years there've been stories of gold coins turning up. Boys—and grown men, too—have been searching the swamp for almost a century, looking for the lost payroll."

"No one ever found it, though," said Annie.

"As far as we know," murmured Hattie slyly.

Hattie and Carrie burst into giggles, and Annie swatted them both with her fan. Verity looked back and forth among the three of them, smiling. "I would like very much to share the joke."

"It's not a joke," Annie said, "only a silly rumor."

"I'm sorry, Verity," Carrie said. "It's just that your father and your uncle were known to be ardent treasure hunters when they were younger."

"My father?"

Annie nodded regretfully. "He spent half his youth trudging through the swamp looking for that payroll."

"Well, boys will be boys," Verity murmured. It did sound like the kind of thing her uncle would do. But her father . . . ?

"Very true. Every inch of that swamp has probably been searched by now." Carrie looked at Verity from beneath coyly lowered lashes. "Some people say the lost treasure isn't really all that lost."

When the sisters were ready to depart, they hugged Verity affectionately, as if she were already a member of their family. Annie, in particular, held her close and kissed her cheek. "I remember your mother as if it were yesterday," she said unexpectedly, glancing at the portrait of Sarah Ann Boone. "I was only fourteen when she died, and I was brokenhearted."

With effort, Verity managed to bite back her questions. *What was she like? Why was she buried that way? What had she done?* She couldn't ask Nate's sisters questions like that on their first meeting. Instead, she thanked Annie for her kind words.

The eldest McClure sister fluffed Verity's curls fondly. "I remember you, too, when you were a baby. Such a beautiful, golden-haired angel! How I loved to come down here and hold you! There were nothing but dark-haired scamps at my house."

"She means us," exclaimed Carrie, putting an arm around Hattie's waist. "Dark-haired scamps!"

Verity laughed. She wished her meeting with Nate had gone half as well as this one had. Still, if she could get along with the sisters, she ought to be able to rectify her gauche mistakes with Nate.

On Friday.

Late that evening, Verity heard a loud thumping outside her room. She rose from the chair at the dressing table where she'd been composing a letter to Polly and went out to the second floor hallway.

The narrow door between her father's room and her

own, which led to the attic stairs, stood open. She poked her head into the cramped, boxed-in space and discovered her father easing a large wooden trunk down the steep, curved staircase. Verity went to help him, grabbing a worn leather handle. It was heavy, and her father called out gruffly, "Watch yourself, child!"

Beulah peeked around the doorway of her room at the end of the hall. She crossed her arms and watched them, her nut-brown face disapproving. After they had managed to get the thing down without injury, she disappeared back into her room.

Verity blew dust off the trunk. "What is this?" she asked. Briefly, she thought of Revolutionary War treasure, but her father didn't seem like the sort of man who would hide a fortune in gold coins in his attic.

Ransloe Boone cleared his throat awkwardly. "I'm ashamed you had to come across your mother's grave by accident," he said. "And I'm sorry you know so little about her. I'd like to make that up to you, if I can."

Leaning over, he briskly unbuckled the leather straps on the trunk, then swung open the lid. Dresses, handkerchiefs, bonnets, little wooden boxes, sachets, and bottles of toiletry items filled the trunk. Verity realized she was looking at her mother's possessions.

"There's more upstairs," her father said. "Dress patterns and fabric and books. Boxes she stored away over the years. You can have anything of hers you want."

He dragged the trunk into Verity's room and looked around while she dusted it off. "Getting crowded in here," he remarked.

"My trunks can go to the attic," Verity said. "I'll have everything I need out of them by tomorrow morning. Thank you, Father. This is a wonderful gift." She hesitated. Her mother's trunk served as an apology, but an actual conversation would make a better one. "I did not mean to accuse you yesterday. I only wanted to know—"

Ransloe Boone backed away, his expression ending their discussion like a shutter closing off a window. "You'll have to trust me, Verity," he said gruffly. "I did the best for her I could under difficult circumstances." Then, with a muttered "Good night," he left and pulled the door shut behind him.

Verity was drawn first to the collection of boxes inside the trunk. Most were made of wood, varying from the size of a prayer book to an egg, but one was inlaid with mother-of-pearl and another was made of silver and had a felt lining. Verity sat down on the floor and opened them all with a sense of awe. Some held pins; one held sewing supplies. The box with the pearl inlay held a stack of calling cards imprinted with her mother's name: *Mrs. Ransloe Boone*. In the silver box she discovered a cache of photographs.

One of the first to catch her eye was a portrait of a very young and surprisingly handsome Ransloe Boone.

In another photograph she recognized Maryett Gaines, seated with a sleeping baby on her lap who was most likely Polly. *Ransloe's cousins,* someone — probably Sarah Ann — had written on the back.

In the next photograph to come out of the box she recognized Uncle John, but the girl with him in the picture surprised her. She'd thought her mother, Sarah Ann, was lovely, but this young woman possessed an astonishing otherworldly beauty. *Asenath and John* — Verity knew it even before she saw the back. Now she understood the dreamy look that had come over her uncle's face when she'd mentioned his first wife, and she felt a pang of sympathy for Aunt Clara. Asenath looked like a princess in a fairy-tale book. The wide-set eyes in her heart-shaped face must have been the lightest blue. Her fair hair, completely colorless in the photograph, was worn in loops and loops of braids that hung down over both her shoulders. Even her dress was white.

She wondered if Liza Thomas had ever seen a picture of Asenath. The girl in this photograph couldn't have been a witch.

EIGHT

ERITY PLANNED on her second visit to the cemetery being more productive than her first. She went armed with a hand trowel and two baskets full of forget-me-nots and ivy from Aunt Clara's garden. When she knelt to arrange the plants, however, she noticed that the stone with her mother's initials lay upside down inside the cage. Puzzled at first, Verity concluded that someone had pried it up and turned it over, perhaps by inserting a crowbar through the latticework.

Shocked and angry, she looked around—at the cemetery, the woods, up the road—as if the culprit might still be lurking nearby. When her eyes landed on the minister's house across the road, she decided the time was right to pay a visit.

Reverend White, a rabbity man of about forty years,

welcomed her readily enough — at least until he learned what she wanted. "Move the graves?" he said incredulously.

"No." Verity sighed. He hadn't been listening. "Enlarge the cemetery. Simply rebuild one end of the wall around those two graves and have the ground consecrated."

The minister shook his head in a worried way. "I don't think that's possible. Our congregation has been saving to build a new church. I wouldn't want to divert funds to some lesser matter now."

"It's not a lesser matter to me," Verity snapped. Then she forced herself to smile politely. Aunt Maryett had always cautioned her about flies and honey. "The current placement of the graves must be an embarrassment to you, Reverend. Surely you'd like to see it rectified? Why were my mother and aunt buried off the grounds in the first place?"

"It was before my time here."

"But surely you must know!"

"My wife grew up in town," he conceded. "She said there were accusations the women engaged in heathen practices. I don't know if there was any proof."

"Then there's no obstacle to rebuilding the cemetery wall around them," Verity concluded. "They cannot remain where they are, Reverend! It's shameful. Why, someone even knocked over the stone inside my mother's . . ." She hesitated, not wanting to use the word *cage*.

"Again?" He sighed. Verity looked at him aghast. "It's the iron cages. People seem to believe they're protecting something valuable."

"Like treasure?" Now it was the minister's turn to look startled, and Verity smiled grimly. "I've been in Catawissa only three days, and I've already heard about that payroll twice. Who would have hidden it under a gravestone?" Her eyes widened as she remembered what Nate's sisters had said about treasure hunters. "*My father?* That's the most ridiculous thing I've ever heard."

"It is indeed."

"Then we are in agreement you'll move the stone wall?" Verity stood up and smoothed her skirt.

The minister stammered and finally allowed that he would "give the matter serious consideration."

Verity eyed him shrewdly. If he thought he could put her off with vague promises, he didn't know whom he was dealing with. "Who has the keys to the locks on those cages?" she asked.

"Why, the groundskeeper does."

"I want the keys. I'll tend those graves myself from now on." Verity smiled politely. "I expect I'll be visiting quite often until things are put right."

The urgent knocking on the front door came late at night, but Verity was lying awake anyway—her mind flitting between the party the next day and the difficulties with her mother's grave. Lighting a candle, she went to the window and looked down. Someone with a lantern stood on the porch.

At this time of night it could hardly be good news.

Throwing a shawl over her nightdress, she hurried down the stairs, rapping on her father's door to rouse him as she passed.

When Verity opened the front door, Clara Thomas held up the lantern. "Aunt Clara!" Verity exclaimed. "What's wrong?"

"Is someone hurt or sick?" Ransloe Boone asked, half stumbling down the steps, befuddled with sleep. From the top of the stairs Beulah peered down at them.

"Yes, but not at my house," Aunt Clara replied. She turned her gaze on Verity. "Have you ever attended a birth?"

A few minutes later, dressed in an old frock, Verity dashed out of the house and met Aunt Clara at her horse and trap. She had attended two births. The delivery of Aunt Maryett's sixth child, when Verity was fifteen, had been quick and simple. But the other—the lying-in of a woman who lived across the street in Worcester—had taken three days. The baby had not survived, and a week later the mother had died of childbed fever.

"Who is it?" she asked as her aunt urged the horse forward.

"Cissy Clayton." When Verity shook her head, Aunt

Clara cast her a sidelong glance. "You haven't met the Claytons yet? Well, prepare yourself. They're not the cream of Catawissa society. Cissy must be in a bad way, or they would not have summoned help. I thought I might need an extra pair of hands, and Liza's no good for this. She hasn't got the stomach for it."

The horse and trap took them past the church and parallel to the river. Her aunt directed the horse into the woods, where the road grew even more narrow and rough. The road ended at a ramshackle one-story house.

With Verity at her heels, Aunt Clara marched up and opened the front door without knocking. Inside, a thin woman with hunched shoulders and greasy hair wrung her hands at the sight of them. "Eli didn't want me to send for you, Clara. But it's been a day and a half . . ."

"That's too long, Idella," Aunt Clara chided.

Verity looked around, trying to hide her distaste. The house reeked of sour milk, unwashed bodies, and liquor. Despite the lateness of the hour, there were children still awake, romping with their dogs amid broken-down furniture. None of them—dogs, children, or furniture—looked as if they'd ever been washed.

The downtrodden woman led them to another room, where the expectant mother—a girl not much older than Verity—lay. She was obviously too tired and weak to scream anymore; each new labor pain left her rigid and helpless. Verity eyed her with worry. She was nothing but skin and bones, her eyes hollowed, her light-brown hair stringy with sweat and tears. The sheets of the bed were fouled, and the stench was unbearable.

"The baby's breech," Aunt Clara proclaimed after a brief examination.

The girl's father hovered in the room like a vulture, his eyes narrow with suspicion and resentment. He was perhaps sixty years of age, reeking of whisky and clothes that might never have seen water. "Meddlesome woman," he muttered, and it was unclear whether he meant his wife or Clara Thomas.

"Bring me a bucket of fresh water," Aunt Clara ordered him, then turned to the wife. "Put a pot on to boil and bring me a cup for brewing tea."

Once they'd left the room—the man mumbling darkly under his breath—Verity's aunt bent over the pregnant girl and plucked a small cloth bag from around her neck, snapping the string that held it there.

"What're you doing?" the girl gasped, her hand flying to her bare throat.

"I can't have you relying on charms, Cissy," Aunt Clara said shortly, opening a window and tossing the little bag out. "You're going to have to work hard tonight." Then she removed packets of herbs and a small glass bottle from her satchel. "I hope you're as steady as you claim," she said to Verity.

A strong draft of tea, heavily laced with a sedative,

made Cissy pliant. Verity held the girl still, comforted her mother, fended off her father's angry protests, and watched with interest while Aunt Clara did her work. A foot emerged, and then another, followed by a skinny wet body—a boy. When the head finally appeared, the girl tried to sit up to see the baby, and Verity, smothering her own gasp of horror, forced her back onto the bed.

The baby didn't have a face.

"Jesus, Mary, and Joseph, protect us!" Eli Clayton shouted from across the room. He clenched his fist and strode forward as if to smite the infant, while his wife fell back against the wall and hid her face.

Aunt Clara wiped her hand across the baby's head, pulling away the sheath of skin obscuring it. "It's just a caul," she said, lifting the child up by his ankles and smacking him on the bottom. The baby, his face now revealed to be as normal as any, inhaled sharply and opened his mouth to cry.

Clayton was not satisfied. "'Tis the Devil's child," he yelled, his fist still raised. Alarmed, Verity let go of Cissy and moved between him and the baby. "The child has no earthly father. My daughters carry the family stain. This one lay with the Devil in the Shades and bears his child!"

"No, Eli, she lay with Tommy Hicks behind Cahill's granary," Aunt Clara snapped. "Half the town knows that, including Tommy's wife."

· · ·

After Cissy's mother had cooed over the baby and handed him back to her daughter, both the elder Claytons left the room. "He'll never die a drowning death," Verity remarked as her aunt packed up the satchel.

"What do you mean?"

"That's what they say. A child born with a caul over his face will never drown." Verity yawned. "It's just a superstition."

Her aunt sighed, glancing at the exhausted girl on the bed with the tiny infant in her arms. "A Clayton bastard, born arse backward, with a caul over his face? I think he stands a fair chance of being drowned in a sack, like an unwanted puppy, before the week is out."

Verity gasped. "You don't mean that?"

"You'd be surprised what the Claytons do to their own." Aunt Clara closed the bag and looked at her niece. "You were very helpful, Verity. You'd probably make a fine midwife, just like your mother."

"Was she?" Verity was tired now, and even her pride could not keep the plaintiveness out of her voice. "I've heard some horrid things since I came back." She didn't say that some of them came from Clara Thomas's daughter.

"Sarah Ann was an excellent midwife," her aunt said flatly. "She just chose the wrong apprentice."

NINE

HE COOL night air was refreshing after the close quarters of the birthing room. Verity yawned again and rubbed her eyes, looking forward to her bed. Aunt Clara climbed into the trap and said before Verity could join her, "The reins are caught on the horse's collar. Will you go and free them?"

Verity nodded and walked around to the horse's head. He sniffed at her curiously as she ran her hands over his collar. The lantern had gone out, and after fumbling around in nearly total darkness, her hands located the bit and then the rein. "It feels free to me, Aunt Clara."

"It's the one on the other side."

Holding the horse's head, Verity stepped in front of him and reached for the opposite rein.

A sudden sharp crack split the air. The horse whinnied

in surprise and lurched forward. Caught off-guard, Verity lost her footing. She hung on to the bridle, but the startled horse shook his head and plunged on, and she lost her hold. She went down hard on her back and was immediately pinned as his front hoof landed on her dress.

Verity shrieked and tried to protect her head. Panicked, the horse bucked in his harness. His back legs narrowly missed crushing her own, and the front wheel of the trap hurtled directly toward her. She had enough time to draw in breath, but not enough to scream.

Inches from smashing Verity in the face, the wheel jerked to a halt. The horse protested once more, stamping his feet, and then was still.

"Verity!" her aunt shouted. "Verity, are you all right?"

She wasn't sure. Her arms and legs were trembling so badly, she could hardly take stock. Only fear of the trap moving again forced her to uncurl herself and crawl out from beneath it. "I'm all right, Aunt Clara," she said, her voice shaking.

"Eli Clayton, what in the name of Providence is the matter with you, frightening my horse like that? You could have killed my niece!"

Verity rose unsteadily to her feet. Aunt Clara was standing upright in the trap. Eli Clayton was holding the horse's bridle. Verity hadn't seen him follow them out of the house.

Clayton glowered at Clara Thomas. "You're mad, woman," he grunted. "Take yourself off my property and don't come back."

Scrambling to obey, Verity climbed aboard the trap. She was still trembling and barely seated when Eli Clayton released the horse and slapped him on the rear. The beast, which seemed nearly as shaken as Verity, started off with a jolt, heading for home.

Aunt Clara stopped the trap in front the Boone house. "Thank goodness you're not hurt," she said. "That man's as crazy as a loon. He and half his kin should be locked away."

"I'm fine, Aunt Clara. I was lucky."

"You hit the ground pretty hard. You might be in pain tomorrow, and it's your party, isn't it?" She opened her bag and felt inside. "Let me give you something to take the ache away."

"Thank you, but that's not necessary."

"Nonsense." Her aunt pressed a paper packet into her hands. "A generous pinch, dissolved in water. Two if you want to be certain you're not stiff tomorrow. Take it before going to bed tonight."

It was easier to accept the packet than to argue. Verity bade her aunt good night, climbed down, and started for the house. Rubbing her eyes wearily, she raised her head and saw a dim glow in one of the upstairs rooms. Her room.

Had she left a candle lit? That was a careless thing to do and very unlike her. Alarmed, she strode briskly toward the house, and the light suddenly vanished.

Verity froze. Someone was in her room.

She marched up the steps of the porch. The front door opened for her readily. Her father never locked his doors. Probably nobody in Catawissa locked doors.

Inside, the house was dark. Verity stood still, listening, but she heard no footsteps, no sound of breathing other than her own. She knew the house well enough by now to find the stairs without a light and creep silently to the second floor. Both her father's door and Beulah's door were closed, and she heard no movement inside either chamber. Her own door was ajar, and she was quite sure she'd left it that way, but her heart quickened as she entered the room.

She tossed the packet of medicine onto the dressing table, then groped for and found the candle she'd left there hours ago, cold and unlit. She struck a match, touched it to the wick, and held the candle aloft. Her shawl and nightdress lay strewn across the bed, just where she'd left them. As near as she could tell, nothing was out of place. Then she turned back to the dressing table.

Nate's letters lay upon the table, and propped up

against them stood the photograph of John Thomas and his very young, very beautiful first wife, Asenath. Verity picked up the photograph, puzzled. She didn't think she had left it out.

She held very still and listened to the house again. At night, too, it was far more silent than her old home in Worcester. Polly and Susan would have been elbowing each other in bed and complaining while Polly's cat burrowed into the covers beside them, purring loudly. Uncle Benjamin's snores sometimes rattled the windows, and two-year-old Alfred frequently cried out in the night.

Verity wondered, as she readied herself for bed, how she could feel so alone here and still have the urge to jam the chair from her dressing table under the knob of her door.

She slept as late as she dared the next morning, but there was much to do. She put on her baking dress and tied up her hair.

Setting aside the untouched packet of medicine Aunt Clara had given her, she put the photograph of her uncle and his first wife back into the silver box and returned it to her mother's trunk. Nate's letters she stored in a drawer out of sight. They didn't have as much appeal now that she knew how many hands had gone into them. She and Nate McClure would have to begin over again, starting today.

Downstairs, she found Beulah carrying two buckets of water from the well pump. Barely five feet tall and ninety pounds, the old woman looked frail, but Verity had already learned enough about Beulah Poole to know better. When she insisted on taking one of the buckets herself, Verity was not surprised to discover it so heavy that she needed both hands to carry it. She could not have carried both.

"Beulah," she said, trying not to slop water all over herself, "I have baking to do for the McClure party today. I'm sorry if that disturbs your plans."

The housekeeper grimaced. "Just tell me what you want, Miss Verity, and I'll make it." She shoved the kitchen door open with her shoulder and held it that way for Verity to pass.

"No, thank you. It's a meaningless gesture if I bring something to the party I didn't make myself." Verity lugged the bucket inside and set it on the floor, then straightened up and faced Beulah. Her aunt had told her to take command of the household, but Verity wasn't used to ordering servants around. *Polish the silver*, she could have said. Or *Beat the parlor rug*. Instead, she blurted out, "You can have the morning off."

Beulah raised her eyebrows. She set down her bucket, then left the house without another word. Verity felt like a fool, trying to bribe the housekeeper into liking her.

She spent what remained of the morning baking four

dozen jam tarts with the preserves she'd purchased in town. It was lonely work without the Gaines girls working beside her and the boys rampaging through the kitchen. Verity consoled herself with the thought that she'd soon have three sisters-in-law for company, and if she really missed rampaging boys, she could visit the Thomas house.

When she looked through the kitchen window and saw Beulah returning, Verity met her at the back door and handed over the tarts in a beribboned basket. "Please deliver these to Mrs. McClure."

Beulah tried to see past her into the kitchen, but Verity stood firmly in the way. "That bad, is it?" The woman glared up at her accusingly.

"I'll have it clean by the time you return," Verity promised. "And then I'll need your help upstairs."

After she'd cleaned the jam-smeared kitchen, Verity devoted the afternoon to curling and pinning up her hair and dressing for the party. She selected her very best gown — a green bodice and scalloped skirt over a full ivory underskirt shot through with gold thread. She'd been lucky to find such a luscious, decadent fabric in postwar Worcester. Verity doubted anyone in Catawissa would have anything as grand.

Beulah appeared as requested and helped lace up the corset. The old woman pulled on the strings so hard, Verity thought it must be revenge for losing control of the kitchen that morning. However, she couldn't complain about the results. While admiring the lines of the dress in the old mirror she'd taken from the parlor, Verity spotted an approving gleam in the housekeeper's eye. "Well, what do you think?" she asked. "Will this make him forget what I was wearing the last time he saw me?"

Beulah's mouth twitched. "Possibly, Miss Verity."

Pleased to have provoked even a glimmer of a smile, Verity laughed and gave her a quick hug, startling both of them.

Verity met her father in the second floor hallway. He was looking uncomfortable in his best clothes—a suit at least ten years old—and he'd been to the barber. Verity was delighted and relieved. She'd been half afraid he would wear his work clothes.

"You're very handsome today, Father," she said, fluffing his outdated cravat so that it looked less squashed and defeated.

"I know it's old," Ransloe said defensively. "I think I bought it for your grandmother's funeral."

"You look nice in it."

"I'll get myself fitted for a new one," he promised, raising his eyes to hers. "For your wedding."

TEN

HE MCCLURE house was everything Verity had imagined: large and rambling, with multiple additions and a huge lawn backing onto the woods. The verandah, which ran around three sides of the house, had been decorated for the occasion with daisy garlands, and when the Boones arrived, a child excitedly rang a giant cowbell hanging from the verandah roof.

The female McClures swarmed like bees around Verity. Towing a reluctant Ransloe Boone behind, they swept her into the back garden, where the party was already under way. Fanny McClure, Nate's mother, nearly babbled her greeting, kissing her future daughter-in-law on both cheeks. Verity thought Mrs. McClure looked exactly like her daughters, red cheeked and bright-eyed with an unquenchable spirit. Annie, Carrie, and Hattie all hugged

Verity and exclaimed over her dress until she was pink with embarrassment. Then the sea of exuberant faces parted to clear a path for her intended.

Nate, too, had been to the barber for a cut and a severe combing, although his hair was already bouncing back to its tousled state. His fashionably cut navy-blue frock coat complimented those dark locks and his blue eyes. He swept one glance over Verity's carefully arranged golden curls and the gown that matched her eyes — and there, at last, was the smile she'd imagined, which turned his stern features into something entirely more attractive. The watching crowd, believing this to be their first sight of each other, sighed with relief when Verity's lips curled upward in an answering smile.

"Verity, my dear," exclaimed Mrs. McClure, looking back and forth between them with eyes alight. "It's my pleasure to introduce my son, Nathaniel."

Ransloe Boone looked confused. "What are you talking about, Fanny? They've already met."

"Days ago," Nate confirmed. Without any explanation, he offered his arm to Verity and led her away.

It seemed the entire town had turned out for Verity Boone's welcome-home party. In her first round of introductions she had no hope of learning which of the half dozen children belonged to which sister. Their spouses were more easily distinguished: Hattie's husband leaned on a cane, and Annie's husband had been deafened in one ear. Carrie's husband was the only one left healthy and hale after the war.

Once she had caught up with the engaged couple, Nate's mother introduced Verity to every prominent landowner in the county. No sooner was that ordeal finished than the minister's wife, Mrs. White, appeared with the church society trailing behind. The one person she wanted to talk to was the one she barely saw. Every time she and Nate had a moment together, one or the other of them was swept away by an insistent guest. Eventually, Verity found herself facing the women she'd seen in the general store and their sour-faced daughters.

Verity was not willing to make false statements such as "pleased to meet you" even for the sake of social nicety, so she simply repeated their names when introduced: "Mrs. Eggars, Mrs. Applebee." Nevertheless, her eyes flashed an unspoken message: *I heard what you said in the store.*

"Welcome home, Miss Boone," said Mrs. Eggars, not bound by the same honesty. Her cold smile conveyed a message too: *You were meant to.*

Mrs. Applebee waited until Mrs. White had stepped away to rake Verity over with resentful eyes. "I must admit, we were all surprised by this hasty engagement," she said. "Not long ago, it seemed Nathaniel was on the point of stating intentions to my Janey."

Janey Applebee simpered, and Mrs. Eggars quickly added, "Or Amelie."

Amelie flashed a set of horsey teeth. "The way Nathaniel used to stare at me in church, you would've thought we were already engaged."

Verity couldn't see anything worth looking at, let alone staring at. "It must have been a passing fancy."

"It's a wonder you even wanted to come back and live in Catawissa," Mrs. Eggars said, "considering . . ."

"Considering what?" Verity snapped, but Fanny McClure reappeared at that point, bringing an end to the conversation. The Applebees and the Eggarses withdrew with shallow curtsies, and Nate's mother carted her off to meet someone else.

Verity felt her smile waver, stretched beyond its tolerance. Now she eyed every friendly face with skepticism, wondering how many of them were false. Were they all seeing her as the daughter of a woman disgraced and buried in shame? As an outsider who stole Nathaniel McClure from their own daughters?

She wanted to talk to Nate, wanted a moment to herself, wanted to *eat*. Although platters of fried chicken and tea sandwiches, along with her own jam tarts, lay under a pavilion tent, Verity hadn't managed to come within a dozen steps of the table.

She saw her father on the edge of the lawn, looking

as if he might disappear into the woods and head for home on foot. She started edging her way toward him, but one of Mrs. McClure's friends pinned her down with a long, dull monologue about charity drives. Then Nate appeared. He clapped Ransloe Boone on the shoulder, exchanged a few words, and led him back to the party. From the way they were looking at the McClure orchards and the manner in which her father perked up and responded, Verity supposed they were talking about their common interest — which was farming, not Verity.

That was a very unworthy thought, and she was ashamed of herself immediately. She was hungry and thirsty, and she wished she were talking to Nate instead of to this tiresome woman, but that was no reason to be petulant. "You can be downright tart on an empty stomach!" Polly had always chided her.

Tart! She wished she had one.

With a determined smile, Verity ended her conversation and turned to follow her father and Nate. If they both loved the farmland of this valley, then she would make an effort to appreciate its virtues. She would ask Nate to give her a tour of his family orchards now. If her father wished to come along, that would be very nice. And if Verity and Nate slipped away from the party and went alone, that might be even better.

Nate looked up as she approached, and once again, she saw that smile she'd been hoping for.

"Miss Boone!" someone called from behind her.

She turned around and found herself presented with a cup of punch by the doctor's apprentice, Hadley Jones. In his other hand he held a plate with a tea sandwich and a cupcake.

"Oh, goodness, how I need this!" she exclaimed, taking the cup and sipping the punch.

"I thought you might." Verity was struck by the young man's laughing eyes, as clear and blue as the sky. "The guest of honor—and you haven't had a bite to eat or a drop to drink." Gazing at him over the brim of the cup, she wondered how closely he must have been watching to know that.

He looked exceedingly smart in a well-cut frock coat and matched trousers, livened by a copper-colored pinstripe vest and a brilliant blue tie. His ginger curls glinted like gold in the late-afternoon sun. Verity looked pointedly at the plate in his hand. "Is that for me as well?"

"Doctor's orders," he said cheerfully, holding it out. When Verity snatched up the cupcake and took a bite, he grinned. "A young lady who eats the cake before the sandwich! I approve!"

Verity tried not to laugh with her mouth full. Here, at least, was someone whose friendliness seemed honest. "I might not have time for both," she said in her own defense. "And how would I feel if I'd eaten the sandwich and never got to the cake at all?"

"A very sensible decision. Please don't let me interrupt your enjoyment of it." He turned his head and whistled while she laughingly ate the rest of the cake and — with a quick glance to see if anyone was looking — licked off her fingers. The doctor's apprentice made a point of peeking to see if she was finished, then turned toward her. "Am I right in believing that the delightful jam tarts were your work, Miss Boone?"

"They were mine." She sipped from the punch cup again and took the sandwich from the plate he still held within her reach. "I don't know if they were delightful or not."

"Every single one of them is gone," he told her. "Would I be endearing myself to you if I told you I ate three of them — or just embarrassing myself?"

She caught her breath in surprise. This young man was flirting with her! Didn't he realize this wasn't just a welcome-home party — that it was an engagement party as well?

Guiltily she looked around for Nate. Her father was talking to the minister over by the tent, and Verity's betrothed was nowhere in sight. Feeling uncomfortable, she looked back at Hadley Jones, meaning to excuse herself — but before she could, three small children darted between them.

Jones's free hand shot out, catching the last one in line by the collar and hauling him back. Piper Thomas wriggled like a trout on the hook. "How's your head?" the young man asked, bending to examine it. "Have you been picking at the stitches?"

"Mama said she'd switch me if I did," the boy replied.

Satisfied with what he saw, Jones released Piper, who threw himself headlong across the lawn and landed on one of Nate's nephews. A wrestling match ensued.

"Oh, my goodness!" exclaimed Verity.

"Let them go," Jones said, taking her by the arm and leading her away. "It's all in a day's work. Between the Thomases and the McClure clan, I knew enough to come prepared." Laying the empty plate aside on a table, he reached into his coat and came out with a handkerchief. Unfolding it, he showed Verity a needle and a length of suture, neatly folded inside.

She broke out into peals of laughter. Whether he was flirting with her or was just a charming young man with an amiable personality, she couldn't help but like him. "I hope you aren't called upon for action," she said. "You deserve an evening off."

"A doctor is never fully off duty," he said with mock solemnity. "It won't be the first time I've done surgery on the field, and I know I can count on you to hold the patient down and not faint." He nodded at the tent. "We can clear one of those tables — sweep the dishes off — and lay our patients out."

"We'd have the church society swooning left and

right," Verity predicted. Then she sobered a bit. "Did you serve in the war?"

The laughter in his eyes dimmed. "I enlisted at fifteen and served as a doctor's aide. It was a far cry from apprenticeship under Dr. Robbins, and not so much doctoring as butchering. We lost hundreds of men simply for lack of clean water and soap."

Verity recoiled, and seeing her reaction, he stepped away from her. "I'm sorry," he said. "That's not a pretty thought for a young lady at her engagement party." So he *did* know. Verity stepped back a pace as well, uncomfortable in the knowledge that she had encouraged his attention.

"Good evening, Miss Boone," Hadley Jones said abruptly, "and best wishes to you. Nathaniel McClure is . . . a very good . . . farmer."

The sun was setting beyond the mountains when Verity finally caught up with Nate. There was no sign of a smile as he looked down on her, his whole demeanor stiff, his eyes dark in the fading light. "Having a good time?" he asked shortly.

"I was," she said, gazing up at him with apprehension.

He nodded. "No one of interest left at the party?"

Verity felt her heart flutter with distress. "There are lots of interesting people here."

"But no one special," he persisted, "now you've finally come over to talk to me."

"I've been looking for you for hours."

"I've been here the whole time."

She knew exactly what had upset him. "I don't know anyone here very well, Nate. I've tried to be friendly to all your mother's guests—"

"Some more than others." He paused, opened his mouth, shut it again, and then went on as if he couldn't help himself. "You knew Hadley Jones well enough to eat off his plate."

She gasped at the unfairness of that. "He brought me some refreshment—which was more than you did."

"Was I supposed to feed you?"

"You hardly have room to talk," she snapped. "How many former sweethearts do you have at this party?"

He stared at her, astounded. "What are you talking about?"

A bell rang—the cowbell on the verandah of the house. Verity and Nate turned as one to find Fanny Mc-Clure pulling on the bell rope. "I hope everyone has had a good time—and a good plateful!" she called out.

"And a good tankard!" shouted one man, raising a mug full of ale.

"Aye!" Mrs. McClure hollered back. "I'm sure you've had that, Amos!" While the crowd laughed, she scanned the various groupings in her yard until she spotted the pair she was looking for. Her features softened with tenderness. "But let's not forget what we've come here to celebrate. One of our Catawissa daughters has come back to us."

Across the wide expanse of the McClure yard, guests turned to look at Verity. She stiffened under the regard of so many people.

Nate drew an uneasy breath. "Verity, I'm sorry," he whispered. She looked up at him, thinking this was an awkward moment to apologize for his fit of jealousy. But Nate's eyes were on his mother, not on her.

Mrs. McClure went on. "Of course, most of you know we're welcoming her not just back to our town but into our family too. My husband, Michael—" She paused and placed a hand against her heart. "My Michael—God rest his soul—saved the ring his father gave his mother for twenty-five years, wanting his son to have it next." She smiled and shook her head. "But then, you know, we had all these girls—"

"Oh, Mother!" cried Carrie, causing a wave of laughter.

"But Michael knew we'd have our boy someday, and there would come a time when that boy would give that ring to a girl of his choosing."

Verity turned and stared up at Nate. "I *told* her I didn't want to do it this way," he whispered.

Fanny McClure clasped her hands together tearfully. "Finally," she said, "that day has come."

Every single person on the lawn turned to watch.

Even in the gathering darkness of evening, Verity could see how uncertain and embarrassed Nate was. He frowned and looked around as if hoping someone might offer him a reprieve or a means of escape. Then, giving a sigh of resignation, he reached into the pocket of his coat and removed a gold band set with diamonds.

With all eyes upon her and her mind on the promise she had made, Verity held out her hand. But Nate was holding the ring between his thumb and index finger, as if he expected her to take it from him. When he realized she wanted him to slip it on her finger, he fumbled and shifted his grip, just as Verity, seeing that he wasn't intending to put it on her hand himself, reached out for it. Their hands collided, knocking the ring out of his grasp. Verity imagined it lost in the grass.

Then Nate's left hand darted out and caught it neatly in midair. He offered it to her on his palm, and she accepted it with a trembling hand and put it on her own finger.

Verity looked up and met his dark, troubled eyes.

This was not a very auspicious beginning.

ELEVEN

ERITY WOKE up around dawn and cried. She lay in bed and examined the ring through her tears, running her fingers over the worn gold band and the three diamonds set in it.

He hadn't wanted to give it to her.

It was one thing for Verity to worry that promising marriage to Nathaniel McClure had been a mistake. But it was crushing to imagine he might think the same thing about her.

Over and over, she revisited her behavior at the party. *Had* she been flirtatious with the doctor's apprentice? It was true she found him easy to talk to—much easier than her intended. He had an affable manner that put her at ease, while Nate was just so stiff!

What was she to do, in any case? Break off the

engagement? Tell her father that she'd *rather not* wed the young man he wanted to take on as his partner?

And do what instead? Return to Worcester, a burden on her foster parents until somebody more pleasing took an interest in her?

When the morning light could no longer be denied, she rose from her bed and dressed. For a long time, she sat at her dressing table, turning the McClure ring round and round on her finger. It was too big for her, and after a while she took a ribbon and her sewing scissors and cut a bit of fabric to wrap around the band so it would fit more snugly.

Sometimes things had to be adjusted before they fitted properly.

With a sigh, she opened the trunk.

When she looked at her mother's possessions, she felt conflicting emotions: sadness and longing, curiosity and protectiveness — and a fair amount of anger and resentment. Because of some sort of scandal, her mother had been buried outside the church grounds. Fearing grave robbers, her father and uncle had erected those cages — which, ironically, had attracted more grave robbers, hunting for treasure.

She examined the assortment of boxes again. They told her little — only that her mother had liked to collect boxes. As for the dozen or so sachets in the trunk, each one wrapped in a scrap of cloth and tied with a ribbon, Verity sniffed at them curiously, but they'd long since lost their fragrance.

One by one, she unfolded her mother's dresses. Some were still in very good condition and could be altered to fit her and trimmed in the latest style. Others were not suitable, too worn or outdated to be worth making over, but they would provide fabric for quilting. Verity thought it might be very nice to have a quilt made of her mother's old clothing.

At the bottom of the trunk she found a thin notebook. It was stuck to the wooden boards, and she peeled it off carefully. She expected it to be a recipe booklet or a church pamphlet. Instead, when she opened it, pages and pages of neat handwriting fell open before her eyes.

> Nov 2 – Mrs. Killgore brought peach preserves today. It was very kind of her, considering she gets the gout so bad she can hardly walk.
> Nov 3 – Asenath has been sick too. I hoped she would be spared that.
> Nov 4 – John helped Ransloe with the fall tillage, and I felt well enough to take Verity to church. They baptized a Warner baby today. I was not asked to deliver this one. They got somebody else.

It was a diary! Verity gasped out loud and leafed quickly through the pages. She turned back to that November fourth entry and read her name again in her mother's neat script — *Verity* — and then she started skimming, looking for the capital letter V . . .

> *Oct 15 – Verity can count to 10 but not in the right order.*
>
> *Oct 17 – Beulah thought Verity needed a spanking but Ransloe would not do it.*
>
> *Oct 20 – Verity rode Ransloe like a pony through the house until he was exhausted and I was dying of laughter.*
>
> *Oct 21 – Verity spilled her milk and then said Papa did it. I put her in the corner and told her she must not lie because verity means truth and that is what she should speak.*

As a child, Verity had resolved to speak nothing but the truth, because of her name. She'd always assumed Aunt Maryett had been the one to teach her that.

It had been her mother, and she hadn't even remembered.

Later that day she worked stubbornly over the grave wreaths in the parlor. They were more difficult to craft than she'd anticipated. Although she could clearly see in her mind what she wanted, the twig-and-ribbon reality was simply not shaping up to meet her expectations.

Beulah brought her tea and caught her muttering unladylike words under her breath. The housekeeper's mouth pursed in silent disapproval as she set the tray on the serving table. Verity flung down the wreath in exasperation and turned to her. "What did I do that made you think I deserved a spanking when I was two years old?"

Beulah looked startled. "What are you talking about?"

"My mother wrote in her diary that *you* thought I ought to be spanked, but my father wouldn't do it." Verity glared at her accusingly. Beulah Poole had been the housekeeper here when Verity was a baby, and no one had told her. Shouldn't Beulah or her father have mentioned it?

Beulah's eyes lit with interest. "You have Mrs. Boone's diary?"

"It was in her trunk. So what did I do?"

"You deserved a spanking half a dozen times a day, but no one would give it to you." Beulah walked toward the doorway. "They made you stand over there instead." She pointed at the corner behind the rocking chair on her way out of the room. "You stood there often."

Verity turned toward that corner and was struck by a sudden, vivid memory of being very angry and of having nothing to look at but a pattern of stripes and purple clover. She remembered reaching out and . . .

She stood up, walked across the room, and knelt down. A foot and a half above the floorboards she found a jagged patch of wallpaper that had been glued back in place after spiteful little fingers had torn it away. Verity shook her head in amazement and returned to her wreath, smiling. She never could abide purple clover, and now she knew why.

The smile faded quickly, however, for nothing she did with the wreath satisfied her. The whole structure looked too flimsy, too sparse and bare, just like the cages themselves. She was beginning to wonder if she should dismantle it and start over when Beulah stuck her head in the parlor door.

"Mr. Nathaniel here to see you, Miss Verity."

She felt her heart leap and thump painfully. "Thank you, Beulah. Please send him in."

Beulah shook her head. "He says he's not dressed to come in."

Verity rose and smoothed out her skirts. "Very well." She didn't know why he insisted on visiting her in the middle of his working day, straight from the fields. In Worcester Polly had accepted calls from suitors, and Verity had entertained an admirer or two. None of those young men had ever shown up unannounced like Nate. At least he hadn't caught her covered in flour this time.

She started toward the kitchen, but Beulah stopped her. "Oh no," she said. "I made him go around to the porch."

Verity dared to smile. "We'll teach him yet, Beulah. Won't we?"

The housekeeper met her eyes briefly, and her lips twitched. "Possibly, Miss Verity."

Nate stood awkwardly on the front porch in his work clothes and a shabby hat, which he whipped off when she opened the front door.

"Good afternoon," she greeted him, then looked around helplessly. There was no porch swing, not even a rocker. She couldn't invite him to sit down.

"Hello, Verity." Nate looked just as confused as she felt. She wondered if he needed to be taught how to pay a call on a young lady. She couldn't imagine that his sisters had failed to give him lessons, but maybe he wasn't an apt pupil.

Or maybe he was determined to do things his own way.

"I came down here to . . ." Nate paused and frowned, fidgeting. "I wanted to apologize for last night. All I've done since you arrived is blurt out the wrong thing and then apologize afterward."

It didn't cross Verity's mind to contradict him. She did wonder if she should agree, but that probably wasn't prudent either. So she smiled.

He apparently found that encouraging. "I'm not always a bumbling idiot," he told her. "You make me nervous."

Verity sucked in her breath, partly indignant, partly hurt. "I realize people may consider me outspoken and some may take offense. But I was taught that a woman has a right to express her opinions, and —"

"You're beautiful," he said bluntly, "and I didn't expect you to be."

He might as well have given her a push. She could have sworn the whole porch rocked while she stood there, her mouth agape.

"So I came down here to find out if you've given me up for hopeless yet," Nate continued, "or if I still stand a chance of not being a complete fool in your mind."

Verity had never before met anyone who could so consistently leave her speechless. Silently, she reached out to him, and he enclosed her slim hand in his much bigger one.

Nate didn't seem to know what to say either, but after a moment he opened his hand and looked down at hers, and she realized he'd just noticed she was wearing his ring. He ran a thumb across it, then turned her hand over to look at the ribbon tied to the underside of the band.

"It's a little big," she explained.

He raised his eyes to hers. "I could take it to a jeweler next time I go to Philadelphia. They could make it smaller."

Verity hesitated at the thought of this family heirloom being altered for her. "Won't there be time to do it later?" If she married him, there would be a whole lifetime to get it fixed. And then she wondered why she persisted in adding the conditional *if*.

"Indeed there will be," he agreed.

While she was contemplating the ring and what it meant, a high-pitched squeak caused Verity to withdraw her hand from Nate's. "What was that?" she asked, looking around in alarm. Last night after the party, an opossum had boldly crossed her path between the house and the barn, startling the wits out of her. Who knew what brazen creature might come up on the porch and make itself at home?

"Oh! I almost forgot." Nate stuck one hand into the pocket of his work coat. "I brought you something. You don't have to take him if you don't want to — but I thought of you when I found him." Verity stepped back as he pulled something bedraggled and furry from his pocket. Then she realized what it was and held out her hands with a cry of delight.

Nate handed over a scrawny gray kitten. "You mentioned in your letters that you had a cat back in Worcester, and I thought maybe you were missing him. This one needs a home. I found him half drowned in a ditch this morning."

Verity tucked the kitten under her chin. "It was Polly's cat, but I do miss him. Thank you, Nate."

He looked pleased. "If I came back tomorrow morning, would you accompany me to church?"

"Yes, I'd like that." She smiled up at him. This gift—this little purring handful of fur—was from Nate, not his sisters. It might take patience, but she *would* get to know him before anybody affixed this ring to her finger forever. "Afterward," she said, "if you have the time, maybe you could show me around your orchards."

He ducked his head as if to hide the grin that spread across his face. "Yes," he said. "I'd like that."

TWELVE

T POURED rain on Sunday, so there was no chance of visiting the orchards. Nevertheless, Nate did escort Verity to the Mount Zion Methodist Church. They sat together in the McClure pew, slipping in after the rest of the family was already seated. In sequence, like gears in a clock, Hattie, Carrie, and Annie all leaned forward to peer at the two of them. Simultaneously, their husbands elbowed the three of them back into their seats. Verity smiled and removed her gloves so that all interested parties could see the ring.

After the service people lingered inside, reluctant to go out in the rain. Some offered their well wishes to the engaged couple; others ignored Verity pointedly or whispered among themselves. Reverend White avoided her, probably afraid she would broach the subject of the cemetery wall.

But she seized the opportunity to mention it to her aunt. "A fine idea, Verity," Clara Thomas responded in her calm, unemotional way. "I noticed the flowers at the graves as well. They make a nice touch."

"Thank you for the cuttings, Aunt Clara. I hope they don't get washed away in all this rain."

"The rain will be good for them. Have you finished the wreaths?"

Verity hesitated. Aunt Clara might offer Liza's assistance again. Her cousin was standing in the doorway, staring out at the rain and occasionally sneaking shy glances at Nate from under her bonnet. "I'm finding them more difficult than I anticipated," she admitted at last and explained the problem.

Aunt Clara pulled on her gloves. "You need something more substantial than the branches you're using. Vines would do—thick ones, mature enough to be brown but supple enough to bend. If you follow the cemetery road past the place where we turned right to the Claytons' and go into the woods, you will probably find what you need."

"Thank you," Verity said, breathing a sigh of relief that she wouldn't have to work with Liza.

The rain fell too heavily and steadily for work in the fields that day. With his afternoon suddenly free of obligation, Nate accepted Verity's offer to take a meal at the Boone house. He paid a visit to the kitten, now named

Lucky, and agreed that his new life, sleeping on a pillow by the stove, was a fortunate change in circumstance for the little fellow.

"Beulah complained at first," Verity confided in a whisper, "but I caught her slipping him cream. I think she likes the cat better than she likes me."

Nate gave Verity a startled look, then glanced over her shoulder at the housekeeper. "Don't let Beulah fool you," he said with a grin.

After dinner, Verity's father astonished her by producing an old chess set and challenging Nate. "You want a rematch, boy?"

"Only if you want to lose again, old man," Nate replied glibly.

Verity was once again left speechless. Apparently, Nate and her father knew each other better than she knew either one of them. Settling in to watch them play with Lucky on her lap, she pledged to change that if she could.

Nate stayed later than he meant to, and it pleased her to think she'd made him lose track of time. True, if it hadn't rained all day, he might have left sooner. But she was happy that they'd enjoyed each other's company. She had no desire to pit herself against his farm for his affection; she was rather afraid she'd lose.

"You like him?" her father asked after Nate had left.

"Yes, of course," she replied without thinking, and then was relieved to realize it was true.

"You don't have to marry him, Verity." Ransloe Boone waved his hand. "Ring or no ring—promise or no promise. I gave him permission to write to you, but I was surprised you agreed to the marriage before you met him."

Verity nodded, embarrassed. She'd been caught up in the romance of the moment when Nate had made his proposal, and that regrettable volume of poetry had pushed her over the edge. Still, Nathaniel McClure was the sort of solid and dependable young man any girl ought to desire for a husband. "*You* think he's a good choice. And you'd like to have him as your partner."

"Not a good reason to marry him," her father replied. "Your mother wouldn't like to think I pushed you into marriage just to make *my* life easier."

"I'm content with the match," she assured him.

He nodded slowly, but as he left the room to retire for the night, he muttered, "Rather see you happy than content."

Verity remained downstairs only long enough to see all the candles and lamps put out, then followed him upstairs. When she entered her bedroom, a gust of wind almost snatched the door from her hand. There was just time enough to see her window wide open, the curtains billowing and snapping, before the candle in her hand went out.

She rushed to the window and threw down the sash. Immediately, the curtains fell back into place.

Who had left the window open? Beulah? But why would the housekeeper open a window on a night like this?

Feeling her way in the darkness, she found a matchbox on her dressing table and relit the candle. Then she surveyed the room with dismay. The rain had drenched the bedclothes, and the floor was strewn with white and pink petals that must have blown in through the window. She bent and scooped up a handful of sodden, sweet-smelling flowers. What a horrible mess!

She didn't want to disturb Beulah, who would probably assume Verity had left the window open herself. She stripped the wet coverlet off the bed and mopped up the puddles on the floor. It was only after she finally sat down at her dressing table that she discovered her mother's diary lying there, apparently blown open by the wind. Worried that the pages might have been damaged, she moved the candle closer.

Nov 10 – Asenath has it bad too.

Nov 12 – Feeling no better today. Very tired of being so sick.

Nov 14 – Asenath pins her hopes on Miss Piper's remedies.

For a moment, seeing the diary unharmed, she felt nothing but relief. Then the significance of the dates sank in.

Her mother had died on November 15.

With a trembling hand, she turned the page to read the last thing her mother had ever written:

> *Pains so bad I fear I will lose the baby*
> *Watering like dog*

Verity clapped the diary closed.

In the morning Verity was just as perplexed as she had been the night before. She knew she'd left the window closed and her mother's diary in the trunk.

She picked up the diary again. Up to this point, she'd read it only in small spurts. As hungry as she was to learn more about her mother, it was painful to read.

On October 24, 1852, Sarah Ann Boone had written:

> *I want to name all my children after virtues. Ransloe*
> *agrees but says please choose Patience this time, because*
> *Verity does not have any.*

Verity smiled; she hadn't known her father had a sense of humor.

A few days later, her mother had written:

*We have decided on Patience for a girl and Clement for
a boy.*

The words caught at Verity's heart, and for a moment she
imagined what it might have been like to grow up in this
house with a brother or sister of her own.

She found other things to smile at besides her father's
joke, such as an unexpected mention of Nate.

*Fanny brought her boy down today, and we let the
children play together while we finished the quilt for
Asenath. He is as smart as a whip, but Verity was shy
with him.*

Verity read through these passages and then shut the notebook. She knew the diary came to an abrupt and unfore-
seen stop in the middle of November 1852, and she was
reluctant to face it again.

An hour or so later, Verity walked down to the church to
inspect the plantings at the two graves. She found them
bedraggled but living and fortified their positions, slap-
ping the wet earth back into place around them. Then she
picked up her basket and walked down the road and into
the woods — beyond the place where the road turned and
headed toward the Clayton house. She could hear the running water of the Susquehanna River and knew that as

long as she continued downhill, she was heading in the right direction. Returning to where she started would only be a matter of walking back uphill.

She examined every vine and likely sapling, looking for just what her aunt had described. She found many dry stalks the right diameter that snapped when she bent them and many green shafts too thin to do her any good.

Verity continued downhill, beyond sight of the road, toward the sound of water. The vegetation grew thicker, and she picked her way past pricker bushes and shiny leaves she suspected might be poison ivy. Yesterday's rain had left everything wet, and soon she felt dampness leaking through her shoes. She'd worn old clothing, knowing she'd be on her knees in the cemetery and wandering through the woods afterward, but she didn't like the feel of water squishing around her toes.

She heard the Susquehanna River gurgling in the distance. Just ahead she could see still water covered with so much green scum that it looked as if someone had thrown a rug over it. A foul odor wafted off the surface, and Verity turned to walk beside the swamp without approaching any closer.

There were more promising vines tangled amid the trees here, thick and ropy and pliable. Verity removed a knife from her basket and sawed through a few of them, finding them green and moist inside. It took some effort to sever them, and then she had to unwind each from its stranglehold on other plants and coil it into her basket. By the time the basket was filled, she was dripping with perspiration.

Wiping her face with her sleeve, Verity wondered how far it was to the river. She would've liked a drink of water before trudging back uphill. But as near as she could tell, the bog lay between her and the river, and trying to walk around it would take her even farther from home. Reluctantly, she decided to wait until she reached the church to quench her thirst; there was a pump adjacent to the cemetery. Picking up the heavy basket, she turned back the way she'd come.

It seemed there were more brambles than ever, and her wet skirt dragged against her legs. Verity panted, sweat rolling down her face as she mounted the hill. The air was heavy and still, and the stench of the bog rose in invisible waves around her, mixed with a sweeter, familiar scent. Eventually she realized it was coming from the shrubs with the pink and white flowers — the same flowers that had blown in through her window the night before.

Verity broke off a branch of flowers and raised it to her face. The scent reminded her of honeysuckle, and indeed, some of the flowers contained a full drop of nectar. She licked her lips.

Suddenly, from behind her came the crash of breaking

underbrush. Verity whirled, but the figure rushing out from behind the trees crossed the distance between them before she could react. The man—dressed in ragged clothes, with dark hair and dark skin—was upon her in an instant, gripping her arm and yanking her out of the shrubbery. Letting the branch fall, Verity stared up in horror at his savage face—the high cheekbones, the scar that deformed one of his eyes, his angry expression. He opened his mouth, but she didn't wait to hear what vile things he might say. She screamed mightily and walloped his head with the basket.

He released her, recoiling. She shoved the whole basket of vines into his face and took off running. Down the incline. Away from him. Back toward the bog.

Running downhill felt almost like falling, and only terror kept her on her feet. She glanced back once, catching a glimpse of movement behind her, and after that she concentrated on dodging low branches and avoiding boulders. She knew she was headed away from safety, but she couldn't put any distance between her and the man—the Indian—if she tried to run up the steep hill. Losing herself in the shrubbery was the best she could hope for.

A vine just like the ones she'd been collecting proved to be her undoing. Her foot caught on a ropy tendril that snaked across the ground between two trees. The loop of vine snagged her ankle, and her leg was wrenched out from under her as the rest of her body plummeted forward. She hit the ground and kept sliding, unable to stop herself from tumbling, the slope dropping away from her.

Verity landed in a heap at the bottom of a small cleft, where a trickling stream had worn away the earth between two massive trees. Feeling the ache of several bruises and a greater, sharper pain in her ankle, she rolled over to look upward, where she now heard loud tramping and the breaking of twigs underfoot. She scuttled backward on her bottom, but there was nowhere for her to go. As the shrubbery parted above her, she did the only thing left for her to do: she screamed bloody murder.

The young man who looked down at her from the top of the cleft threw both his hands out in a gesture of innocent intent. "Whoa! Easy there!" Then he blinked and stared at her in disbelief. "Miss Boone?"

Verity could hardly believe her eyes. "Dr. Jones?" she said incredulously. Then, with relief, she repeated "Dr. Jones!" and burst into tears.

Hadley Jones jumped down into the cleft. He was dressed in work clothes, an old torn hunting jacket, and a wide-brimmed felt hat, but he was not the person who'd assaulted her. She could still picture the dark, angry features of the Indian who'd loomed over her so menacingly.

"What happened to you?" Jones asked. "Did you fall?"

"I was running!" she gasped. "There was a man . . . chasing me . . ."

"Chasing you?" He looked up in alarm, scanning the area around them.

"An Indian!" she exclaimed. "He leaped out of the woods and grabbed me! I hit him with my basket and ran —and then I tripped and fell." Jones helped her up, and she winced when pain shot through her ankle.

Jones craned his neck to look out of the cleft. "Chased you?" he asked again. She nodded.

He tightened his arm around her waist, and she threw her own arm over his shoulder for support, easing her injured foot off the ground. "Let's get you out of here," he said, surveying her with worried eyes. "What in the world are you doing in the Shades of Death?"

THIRTEEN

HIS IS the Shades of Death?" Verity gasped.

"It's just a name," Jones said in a soothing voice. "Nothing to be afraid of. I don't know why they call it that instead of, say, the Sunny Swamp of Happiness."

She laughed without much humor, grabbing hold of exposed tree roots as Jones maneuvered her into position to be lifted out of the hole. This was a dark, miserable, foul-smelling place, and she hoped never to venture here again — but he was right. It was just a swamp. The person who'd accosted her had been a living man, not some specter lingering here from the Revolutionary War. "I was collecting vines for a wreath," she said. "And now I've lost my basket."

He lifted her out of the cleft, clambered up himself, and helped her limp to a seat on a boulder. "Shall I go look for it?"

"No! Please don't leave me alone!"

He smiled, kneeling down beside her. "I won't leave you," he promised. "Now, with your permission, I'll examine your foot."

Verity nodded, feeling her heart race as he carefully lifted her sodden skirt and took her foot in his hands. Adeptly, he unlaced her shoe and slipped it off. To distract herself while his gentle fingers probed at her ankle, she asked, "What are *you* doing out here?"

He shrugged off a canvas haversack he'd been wearing over his shoulder, then removed his hat and laid it on top. "I was gathering some plants," he murmured, bending over her foot again. "Roots and herbs. That apothecary at Dyers doesn't always have a fresh supply, and sometimes I just like to know where my remedies are coming from. Does this hurt?" He rotated her foot carefully, supporting her leg with one hand under the calf.

"Yes, it does," she said between gritted teeth.

"It's not broken, though. Just a sprain."

"How can you tell?"

He looked up, his blue eyes twinkling. "If it were broken, you wouldn't be telling me it hurt in complete sentences, or even in words." He slipped her shoe on again but left it unlaced, pulling out the tongue so it fitted as loosely as possible. "Now," he said, putting his hat back on his head and slinging the haversack over his shoulder, "I'm going to carry you out of here."

"Oh!" She blinked, startled, and glanced up at the steep wooded slope.

"You can't walk on it, and certainly not up that hill."

He was right, of course. Verity stared at him, embarrassed. "I'm sorry."

The young man grinned. "I don't mind."

She could see quite plainly that he didn't. He bent over her, and, uncertainly, she put her arms around his neck. He slipped one hand under her knees and the other around her back and hefted her into his arms.

Hadley Jones was not as tall or as broad-shouldered as Nate, but she could feel the strength of his arms as he tested her weight and shifted her so that she was cradled against his chest. Then he started up the hill without another word.

Verity had never been so close to a man in her life. Jones was overwarm and sweaty, but so was she, and somehow it wasn't unpleasant. She could feel his heart beating and hear his increasingly labored breaths as he climbed the hill. Her head was so close to his that she kept bumping his hat. The third time she almost knocked it off, he said, "Just take it and shove it into my haversack."

She removed his hat, leaned over his shoulder, and reached down until she could grab the strap of the bag and pull it closer. As she fumbled the bag open and folded the hat inside, her upper body was entirely pressed against his. By the time she let go of the sack, her heart was beating as fast as his—for no good reason at all.

When they finally reached the road, he set her down on a fallen log and bent over, his hands on his knees. "Let me catch my breath," he gasped. She nodded guiltily. He grinned and wiped his forehead with his sleeve. "It's not you, of course. It was the climb. *You* weigh less than a feather."

Verity smiled wryly. Catching a whiff of sweet fragrance, she looked up and saw another of those flowering shrubs above her, the petals nearly dripping in nectar. She plucked a bunch of flowers and brought it down to her lips.

"Miss Boone! Don't!" Hadley Jones snatched the flowers out of her hand. "That's mountain laurel!"

She was taken aback. "It smelled like honeysuckle."

"Well, it's not. It's poisonous." A look of alarm passed over his face. "Did you eat any of this nectar earlier?"

She shook her head. "No, I didn't. I—" She gasped in understanding and stared up at the doctor. "I was about to—right before that man jumped out of the woods and grabbed my arm."

"Right before—" Jones made a sound of exasperation and looked out at the swampland below them. "He grabbed your arm and stopped you from eating it."

"Yes," she said in a small voice.

"And you—"

"Hit him on the head with my basket and ran away," she finished glumly.

Her companion gave a short bark of laughter. "This isn't the eighteenth century, Miss Boone, and the Indians here don't make war on the white settlers anymore. You just met one of the Pooles," he said. "They hunt and fish in these woods. You probably scared him half to death."

"It was mutual." Verity cringed with embarrassment. Yes, the man had startled her, but she'd run screaming from the sight of him like a half-witted female in one of those dime novels Polly Gaines liked so much. Verity had taken offense when her uncle belittled the Pooles, but she'd behaved no better today. She hung her head in shame.

Hadley Jones looked at the flowers in his hand and then shook them in her face. "You can't eat things when you don't know what they are. Didn't anybody teach you that?" She glared at him, but she knew he was right. "It would have made you very sick at best," he went on, flinging the flowers to the ground. "At worst—well, that doesn't bear thinking about."

Suddenly he sat down beside her and took her hand.

And although she knew it was imprudent, she let him. Her hands were trembling with reaction, and his grip was strong and comforting.

After a long moment of silence, Jones uncurled his fingers and looked down at her ring, as Nate had. Then he looked up at her, and she winced at the beseeching expression in his eyes.

"You're really going through with this . . . business arrangement?" he asked.

"It's not business," she whispered.

"I think it is. It's a land deal."

Her breath caught in her throat. "That's an unkind thing to say."

He frowned. "Seeing this ring on your finger makes me feel unkind, Verity."

"Don't," she murmured. How had they come to the point of first names? She barely knew him. Why was she sitting here, letting him hold her hand?

She couldn't take her eyes from his face—the light spattering of freckles across his nose, his fair blue eyes. "I don't want you to do it," he said.

"It's none of your business." She pulled her hand free.

"All right. *As your doctor*, I don't think you should do it."

"You're not my doctor."

"Huh," he grunted. "If you're going to live in Catawissa, then I *will be* your doctor. Trust me, you don't want Dr. Robbins." He raised his hands in the air and made them tremble.

"Palsy?" asked Verity.

"That's right," he agreed. "The kind you get from drinking whisky before noon." He stood up. "Let's get you home."

When he reached for her, she leaned away, shaking her head. "I don't think you should carry me anymore."

"I won't say anything else personal. I promise."

Verity kept her hands on the log and her face turned away. "The minister's house is just a little way up the road. Can't you please go and bring help back?"

"I'd have to leave you alone."

"You said it yourself—my 'Indian attacker' was just some fisherman trying to save an empty-headed city girl from poisoning herself." She refused to meet his eyes, staring steadfastly at the road. "I'm perfectly safe. Humiliated, but safe."

He stood there a moment, but she would not look up at him. Finally he opened his haversack, removed his hat, slapped it against his knee to reshape it, then put it on his head and started up the road.

Reverend White immediately brought his horse and carriage to her aid. Within half an hour she was sitting in the Whites' parlor with her foot propped up and a glass of iced tea in her hand, glaring at Hadley Jones, who'd just asked her to remove her stocking.

"Your ankle is swelling," he said, sipping his own iced tea and regarding her with professional detachment.

"It's all right, dear," said Mrs. White, setting down a bowl of water chilled with chips of ice. "Our apprentice is shaping up to be an excellent physician."

Explaining why she didn't want to bare her ankle for him would have been embarrassing. The men turned their backs, and she reluctantly freed her stocking from her garter and rolled it down. Mrs. White and Hadley Jones together bathed her ankle in cold water, while Verity sat back in her chair and pretended she didn't know when it was *his* hands on her bare skin.

Meanwhile, Reverend White fretted. "You can't wander around in the Shades, Miss Boone," he said. "That place has claimed many lives over the centuries. It's not a safe place for a young lady to gather flowers, if that's what you were doing."

"Were you lost, my dear?" asked his wife.

"No. I *was* gathering plants—for grave wreaths." Verity turned her gaze on the minister. "Reverend White, have you given any thought to my request?"

He mumbled something inaudible and refused to meet her eyes. "What request?" Mrs. White asked, looking back and forth between them.

Perhaps the wife would be more decisive than the husband. "I want the cemetery wall moved to enclose the graves outside," Verity said. Mrs. White's eyebrows shot up, and she turned to look at her husband.

Jones wrapped a cool cloth around Verity's ankle. "Are we talking about the two caged graves?"

"Oh, we don't like to call them cages," whispered Mrs. White.

"No one's ever been able to tell me what purpose they serve," Jones went on.

The minister and his wife shared another glance.

"Protection against grave robbers," Verity said.

Mrs. White gave a little gasp, and the minister murmured in alarm, shoving his hands into his pockets. Jones looked up and met Verity's eyes for the first time since he'd spoken his mind by the side of the road. "Are you serious?" he asked. "What — were they buried with the family jewels?"

"We're talking about my mother and my aunt," Verity said tersely. "And getting them a proper, dignified burial."

Mrs. White wrung another cloth over the bowl and avoided meeting Verity's eyes. "Miss Boone, you don't want to stir up old trouble. Everyone's accustomed to those graves where they are, and trying to make changes will only resurrect the old stories."

"What stories?" Verity demanded.

"Nothing you want to hear, my dear."

Verity didn't like being told what she did or did not want. "Perhaps I do."

"Trust me; you don't." The minister's wife handed Jones the fresh cloth and leaned forward to whisper to Verity: "There was talk of *witchcraft* and other, nastier things. Best to let sleeping dogs lie. I'm sure you can make a very happy future with Nathaniel McClure, if you'll just leave well enough alone."

Hadley Jones slapped a discarded cloth into the bowl, splashing water everywhere and letting Verity know exactly what he thought of that future. But her mind was elsewhere.

Well enough did not describe the manner in which her mother had been buried, and she did not intend to leave it alone.

FOURTEEN

ERITY'S BASKET turned up outside the kitchen door the next morning. It had been re-filled with the vines that had spilled out when she threw it, although her knife was missing.

"Do you know anything about this, Beulah?" she asked.

"No, miss." The housekeeper seemed almost cheerful now that Verity's mobility had been reduced, along with her ability to wreak havoc in the kitchen.

"I have reason to believe it might be one of your relatives who returned it."

Beulah's eyebrows rose. "You mean a Poole?" She went back to washing dishes. "I have a lot of kin," she said. "And I don't know what they're all up to at any given time — any more than you do."

With a shrug, Verity put the mystery of the basket aside. There were more worrisome things on her mind: the caged graves, the treasure, stories of witchcraft and nastier things — although what could be nastier than witchcraft she had no idea.

And since no one worth believing wanted to tell her the truth, she was left with only one source of information — her mother's diary. She wondered if she could find anything of significance amid things like:

> Oct 25 – Loaned dress patterns to Miss Piper.
> Nov 6 – Verity skinned her knee playing with the McClure children.

There was only one diary entry Verity thought might be important. On October 30, her mother wrote:

> Went to Mrs. Needham's house for a sewing bee but did not stay. They kept talking about what happened at the cemetery last August, and I cannot abide it.

That was interesting, but not nearly informative enough.

As she searched for something to explain the accusations made against her mother, she got closer and closer to the end of Sarah Ann Boone's life.

> Nov 8 – Mrs. Cahill was by today and brought cabbage juice. Could not keep it down.
> Nov 9 – Ransloe held my head while I puked today.

I was not sick for this long carrying Verity. Everybody
says it must be a boy this time.
Nov 10 – Asenath has it bad too.

And then there were the last entries in the diary. Her mother must have been very sick when she wrote her final lines, and Verity did not turn the page to look at them again.

When Nate arrived that afternoon, he found her sitting in the dining room with her foot wrapped and propped on a neighboring chair. Vines and ribbons covered the table, and the kitten was batting his paw at anything that dangled over the edge and then fleeing if the item bounced back.

Nate carried a basket of fresh strawberries in one hand and a small bouquet of flowers in the other. "This is from my mother," he explained, setting down the basket. He handed the flowers directly to Verity. "These are from me."

"Thank you," she said, bending her head over the blossoms.

But Nate had spotted her reddened eyes. "You've been crying," he said, dropping down to squat beside her so their faces were level. "Are you in pain? Do you want me to fetch a doctor?"

"No." Heaven help her if she had to deal with Hadley Jones in the same room as Nate!

"Then what's wrong?"

Verity sighed. She slipped the notebook out from under the vines on the table and handed it to him. "It's my mother's diary."

Nate met her eyes with a startled expression. He immediately turned to the back of the diary. "Oh, Verity . . . why are you reading this? Why would you torture yourself?"

"Because no one will tell me what happened!" She couldn't keep the frustration out of her voice. "Nate, won't you—?"

"I was three years old when she died. I don't *know* what happened. I've heard stories," he admitted. "Every child in this town has heard stories about those graves— ghosts and treasure, the walking dead, and—" He faltered a bit. "Witches. But I haven't believed any of that since I was seven. And I don't think you can find out what really happened by reading this." He held up the notebook.

"You can't be sure of that. Besides, I never knew my mother. This diary is all I have of her. Oh, Lucky, stop." She made a grab at a coil of vine that was sliding toward the edge of the table and missed. The pile went over, spilling onto the floor and narrowly missing the kitten. He shot out of the dining room like an arrow.

"That's right," Nate called after Lucky. "Make a mess and run away." He scooped up the vines and ribbons, put them back on the table, and then fetched a chair from the end of the table to sit next to Verity. "I understand what you're saying," he said, laying the notebook down on the table, "but this must be painful for you to read."

"You used to visit here." Verity retrieved the notebook and opened it to the right page. He leaned forward to look, and they both read the entry, their heads close together.

After a moment he sat back in his chair and graced her with one of his rare smiles. "I remember that," Nate said. "I remember coming to this house to play with a girl who had golden curls. Several times. And then she wasn't here anymore."

"I don't remember *you*."

"It's probably for the best. I'm told I was a terror." Suddenly a thought seemed to cross his mind. "If you want to know more about your mother, why don't you read her other diaries?"

"Her *other* diaries?"

"This probably wasn't the first one. My sister Carrie kept a diary for years and filled up dozens of notebooks. I peeked into them whenever possible."

Verity flipped back to the first page, where the entries began quite suddenly in the October before her mother died. It had not occurred to her that keeping a diary was a lifetime practice. Hadn't her father told her there were more of her mother's belongings in the attic?

"Nate," she said, "would you do something for me?"

FIFTEEN

ERITY PEERED up the cramped and narrow attic staircase. Above her, objects shifted, scraping across wooden planks. She heard Nate's footsteps, the unmistakable sound of him barking his shin, followed by muffled swearing.

"Are you all right?" she called up. Receiving only silence for an answer, she raised her voice. "Nate?"

His voice carried down from above. "Found 'em."

She heard his footsteps descending, and then he appeared around the curve of the staircase carrying a wooden box. Nate set it on the floor, and Verity knelt to lift the lid. Two piles of notebooks had been carefully stacked inside with newspapers between them. There were at least two dozen diaries—years and years of her mother's life for Verity to read. She raised a tearful face to Nate and smiled.

He looked perplexed. "Does this make you happy?"

"Yes," she said, standing and plucking a cobweb off his shoulder.

"Good." He captured her hand and brought it to his mouth, brushing his lips against the backs of her fingers. But his eyes were on her face, as if he was seriously thinking about leaning forward to give her a more intimate kiss.

Verity froze. She'd come to the conclusion that Nate was everything his sisters said he was—earnest and kind and hard working, and sometimes rather sweet. But the memory of Hadley Jones's arms encircling her as he carried her out of the swamp was still too vivid. If Nate kissed her now and she felt nothing . . . she would know something about herself she really didn't want to know.

Nate let go of her hand. "I should get back to work," he said, backing away.

She watched him take the stairs down to the front door with a strange mixture of feelings: relief that he hadn't tested her affection; disappointment that he'd chosen prudence over passion; and guilt, for she felt certain he *would* have kissed her, given the slightest encouragement.

Sarah Ann Boone could not abide cruelty, and when the townsfolk were unkind to her sister-in-law, it raised her ire.

Sept 20 – Mrs. Applebee cut Asenath dead on the street yesterday, and today I gave her a piece of my mind.

As far as Verity could tell from the diaries, her mother had been Asenath Thomas's sole defender and friend. For some reason the townfolk of Catawissa had despised the pure-faced, fair-haired beauty. Entry after entry recorded slights to Asenath that angered Sarah Ann Boone. Verity was gratified to see that her two-year-old self had been less judgmental.

Sept 17 – Asenath sang Verity to sleep today. She has the voice of an angel.

Nevertheless, her uncle's first wife had been a little strange, and even Sarah Ann's patience wore thin at times.

Sept 21 – I had to scold Asenath for giving out her charms. It was like kicking a puppy. She does it out of generosity, and I cannot make her understand how it looks to others.

Charms? What kinds of charms?

Sept 30 – Asenath came to me because she thought she might be expecting, but she was not sure of the symptoms.

She can count no better than she can read or write, but as
near as I can calculate, she must be due six weeks after me.

Verity became so curious about her young aunt that she leafed back through the pages seeking her name until she finally found the passage where Asenath appeared in the diary for the first time.

In April 1852, Sarah Ann Boone wrote:

John has taken up with one of Eli Clayton's daughters.
Mother is beside herself!

A few days later she added:

John is still seeing Asenath Clayton. He brought her
to church on Sunday. She held the hymnal upside down
and John had to turn it around. We thought Mother
might faint.

Verity opened her mother's trunk and dug out the picture of Uncle John and Asenath. This sweet-faced, fairy-princess creature had been a *Clayton*? No wonder her grandmother had been upset! Knowing Asenath's origin didn't make the girl in the photograph any less beautiful. Verity couldn't tell if she had all her teeth; Cissy Clayton was missing several of hers.

According to the diary, John Thomas's courtship of

Asenath Clayton turned the town on its ear and blighted many hopes.

> *Half the girls in Catawissa had their sights set on John.*
> *He has broken all their hearts — from Miss McClure*
> *to Miss Piper. Mother wishes he would pick any one of*
> *them over Asenath.*

Verity's grandmother dragged every eligible girl in Catawissa up to the Thomas house for tea, hoping to tempt her son into choosing one of them. Sarah Ann, by contrast, made it a point to welcome her brother's sweetheart and claimed to be the only person unsurprised when John married Asenath before the end of May. *Everyone will be watching her waistline carefully,* Verity's mother predicted, *but John swears to me he has not done what everybody thinks he has done.*

After the wedding, Verity's grandmother resigned herself to the new daughter-in-law.

> *Father had a word with Mother, and she is now behaving herself.*

Sarah Ann Boone coached her sister-in-law in the social niceties she was lacking. It was hard for Verity to imagine the dainty girl in the photograph eating with elbows on the table and walking barefoot through town, but she had no trouble believing her uncle found it highly amusing.

*John says Asenath is his unspoiled angel and has no
pretensions. Mother replied that she wished Asenath
would at least pretend she was not raised in a barn.*

Although Verity's mother agreed her sister-in-law had ap-
palling manners, she wrote in her diary that she was willing to forgive Asenath anything if the girl provided a solid
foundation for her brother's life.

*June 10 – Thank heavens John has finally found
something he loves more than his ridiculous treasure
hunting.*

So it was true! Ransloe Boone's involvement was confirmed by an entry made a few days later.

*June 17 – Asenath hungers for that cursed gold as much
as my brother. I could shake her! I suppose John will be
dragging Ransloe out to the Shades all summer when he
is supposed to be working our land. And I thought I had
finally convinced Ransloe to give it up.*

As hard as it was to imagine, her father had once been an
adventurer, hunting for a legendary payroll of gold coins.
Furthermore, it was common knowledge in Catawissa,
and according to Nate's sisters, some people believed he
and his brother-in-law had actually found the treasure.

Looking around the sparse household kept by Ransloe Boone, Verity couldn't imagine why anyone suspected her father possessed a fortune in gold.

Then, she remembered they *didn't* think that. They thought he'd buried the gold with his wife inside an iron cage. Why? Out of guilt, grief, maybe regret?

It couldn't be true.

Could it?

SIXTEEN

UNT CLARA paid a social call the next day. Verity would not have minded the visit if Liza hadn't come with her. The girl's sullen expression showed that she had been dragged along against her will. Liza eyed Verity's wrapped ankle with a frown, and Verity thought her cousin was probably wishing she had twisted her neck instead.

Aunt Clara inquired about the grave wreaths, and nothing would do but for Verity to bring them out for her inspection. When she limped back to her seat and put her foot up on a stool, Aunt Clara shook her head. "If you want to be a farm wife, you're going to have to toughen up. Nathaniel has ambitions for this land. He's going to expect you to do your part."

"I *will* do my part," Verity replied indignantly, but her aunt talked right over her.

"He doesn't need a coddled city wife any more than a farm needs a cat that doesn't catch mice." Aunt Clara waved a hand at Lucky, curled up asleep on the cushioned back of the settee. "Nathaniel's had his eye on this property ever since he got a taste for running it when your father went to war. He's only been waiting for you to grow up enough for marriage."

Verity bit her lip. According to Nate's letters, his mother had been the one to suggest the marriage — and he hadn't been keen on it. *I expected a brief correspondence with you would put an end to the whole foolish plan*, Nate had written shortly before he'd proposed. *Instead, I find myself wanting to shake the postmaster every day he does not have a letter from you.*

"Not that I fault Nathaniel, of course," her aunt went on. "When you recognize the best of what's available, you shouldn't let anything prevent you from obtaining it."

Verity cast her eyes down, stung for reasons she couldn't explain. She knew very well that her land was more valuable than her person, except perhaps to Hadley Jones.

Liza looked particularly sour at the mention of Verity's impending marriage. She couldn't contain her hands any longer. Snatching one of the wreaths off the table, she began to untie Verity's ribbons and rearrange them. Verity opened her mouth to object, then closed it. Liza's work was sure to be better than her own.

"If your ankle pains you, take some of the medicine I

gave you," Aunt Clara continued. "Do you still have it?"

Verity hadn't been able to find the packet her aunt had given her. She'd searched for it just last night, when her throbbing ankle had kept her awake. Even though she knew she'd look like a featherbrained fool, she had no intention of lying. "I—" she began.

The front door slammed. "Mama! Are you here? Liza!"

Samuel and Stephen burst into the parlor, tousled and dirty and indistinguishable. "Mama! Mama!" they cried in tandem.

"You'll never guess—"

"—what happened to Piper!"

Aunt Clara eyed them over her cup of tea. "Is the blood dripping or gushing?" she asked, unperturbed.

"No blood, Mama! He was grabbed by bandits—"

"—but he got away!"

Liza reached out and cuffed the nearest twin in the ear. "What have we said about telling fibs?"

"Ow, Liza!"

"It ain't a fib, neither!"

"It's true!" Piper appeared in the doorway, his face flushed with excitement. "Two men grabbed me in the woods! They tried to catch Samuel and Stephen, but—"

"I went up a tree!" shouted one twin.

"And I got clean away!" hollered the other.

Aunt Clara frowned and set down her cup. "Are you telling me the truth?"

The twin who'd been in the tree pointed a finger at Piper. "The one with the scar picked him up and held him in the air—asked him where Papa has the treasure hidden!"

Their mother hissed in aggravation. "I should have known!"

"I kicked him in his ugly old mug!" Piper said proudly. "And he dropped me! I ran like the dickens and hollered I was gonna fetch the sheriff. Then they left Sam in the tree and run off in the woods."

"Was it a scar across his eye, like this?" Verity drew a line with her finger across the corner of her left eye and down her cheek.

Piper wrinkled his brow and looked at Verity as though she'd lost her mind. "You mean Hawk? Nah, it weren't him. This fellow had one side of his face all puckered."

"Former soldiers, most likely," Aunt Clara said. "It's been like this ever since the war ended—people drifting through, looking for jobs. Worse, some of them are deserters, can't go home, and *they're* mostly looking for what they can steal—thinking a fortune is going to turn up at their feet."

Verity wondered what her aunt thought of her husband's youthful treasure-hunting days. "Like Revolutionary War gold?"

"Or Confederate silver," Aunt Clara said. "Or a chest

of Blackbeard's jewels. According to the foolish and the ignorant, we've got everything stashed in these mountains except Queen Victoria's crown." She pierced her sons with her no-nonsense gaze. "Keep close to home and out of the woods for a few days. Drifters will pass on soon enough."

Liza put the improved wreaths back on the table. She stood up and left the room, shooing the boys before her. Verity turned to her aunt and asked, "Who's Hawk—the man with the scar across his eye?" Piper apparently knew the fellow who'd frightened her in the Shades.

"Hawk Poole. Where did you meet him?"

"In the woods. On the day I hurt my ankle."

Her aunt nodded. "Hawk works for Dr. Robbins—keeps his horses and his carriage. I suppose he was with Jones when they found you."

"What do you mean?"

"Hawk guides that apprentice through the swamp, to make sure he doesn't get lost. That's what they were doing when they found you, isn't it?" asked Aunt Clara. "Collecting herbs?"

Verity narrowed her eyes. "I suppose it was."

As soon as her aunt left, Verity forced an unlaced short boot over her swollen foot and took her father's horse and wagon to Catawissa. She'd never driven such a large conveyance before, but she managed well enough, tied up the horse, and marched directly into Dr. Robbins's waiting room.

She would have spoken her mind in front of witnesses if necessary, but by chance she found Hadley Jones alone, seated at a desk. His face brightened on seeing her, and he stood up. "Miss Boone! How's your ankle?" His eyes fell to her foot. The tongue of her boot flapped open at every step. "I wish you weren't walking on it yet, but —"

"Hawk Poole," Verity said between clenched teeth.

Jones looked confused. Then he looked around the room as if expecting to see the man. "What about him?"

"You were together, the day you *found* me in the woods. The day you *rescued* me from the *Indian* who attacked and chased me. But it was your servant, Hawk Poole, who attacked me, and *you* were the one who chased me!"

His eyes widened in surprise, and he held up his index finger, defending himself. "I wasn't chasing you. A girl was screaming in the woods, and I wanted to find out what was wrong."

"But it was your man who frightened me!"

"I didn't know that! You told me somebody assaulted you. I knew Hawk wouldn't have done that." Jones blew out an exasperated breath. "And I thought we established that he didn't attack you at all but saved you from doing something foolish!"

"But you realized later who it was," Verity persisted.

He nodded. "After you told me about the mountain laurel."

"And you didn't tell me!"

"What did it matter?"

It mattered. He'd played the hero, carrying her out of the terrifying Shades of Death—but it was his fault she'd fallen and hurt her ankle. The Shades hadn't been terrifying until Jones and his companion had frightened the wits out of her. In the back of her mind she knew she might have poisoned herself if they hadn't been there, but that was an entirely separate matter.

"Now I know how I got my basket back," she muttered.

"Oh!" He snapped his fingers and opened a desk drawer, from which he removed her garden knife. "Found this later," he said sheepishly, coming out from behind the desk and holding it out to her, handle first.

When she limped forward to take it, he caught her by the hand. "Tell me you didn't come here to be angry with me." His eyes swept over her. "Why don't you sit down, and I'll take a look at your ankle."

She wrenched her hand loose and backed away. "Touch my foot and I'll box your ears."

He just grinned and shook his head. "You can be indignant, and I'll apologize profusely." He crooked a finger at her. "Come here. Let me apologize. Please."

Verity took another step backward. She knew the

look of a young man planning to steal a kiss. She'd been ducking ornery lips since she was fifteen years old. She'd even been caught a few times, and that hadn't been too terrible — rather like cupcakes: sweet and finished quickly. But now she was spoken for, and she absolutely could not indulge in cupcake kisses with Hadley Jones.

"You are entirely too forward," she said.

"I have to be," he said. He dropped a little of the playfulness, but he still watched her intently. "You're engaged to another man, and I have only a short time to plead my suit with you."

"You have no suit with me," Verity replied. And when she realized how dangerously close that came to being a lie, she turned and fled.

SEVENTEEN

ERITY PUT Hadley Jones out of her mind and returned her attention to her mother's diaries. She had started reading to better understand her mother and what had happened to her, but now she felt a growing fascination with the young woman who would be her aunt for such a short time.

Asenath never fitted into the Thomas family. Her mother-in-law tried to teach her to read, but the girl wasn't interested; she thought the best use for books was pressing flowers. Sarah Ann wrote:

> *Father says that when you pick up any book in the house,*
> *a very flat bouquet falls out.*

Verity's mother was the one family member who made the greatest effort to include Asenath. She started bringing the girl along to assist in midwifery, which probably explained Aunt Clara's comment about choosing the wrong apprentice.

> *June 15 — Took Asenath with me to Mrs. Harper's lying-in because I knew it would be a simple one. She was cheerful and helpful and said she would come again.*

Sarah Ann seemed tolerant of Asenath's strange ways, perhaps more than she should have been.

> *Asenath keeps giving me sachets she has made with herbs and dried flowers. Mother calls them "spells" and hates the sight of them, but they are only superstitious little charms. One is supposed to protect the house, another is supposed to bring good luck, and today she gave me one to put in Verity's cradle to keep "evil spirits" away.*

Verity realized that the little bags she had found in her mother's trunk were not scented sachets, but charms made by Asenath.

In the middle of July, after several days without any entries at all, Sarah Ann wrote:

> *Thank the Lord Verity's fever broke at last and the coughing has lessened. We are all grateful and tired and a little irritable. Poor Asenath put a red ribbon around*

Verity's wrist to "keep the illness from coming back," and
Mother ripped it off. Asenath cried.

It seemed Verity's grandmother despaired of trying to edu-
cate her daughter-in-law and simply tried to prevent her
from embarrassing the family. According to Sarah Ann's
gently phrased summaries, she was not very successful.

We had a visit from Mrs. Eggars today. She brought
back the charm Asenath gave to her sister at her lying-in
and said making them was a heathen practice. Asenath
did not know what the word meant.

Cissy Clayton had been wearing a charm at her lying-in.
Verity felt a chill when she considered how the practice
of making and wearing charms — especially by folk as wild
and strange as the Claytons — might be misconstrued. This
was almost certainly the beginning of her mother's ruined
reputation.

The diary was emotionally fatiguing. Verity read
only a few pages at a time and was happy to put it aside
for visitors. When Nate appeared on Saturday, offering
to take her out of the house, she gratefully accepted. After her trip into town to give Hadley Jones a piece of her
mind, her foot had swollen so much that she couldn't fas-
ten her shoe, and she'd remained at home ever since. It

wasn't until she'd limped outside that she realized what Nate had in mind.

"It's a beautiful day to look at the orchards," he suggested.

"Oh, but I can't walk very far," she said apologetically. They couldn't drive a carriage through the fields. Then she saw he'd come on horseback and froze. "I'm not very good on horseback." In fact, she'd never ridden anything larger than a pony, and that only at a fair where she'd paid a penny to be led around a corral.

"The mare does all the work," Nate said calmly. He put his hands around her waist and lifted her up. Finding herself perched sideways five feet in the air, Verity clutched the saddle and a fistful of the horse's mane. A second later Nate mounted up behind her, taking the reins in one hand and putting his other arm around her waist. "You're safe," he assured her. "Sally's very gentle. Hold on to me if you're scared."

Hold on to him *where?* Verity couldn't bring herself to put her hands on his thighs, so she grasped the arm he had around her waist with one hand and kept her grip on the saddle with the other. Her heart beat rapidly, and she sat as stiff as a board in front of him.

Nate clucked at the mare, and she started off across the Boone property. "Let's take a look at your father's fields first."

Of course he wanted to see her father's fields. According to Aunt Clara, he'd had his eye on them for years. Verity twisted her head to look up at him, expecting to catch him gazing at the land.

He was smiling down at her. "Don't worry," he said. "I promise you, I won't let you fall." She faced forward again, suddenly very conscious of every part of her body that touched his.

They found her father pruning trees in his apple orchard with his two hired hands. Ransloe Boone pushed his hat back on his head and gazed up at them, surprised. "Well, look at this."

"I thought I'd show her around a little," Nate explained.

"Good," said her father. "She could use some airing out."

"What does that mean?" Verity called indignantly over her shoulder as they rode on. Nate didn't say anything, but she could feel him chuckling.

Her father's workers raised their heads as the horse passed. "Enoch," Nate said to the older of the two, who waved a hand and went back to work. The younger one laid down his pruning shears and walked over, and Nate stopped the horse to wait for him. Verity was fairly certain this young man was either Beulah's grandson or her grandnephew. She hadn't quite worked out the complexities of the Poole clan yet.

Nate greeted him. "Hello, Daniel."

"Afternoon, Nathaniel," the young man said, taking off his hat. "Miss Boone." He was about Verity's age, slender and muscular, with dark hair and eyes.

"Good afternoon," she replied.

"Heard from your brother lately?" Nate inquired. "My mother's been asking about him."

Daniel Poole nodded, wiping the sweat from his brow. "He doesn't like Philadelphia much. Misses the mountains. But he's near the top of his class and fixin' to beat the ones ahead of him. He won't waste a penny of that money, you can be sure."

"Father would've been pleased." Nate looked down at Verity. "When my father was too ill to serve in the war, Daniel's brother went in his place, and my father set up a bank fund to pay his fees at the University of Pennsylvania."

Verity nodded solemnly. It was an unusual bargain between a man and his paid substitute but, in her mind, an honorable one. "I wish him good luck at his studies," she told Daniel Poole.

Nate gathered the reins and nudged the horse forward. "Send your ma greetings from mine. And if she makes any of her cabbage beet relish . . ."

"I'm sure she'll save some for you!" Daniel called after them.

"Cabbage beet relish?" Verity looked up at Nate and wrinkled her nose.

"Every man's entitled to one vice."

They rode past the apple trees and through a narrow wooded strip of land, and then they were on the more expansive McClure property. Nate talked casually about the land, the workers, and the season, and Verity relaxed, growing accustomed to the horse's movement and Nate's presence behind her in the saddle. When there was tricky terrain ahead, he leaned forward and said "Hold on" in a calm voice, tightening his grip on her in a way that made her feel something warm and delightful.

They toured more apple trees, then the peach and plum orchards. Nate pointed out the field crops in the distance, and Verity eased back against his chest, listening to the sound of his voice and admiring the sunlight on the leaves and the azure sky streaked with white clouds. The land was lovely, richly green and productive. He had every reason to be proud of it, as did her father, and seeing it this way for the first time, she was proud of it, too.

Did it really matter whose idea this union had been — or when it had first been suggested? Yes, it was an arranged marriage, but wasn't it possible to be happy with a man who came to her this way — just as much as she would be with someone who took a liking to her at first sight and pursued her against all reason?

When Nate brought her home, he dismounted and turned to assist her. She transferred one hand to his shoulder, and he guided her as she slid to the ground. So cheered was she by the entire outing that she stood on tip-toe and impulsively kissed his cheek. "Thank you, Nate."

That brought on one of the smiles she liked so much, and a second later, Nate bent down and returned the favor by kissing her on the mouth.

It wasn't a quick smack on the lips while she tried to wriggle away, which was the only kind of kiss she'd ever known. This was a kiss a man gave his intended bride. After a moment he put a hand behind her head, not to prevent her from getting away but to steady her. Verity wondered, in a faraway part of her mind, if she'd swayed a little bit. Better safe than sorry—so she reached up and held on to a handful of his coat. She'd just discovered that this kind of kiss invited her participation, and she felt a little dizzy. When they finally stepped apart, they were both breathless. He looked just as startled as she felt.

After that, Nate came to see her every day he wasn't away at market. Sometimes he came in the evening and sat with her in the parlor like a proper visitor; sometimes he showed up for only a few minutes at the back door. It didn't take long to rediscover the cordiality they'd once enjoyed in their letters, and this time Verity knew that no one was telling him what to say.

One evening her father found Nate kissing her good night on the kitchen stoop. Neither one of them had any idea he was there until he took off his hat and snapped it against the door frame loudly enough to make them jump apart.

"That's enough of that," Ransloe Boone said sternly.

"Yes, sir," Nate agreed, promptly retreating.

Ransloe Boone took his daughter by the back of the neck and marched her into the house. She did her best to look remorseful, but she didn't miss the smirk her father couldn't quite hide.

He seemed rather pleased that Verity and Nate were finally getting along.

Verity was discovering a number of things about her father she'd never known before.

In late July Sarah Ann Boone had written:

> Rained hard, but John and Asenath walked up to the house and we had an enjoyable evening. Ransloe played the fiddle and Verity danced.

The fiddle?

And:

> John wants to go to the church social, but Asenath does not know any dance steps. Of course, he asked Ransloe to teach her.

What did she mean, *of course?* Was John Thomas a terrible dancer, or was her father an exceptionally good one?

If Ransloe Boone and John Thomas were spending their time searching the swamp, Verity's mother did not dignify it with a mention in her diary. Only one entry in early August hinted at such an occupation:

> *Argued with Ransloe again about the time he spends*
> *with John, but we made amends in the usual way.*

The usual way? Verity clapped both hands over cheeks that suddenly felt very hot.

Then she turned the page, and the death of Asenath's sister Rebecca claimed her attention. *Asenath was called to the Claytons' today. Her sister was gravely ill,* Sarah Ann wrote on August 13, 1852.

> *I drove her in the carriage, but by the time we arrived,*
> *Rebecca had already passed. They waited too long to call*
> *the doctor in. The apothecary's daughter was there and*
> *did what she could, but the girl was beyond help. They*
> *say she had terrible stomach pains and then fell down in*
> *a stupor. I do not like to think ill of anyone, but it was*
> *very foolish not to call for Dr. Robbins at once.*

The following day, she added:

> I helped lay Rebecca out for burial. The poor thing was
> barely 15. I thought it strange that her arm was badly
> swollen, and there were marks that might have been bee
> stings. Ransloe says he knew of a man who died from bee
> stings. But stomach pains are not usually a symptom of
> bee stings.

Sarah Ann Boone offered her sympathy to Asenath's relations, even though the Claytons were the outcasts of Catawissa society and difficult company.

> Ransloe and I paid a condolence call after the funeral,
> but Eli Clayton was so unpleasant, we did not stay. I felt
> sorry for poor Idella, trying to serve honey cakes and tea
> while her husband ran guests off the property.

Asenath's grief verged on hysteria, leaving her prostrate and bedridden. Verity knew her mother must have been reaching the end of her patience when she wrote:

> Asenath would not get out of bed, not even to attend Rebecca's funeral. She supposedly saw 6 crows sitting together and believes it is a sign of more deaths to come.
> I thought Mother might slap her, and I almost wished
> she would.

That entry was dated August 15. Verity felt a chill up

and down her spine when she realized that in exactly three months' time, both her mother and Asenath Thomas would be dead.

EIGHTEEN

ERITY FELT she knew her father better through her mother's diaries than from living with him for three weeks. Every morning, Ransloe Boone came downstairs for breakfast and looked at his daughter as if he was surprised to find her there. The man who'd once romped through the house like a pony for her amusement seemed uncomfortable conversing with the young woman she'd become. When she tried to talk to him about wedding plans, he tugged on his shirt collar and suggested she take such matters to Nate's mother and sisters.

"Aren't you interested?" Verity asked, hurt.

Her father cringed. "Of course I am, Verity. Anything you want—I'll purchase it for you. If you'd like a fancy arbor on the lawn like your Aunt Clara has, I'll build it. But if you want to plan a party . . ." He spread his arms wide in a helpless gesture. "You're better off asking Fanny McClure."

Verity wasn't averse to asking Nate's mother for help; she'd already determined that Fanny McClure was the queen of Catawissa society. But planning an event with Nate's mother bore some resemblance to being run over by Clara Thomas's carriage. No sooner had Verity broached the subject than half a dozen *Godey's Lady's Books* were dumped in her lap.

Mrs. McClure turned the pages so quickly that Verity could hardly take anything in. "White satin and lace for the dress, don't you think, dear? Just like Queen Victoria."

Verity hesitated. A dress made especially for the wedding would be a great expense, and she didn't want to impose on her father's generosity. "I thought I would put a new overskirt on the gown I wore to the party and change the trim on the bodice." One of her mother's old dresses had a lovely velvet ribbon trimming the sleeves, and Verity thought it might be nice to put something of her mother's into her wedding gown.

"Oh no, dear. This is the wedding of my only son, and you shall have a new dress! I'll buy the fabric and take you to my seamstress." Verity started to protest, but Mrs. McClure didn't give her a chance. "Don't say a word. It's my pleasure. Of course, it doesn't have to be white. Now that I think about it, blue silk would be lovely with your hair. And we should consider the date. We harvest rye in July, peaches and plums through September, and then the apples start. We *could* have the wedding in August, or wait until November. No later than that, or snow might prevent your Massachusetts relatives from coming. What do you think? August or November?"

Verity blinked, feeling dizzy. She opened her mouth to reply, but Mrs. McClure didn't wait for an answer. "November," her future mother-in-law decided. "It will give us so much longer to plan."

"Nathaniel might have an opinion on the matter," Verity said.

Fanny McClure graced her with a confident smile. "Nathaniel will do what I tell him to do."

A day later, Nate announced that he and Carrie's husband were traveling to Lancaster County to look at a new variety of plum tree, and Verity accused him of making a cowardly retreat. "You're escaping your mother."

"I am not," Nate protested. "Timothy and I have planned this trip for weeks. It has nothing to do with being forced to look at wedding invitations in *Godey's*."

"He's a terrible liar, isn't he, Beulah?"

"I couldn't say, Miss Verity." The housekeeper sat in a corner of the parlor, sewing. After Ransloe Boone had caught Verity and Nate on the back stoop, he'd asked Beulah to chaperone their visits. No matter. Verity was certain

Nate could slip in a kiss when she walked him to the door.

"I'll miss you while I'm gone," Nate said. "And that's the truth."

"You'll probably forget all about me, you fickle thing," Verity chided him. "The way you forgot all about poor Amelie Eggars after staring at her in church."

"I did stare," he admitted ruefully, "when the sermon was really dull. I used to wonder why her eyebrow grew straight across her forehead the way it does."

"Shame on you," Verity said, although she couldn't smother her grin.

"What are you going to do while I'm gone?" he asked then. "Promise me you won't spend the whole time with your nose in those diaries. I'm almost sorry I fetched them for you, they make you so sad."

"I don't think it's a bad thing for me to want to know my mother."

"No, but that's not all you're doing. The past is the past. I wish you'd let it go." Nate sat up straight and eyed her with firm command. "See here. I want you to visit my sisters while I'm gone. If you want something to read —why, Annie can lend you a dozen books of poetry. For pity's sake, Verity, if you'll promise to put those diaries away for a while, I'll—I'll read one of those books myself. I'll even"—he looked mildly panicked—"memorize verses and recite them for you."

She raised her eyebrows in a challenge. "I'll give you back the one you sent me. You can learn a few verses by Barrett Browning while you're away."

"Timothy will think I've gone stark raving mad," Nate groaned, overlooking the fact that she'd promised him nothing.

Two days later, Verity stood on the front porch of the Boone house after dark, calling "Lucky" and "kitty" and "puss-puss" just as she'd been doing for the last two hours. The kitten, who normally kept pretty close to the house, was nowhere to be found. Verity was beside herself with worry—and angry that no one else seemed to care.

Her father stuck his head out the front door. "He'll come back when he's ready, Verity. And if he doesn't, we've got plenty of cats living around the barn. Pick another one to pamper and fatten up on cream. Nathaniel won't care." Verity shot him a resentful look, both for assuming Nate didn't care about the kitten he'd given her and for suggesting her pet could be replaced by any barn cat. Ransloe Boone shook his head at her expression and climbed the front stairs to retire for the night.

She called for Lucky again, peering into the dark. She didn't want to leave him outside all night with bears and bobcats. For all she knew, opossums might eat kittens. There was no use trying to sleep when she was so worried, so she fetched a lantern and started walking down the road toward the woods.

It was only a little after ten o'clock. In Worcester people would still be walking or riding home from social events, their way lit by gas streetlamps. On the Pennsylvania mountainside, however, there was little difference between ten o'clock in the evening and the dead of night. The sky was deep indigo, the trees black against it, and the only thing she could hear besides her footsteps was the rustle of nameless things in the woods. Verity wondered if she would ever be at ease with this isolation. She felt a little like Lucky, small and helpless in a wild world.

It wouldn't have been so bad in town. Catawissa might not be a city, but she could grow accustomed to its picturesque homes and little shops. For a moment she imagined herself living in a clapboard house with a gable front near the center of town and felt a flicker of cheer. But Nate would never agree to live that far from his property. Verity was marrying a farmer, not a doctor.

She frowned, unhappy that thought had even entered her head. "Kitty, kitty, kitty," she called. She reached the place where the road divided in two and stopped, reluctant to venture farther. It occurred to her that bears and bobcats might not find a kitten worth their trouble, but a foolhardy city girl would make a tasty meal indeed.

She was about to turn around and head home when

she heard a distant meow. "Lucky?" She stood still, listening. A thin, mewing sound answered her. Verity promptly started down the road toward the church, putting bears out of her mind. Was Lucky hurt? This was exactly what she'd feared all day—that he was injured and lying helpless somewhere, unable to come home.

Her sore ankle protested as she descended the hill, and she held the lantern up to light her way, not wanting to turn her foot and injure it all over again. She imagined the embarrassment of appearing a second time at Reverend White's house, where she would be chastised for another foolish excursion. Every few yards she stopped at the edge of the road and peered into the woods, calling for her cat.

About halfway down the hill she spotted a light near the cemetery—a lantern, if she wasn't mistaken. Verity paused, wondering if Reverend White had heard her voice and come outside to see what the problem was. But the White house was dark, and this lantern wasn't moving. Whoever held it was standing still, or else it was resting on the ground outside the cemetery wall.

Verity drew in her breath as she remembered finding her mother's marker overturned. Was somebody tampering with the graves again? With an unladylike exclamation, she marched the rest of the way down the hill, meaning to surprise the culprit in the act.

When the light near the graveyard went out, she knew she'd been seen. The person and the lantern had both vanished by the time she arrived at the cemetery wall. She looked left and right, glanced over her shoulder, and peered around the corner of the church. The light proved she hadn't been alone here a minute ago; but the darkness did not prove she was alone now.

The caged graves cast long, latticed shadows on the ground. She walked around both of them. The doors were closed and padlocked. The stones marking the resting places of her mother and her aunt looked the same as ever, the ground around them unbroken.

Her lantern radiated a circle of light all around her, but on the other side of the low cemetery wall, headstones threw oblong shadows that stretched blindly toward the darkness. She saw no sign of movement and no evidence of mischief, but then her eye was caught by a dim glow in the grass some yards away from Asenath's grave.

Embers. A few dying embers, growing cold and gray even as she watched. Verity walked over and poked them with the toe of her shoe, smelling the sharp odor of pipe tobacco. Someone had stood here with a lantern a few minutes ago, emptying a pipe. Who would visit a graveyard in the night to smoke a pipe? Verity raised her own light and for the first time saw that there were two other graves outside the cemetery wall, their rectangular stones set flush against the earth and overgrown by grass.

The inscription on the older of the two was worn nearly to illegibility. Verity could make out only the last name, CLAYTON, and a death date beginning with the numbers 17–.

The other was not as old, but strange indeed.

CALEB CLAYTON
1780–1832
STAY PUT NOW

"Begone, you foul creature!" boomed a voice from the darkness.

Stifling a shriek, Verity whirled around. She thrust the lantern in front of her in defense.

Eli Clayton loomed over her, his hair awry, his brow bunched in anger. He held a walking stick in the air as if he was about to strike her with it. She gasped and stepped backward. He watched her, his expression slowly changing from fury to astonishment. "You!" he gasped. "What are *you* doing here?"

Verity didn't need to explain her presence to this man. "Who did you think I was?" she countered, her heart pounding.

He clamped his lips shut, but his eyes skittered sideways toward the caged grave of his daughter Asenath. Verity felt a prickle of horror crawl up her spine.

Eli Clayton turned his malevolent gaze back on her and growled, "What are you doing *here*?"

She glanced down involuntarily at the stones in the

ground between them. "Who were these people?" she asked. "Relations of yours?"

"Get out of here!" Clayton snarled, his voice low and angry. "Stay out of my family matters, or worse will befall you than being trampled by a horse!"

He stepped menacingly toward her, and Verity suddenly awakened to her danger. This man had nearly gotten her killed once before. She bolted from the church grounds, taking the hill at a breakneck pace. Shooting pains in her ankle didn't slow her, nor did the fall of darkness when her lantern blew out. She was gasping for air by the time she reached the top of the hill and staggering by the time she stumbled up the front steps of her father's house. She locked the front door behind her.

When she reached her bedchamber, she found her mother's last diary lying on her bed, open to the very same page as before:

> *Nov 10 – Asenath has it bad too.*
> *Nov 12 – Feeling no better today. Very tired of being so sick.*
> *Nov 14 – Asenath pins her hopes on Miss Piper's remedies.*

Beside the open diary lay the photograph of John and Asenath Thomas.

Verity recoiled. "Who's doing this?" she cried,

turning around and looking at the four walls of her room as if they held some answer. "Why?"

This time she didn't just think about jamming a chair under the knob of her door.

She did it.

Brisk knocking startled her awake in the morning. Verity leaped out of bed, pushed aside the chair, and threw open the door. Her father was standing in the hallway, holding her kitten in the air by the scruff of his neck. Lucky curled his tail toward his belly and looked repentant.

"Oh!" she cried, reaching out.

Ransloe Boone handed the kitten over. "He was hollering for breakfast at the back door. Lazy thing should be catching his own meals."

His gruffness didn't fool Verity at all. "Thank you, Father," she said, throwing one arm around him and kissing his cheek. He grunted in surprise, and when she stepped back, he left wearing the biggest smile she'd seen on him since she'd come home.

Cuddling the kitten under her chin, she turned to face her room. In the bright morning light, with her pet safely home just as her father had predicted, her fears and fancies of the night before seemed silly. Eli Clayton had frightened her in the cemetery, staring down at her with wild eyes as if she were Asenath out of her grave. But he was crazy; everyone in town knew that. She certainly wouldn't go walking alone at night again, now that she knew he might be out there.

As for the diary and the photograph left out for her to find—Verity had thrown them both into her mother's trunk last night and buckled it closed, convinced that Nate was right and she needed to leave the past alone. But what if she wasn't supposed to leave it alone?

What if that was the message contained in the photograph and the diary?

Her courage rekindled, she set Lucky on the bed. She pulled the trunk's leather straps free of the buckles and threw open the lid.

Verity reread the final entries of her mother's last diary, hoping to see something she'd missed. The days leading up to her mother's death were ordinary and unremarkable. And the final page was heartbreaking. Verity closed that book, puzzled and no more enlightened than before. Then she returned to the one Sarah Ann Boone had written in the summer of 1852 and took up reading from where she'd left off.

Rebecca Clayton's death had been only one of several that August.

The night of the funeral, other members of the Clayton family sickened, succumbing to the same ailment that had felled Rebecca. And the day after that, Asenath took ill too.

Aug 16 – Mother sent for us at once. Asenath fell ill
in the evening — cramps in the stomach and gut. We all
knew it was the same thing that has taken her family,
even though we did not want to say it.

Dire stomach pains followed by lethargy and stupor resulted in the death of Rebecca's grandmother, a baby, and
an aunt, and the Thomases feared for Asenath's life.

Every person in this town with the name of Clayton has
fallen to it. What nature of illness can pick out people
by their name? It is no wonder people are remembering
the stories about a curse on that poor wretched family!

Verity's mother didn't think it was a matter of contagion.
Asenath had not visited her family home since the day of
Rebecca's death.

On August 17, the entry read:

Heart beats slow. She waters from the eyes, nose, and
mouth. Chokes if we lay her down. She is very sleepy,
but we are afraid to let her sleep. Those who died fell
into a stupor before they passed.

Sarah Ann Boone's hands had shaken as she wrote those
words.

However, later that evening, she wrote:

There is no more drool and her heartbeat is stronger.
I dared not write it before, but praise the Lord, I think
she will live.

The following day's entry reported:

Asenath is much better today, John is prostrate with
exhaustion and relief, and Mother broke down and re-
pented of every unkind thing she has ever said. Ransloe
took us down to church to pray, where we heard disturb-
ing gossip from town. Sometimes I cannot credit what
ignorant people will stoop to believing.

Verity wondered what the townsfolk had been say-
ing, but her mother did not record it. *I heard it again today,*
and it is not worth repeating, she wrote on August 19.

And then, on August 20:

When I heard about Rebecca's grave being opened last
night, I ran from the room and emptied my stomach.
What has the world come to? How could anyone des-
ecrate the dead in such a vile manner?

There it was. Verity could draw only one conclusion—
this was the incident her father had mentioned. Rebecca
Clayton's grave had been robbed, her body stolen and sold
to medical students.

Verity closed the diary. An illness that took only Claytons? Ignorant gossip in town and pillaged graves?

If she wanted to know what had really happened in the summer and fall of 1852, she was going to have to seek more information from people who liked to gossip and tell stories, even when it wasn't prudent to do so.

NINETEEN

ARRIE," VERITY ventured, eyeing Nate's sister over her cup of tea, "I was at the cemetery yesterday, and I realized that there are two other graves outside the wall. One of them has the strangest inscription . . ."

Carrie's blue eyes twinkled. "I'll bet you mean the Clayton stones."

Annie and Carrie had been delighted to receive Verity's calling card and promptly invited her for afternoon tea. They welcomed her in the family library, a much cozier room than the front parlor, where Verity had looked through countless issues of *Godey's* with Mrs. McClure. The sisters expressed regrets from Hattie, who was unable to join them. The youngest McClure sister was nursing her husband, whose war injury had flared up.

"Yes, those two," Verity agreed, smiling as if her

interest in the subject were only a passing fancy. "I said to myself, if anyone knows the story, Carrie will."

"She does indeed." Annie sniffed with mock disapproval. "It's her favorite story after the Battle of Wyoming."

Carrie waved a hand dismissively at her older sister. "All part of the *same* story, as it happens. The older stone belongs to the fellow I told you about: the Clayton who survived the massacre and might have escaped with the soldiers' gold. Some say he made a bargain with the Devil to get out of the swamp alive; others say he murdered another soldier for the gold and brought a blood curse down upon his head." Carrie seemed to find both possibilities equally thrilling. "Whichever it was, he didn't make out well in the end. He lived in Catawissa for a while, but somebody turned him over to a regiment of Continental soldiers at Forty Fort and they shot him for desertion. Repeatedly."

"Once wasn't enough?" Verity asked.

"They say it took five musket balls to put him down. Even that wasn't enough. They took their eyes off him, thinking he was dead, and he almost got away — staggered to his feet and into the woods. They had to—" Annie cleared her throat loudly, and Carrie changed whatever she'd been going to say. "Take more drastic methods after that. If you ask me, they should have made him give up the gold before they killed him!"

"I don't believe he had any gold," said Annie. "The Claytons live like paupers."

"Well, he couldn't use it openly, could he?" Carrie protested. "People suspected him, and he kept it hidden somewhere. Drove his son, Caleb, crazy looking for it."

"Caleb Clayton didn't have far to go," Annie said.

"And the other grave belongs to the deserter's son?" Verity asked. "What relation was he to the present Claytons?"

"Caleb, the son, was Eli's father," said Carrie. "My father said Caleb was the meanest, craziest wretch the town has ever known—and that's saying a lot, when you consider Eli."

"What's the meaning of that epitaph—*Stay put now?*" Verity asked.

Carrie leaned forward eagerly in her chair, her carefully curled hair bobbing on her shoulders. "They had to put him in his coffin *twice*. Father saw it." Annie clicked her tongue in annoyance, and Carrie darted a look her way. "Well, he *did*, Annie!" She turned back to Verity and lowered her voice. "Our father was about fifteen when Caleb Clayton died, and he went to the wake out of curiosity—just to make sure Caleb was really dead, he said. About halfway through the evening, everyone heard a moan . . . and a rustling . . . and the coffin began to shake. Father said the hair stood up on the back of his neck, and if he could have gotten out of the house, he would have! But the coffin was between him and the door. Then the whole thing fell off the table—and Caleb kicked his way out of it!" Carrie's eyes were alight with gleeful horror. "He staggered to his feet . . . then turned and grabbed his wife by the neck and started strangling her!"

"No!" gasped Verity.

"He did!" insisted Carrie. "And people were too stunned and frightened to stop him, except Eli, who grabbed up a shotgun and emptied both barrels into his father. Then, when Caleb was down and still, they rolled him back into the coffin, closed it up, put it back on the table, and went on with the wake. My father swore to it."

Verity looked back and forth between the sisters, wide-eyed. "He wasn't dead."

"Not the first time," murmured Annie. "Father thinks he must have been in a drunken stupor, and his wife knew it. She probably hoped they'd put him in the ground before anyone noticed—he was such a hateful cuss."

"But Eli Clayton wasn't punished?" asked Verity. "He killed his father in front of half the town."

"You can't kill somebody who's already dead," replied Carrie. "And none of the Claytons rest easy in their graves. I've heard lots of people say as much."

"Is that true of my aunt Asenath as well?"

The teasing light in Carrie's eyes died out. "Oh, I—"

Annie gave her sister a withering look, and Carrie winced. "I'm sorry, Verity," she said earnestly. "I forgot she was a Clayton. I was only a child when she died, and I don't remember her very well."

Verity nodded, accepting the apology. She could hardly be offended when this was what she'd come to hear.

"Your uncle could have had the pick of any girl in town," Carrie declared, then cast a sideways glance at her sister. "Including Annie, I think. If he chose Asenath Clayton, she must not have been like the others."

"Why were she and my mother buried with those two Clayton men outside the church?" After regaling her with those other horrible stories, they could hardly refuse to tell her now.

Annie, still red cheeked after Carrie's comment, looked pained. "Very few Claytons ever made it into the churchyard, and when they did, parishioners complained. There was trouble."

Trouble with the parishioners or with the dead Claytons? Verity wondered. But instead of pursuing that, she asked, "Did my mother die of the strange illness that otherwise made only Claytons ill? Asenath survived it once, but it came back, didn't it?"

"Yes, and when your mother caught it, people believed she was somehow tainted by their—"

"Curse," Carrie concluded.

"I'm sorry, Verity." Annie sighed. "The sickness came upon your mother suddenly; she fell into a stupor and died. Ransloe was terrified you'd contract it too, so my mother and I took you out of the house. We brought you here and kept you for a few weeks, until your relations from Worcester came to get you."

Verity looked at Annie with surprise. "I didn't know that."

Annie's eyes filled with tears. "I was very upset when they took you away. I thought we were going to get to keep you." She pulled a handkerchief out of her sleeve to wipe her eyes. "Your father was devastated. I think that's why he gave in when people wanted to keep your mother out of the cemetery. He didn't have any fight left in him."

Verity wanted to know who had demanded that her mother be buried outside the cemetery, but Annie was in tears. Moreover, she felt quite certain she knew two of the names already.

"Nate suggested I ask you to lend me some poetry," Verity said instead.

"Oh!" Annie pressed the handkerchief to her eyes, then folded it away, obviously grateful for the change of subject. She rose and beckoned Verity toward the bookshelves. "Did you like the one he gave you?"

"I did." She couldn't stop herself from adding, "I

admit I liked it better when I thought Nate had chosen it."

Annie glanced back at Carrie. "Oh, dear. Well, you couldn't expect *Nate* to pick out poetry for you. He asked me to do it."

"Nate was very particular in his instructions." Carrie put in her two cents. "I know he had poor Hattie doing his bidding, fetching gloves and whatnot for you, making her take them back if they weren't what he'd asked for."

Verity felt herself blushing and hid it by pretending to peruse the poetry titles. "I didn't realize he gave it much thought," she murmured.

"On the contrary, I think he read your letters very carefully and sent Hattie out to purchase things you might like," Annie said. "I was chosen to select the poetry, and I viewed it as quite an honor."

With a sinking heart, Verity realized how she'd misjudged his words on their first meeting. "Did you advise him on his letters?"

"Well, I *offered* advice," Annie said with some exasperation. "We all did! Heaven knows if he took it."

Carrie flashed a mischievous smile. "I searched his room from top to bottom but didn't find a single letter from you. He must have hidden them well or kept them on his person."

Verity wanted to laugh and cry at the same time. The young man who'd stolen her heart in those letters and the young man she'd been kissing on the kitchen stoop and behind the parlor door — they were the same person. How could she not have known?

"You don't have to take a poetry book, you know," said Annie. "Let's see — Hattie's shelf is full of really dreadful dime novels. And Carrie has three shelves filled with even worse ones!" Her sister sniffed but didn't deny it.

"Does Nate have a shelf?"

Annie smiled triumphantly. Clearly, she'd been waiting for Verity to ask. "Nate has a *wall*."

As Annie dragged her to the opposite end of the room, Verity was regretting her self-righteous assumption that a person who didn't read poetry didn't read anything at all. In fact, Nate's shelves were filled from floor to ceiling with travel histories, from Melville's *Typee* to Kane's *Arctic Explorations*, and adventures such as *Robinson Crusoe* and *The Last of the Mohicans*.

She scanned the titles and felt humbled. If Nate had truly read all of these, he was better read than she was! "Which one is his favorite?" she asked.

Annie plucked a book off the shelves without hesitation.

Gulliver's Travels.

"I'll take that one, then," Verity said. "If I may."

Suddenly Annie turned toward the door and exclaimed, "Hattie! How is William?"

Verity guessed the answer by the way Nate's youngest

sister leaned her head against the door frame as if she could not hold it up. "He's very uncomfortable." Hattie looked drawn and strained, her pretty face pale and her hair bedraggled. "The pain has not let up since last evening, and the swelling is no better. You can imagine how frustrated he is." Then she added in her characteristically audible whisper, "And how irritable."

"Poor Will!" exclaimed Carrie.

"I'm so sorry," Verity exclaimed. "Would you like me to sit with him while you lie down?" She barely knew Hattie's husband, but sometimes a visit from an acquaintance would encourage a patient to perk up, just out of pride.

Hattie smiled gratefully. "Thank you, Verity. That's very kind. But I've sent for the doctor, and I saw from the upstairs window that he's arrived. I've just come down to meet him." She turned and disappeared into the hallway.

Annie followed her sister. Carrie hooked her arm with Verity's in a companionable manner and drew her along in their wake.

Verity was distressed by how loudly her heart thumped and how weak her knees suddenly felt. She clutched Nate's book to her bosom, as though to remind herself where her heart was supposed to lie, as Carrie dragged her toward her first meeting with Hadley Jones in two weeks.

TWENTY

HE DOCTOR stomped into the house with ill humor, grumbling and looking around impatiently. His eyes passed over Verity without recognition and caught sight of Hattie. "Did you use the poultice the way I told you last time?" he demanded.

"Yes, doctor, I did."

Verity tried to calm the pounding of her heart. It was Dr. Robbins—not his apprentice. He was a big man, well over six feet tall, with wild gray hair and a puffed-out beard under florid cheeks. His shaggy eyebrows might as well have been a pair of mustaches hovering over his eyes. He mounted the stairs, leaning heavily on the banister.

Verity bade the McClure sisters a hurried farewell, and they were too caught up in worry about Hattie's husband to notice how shaken and embarrassed she was. She didn't know why she cared so much whether it was

Hadley Jones or not, but she did know it would have been an awkward meeting and not one she wanted Nate's sisters to witness.

Leaving the house, she had to pass the doctor's horse and trap. The man in the driver's seat sank down as she descended the front steps, tilting his hat over his face — as if planning to nap while he waited for his employer. She considered walking by without stopping, but her sense of duty did not permit it. Taking a determined breath, she strode directly to the trap and called up to him, "Good day, Mr. Poole."

"Good day, Miss Boone," the driver replied in a soft voice. At least he didn't pretend not to know her.

"I believe I owe you my thanks for your timely assistance in the Shades two weeks ago." He made no move to lift his hat from his face; nevertheless, she could see the scar that had frightened her that day. "And my apologies for hitting you on the head with my basket."

"No harm done" was his mumbled response.

No harm done except Verity's injured ankle, and that was her own fault for behaving so foolishly and running from a man who was trying to help her. However, as Verity continued down the lane toward home, she reminded herself that she wouldn't have run so far or fallen at all if Jones hadn't chased her. Placing blame for the entire incident on the impertinent Hadley Jones gave her a certain measure of satisfaction.

When she got home, she took Nate's letters out of the drawer where she'd consigned them after deciding that he hadn't written them himself. If she hadn't been so pig-headed, so quick to judge him — if she'd just *looked at* his letters after meeting him — she would have known they were his by his turns of phrase.

> I told my mother, see here, I will write her myself, and that is how I came to this unlikely point of courting you by letter. . . .
>
> If you don't think it is too forward, I would be pleased if you called me Nate. Otherwise you can use Nathaniel, but when you address your letters to Mr. McClure, I feel like you are writing to my late father
>
> . . .

She could hear his familiar voice in every line, and the next day, when a late-evening knock on the door proved to be one of the Poole men sent down from the McClure house with a basket for her, she beamed with joy.

"Sorry to disturb you so late, Miss Boone," the man said. "But Mr. Nathaniel bade me deliver this with his greetings."

The basket held fresh cherries, no doubt carried all the way from Lancaster, as well as a short length of sturdy red ribbon fitted with a bell. Verity laughed. Nate knew her father thought Verity was spoiling what ought to have been a good mouser. A bell around her cat's neck would make him useless for hunting and identify him for what he really was: a very lucky, pampered house pet.

She found a brief note tucked along the side of the basket: *I will see you tomorrow, when I will count all the ways I love thee — even if I don't understand most of them.*

He'd memorized Barrett Browning's poem for her, just as he'd promised. It shamed her to realize how she would have misunderstood his words before seeing his own books. Just because he didn't understand every line of the poem didn't mean he lacked intelligence. Verity had been struggling with *Gulliver's Travels* and felt thoroughly chastened.

She could explain the poem to him, and he could explain the book — if they didn't have anything better to do with their lips.

Beulah bristled the next morning when Verity announced her intention to make cherry pies, but Verity was prepared for this. "I'll make the filling, and I wondered if you would make the pastry. Your pie crust is much better than mine." Verity hoped Beulah knew her well enough to realize this wasn't empty flattery.

If she did, it didn't seem to mollify her. "I found jam everywhere after you made those tarts," the housekeeper said with a frown.

"I cleaned up all the jam."

"I'm sure you thought you did," Beulah muttered.

Verity blinked in surprise. "I'm sorry. I'll be more careful in the first place, then," she said contritely. "I promise."

The old woman didn't reply but brought out the flour and her rolling pin. Verity took that as evidence of a truce between them and commenced pitting the cherries. They were working together in silence when Johnny Thomas burst in through the back door, his eyes alight with excitement. "Cousin Verity!" he cried. "Have you heard what happened at the cemetery last night? Someone tried to dig up your mother's grave!" And having delivered this devastating news with the innocent callousness of a twelve-year-old boy, Johnny turned and darted back outside.

"Miss Verity!" Beulah exclaimed, and stepped between her and the door. Verity dodged around the housekeeper and took off in her cousin's wake.

Several yards ahead of her, Johnny vanished at the turn of the road. As soon as she reached the top of the hill, Verity could see carriages stopped at the bottom, all in a row as if it were a church day. People milled around outside the cemetery, congregating by the two graves marked with iron cages. At Johnny's arrival, people turned and looked up the road. No sooner had Verity been spotted than a familiar figure separated from the group and started toward her.

By the time Nate intercepted her, Verity had slowed her perilous run to a breathless trot. Her fists were clenched at her sides. "Don't you dare try to stop me!" she said.

Nate held both his hands up placatingly. "I know better than that." His brow was furrowed with anger and worry. "Just — take my hand, Verity."

His fingers gripping hers tightly, he walked her toward the cemetery. Ransloe Boone looked up with an anguished expression. Nate stopped at the edge of the crowd, and although Verity wanted to approach the grave, she could not induce her feet to move forward without him.

She was close enough to see that the cage had done its job.

The flowers and ivy she'd planted had been ripped from the ground and tossed aside. A hole had been dug at one of the corners of the cage and extended into a trench along one side and around the back. It looked as if someone had been testing to see whether the framework extended below the casket, which apparently it did.

The township sheriff stood at the foot of the grave, his hands on his hips, and Reverend White was explaining what happened. "After the voices roused me," he said, "I came downstairs with a lantern and looked along the road. I didn't see anyone and thought perhaps it had just been an open carriage passing by. This was around two or three in the morning."

"But they were arguing, you said. Loudly and

violently." The sheriff glared down on the tremulous clergyman. "This is not the first . . . incident that has occurred in this cemetery. Why didn't you come out to take a closer look?"

"I was in my nightclothes!" the minister exclaimed indignantly.

The sheriff looked down at the iron framework. "Was it the same grave last time — or the other one?"

"It's always Sarah Ann they come after," growled Ransloe Boone. "Never Asenath."

Verity shuddered to hear it. *They always come after Sarah Ann.*

"I'm sorry, Ransloe," John Thomas said in a voice hollowed with sadness and regret.

Nate whispered into her ear. "You're upsetting yourself *and* your father *and* me by being here. Have pity on your father, if no one else, and let me take you home."

She nodded without speaking. Putting one arm around her shoulders, Nate turned her away from the graves. People stared at her as she passed, most with sympathy, some with bold curiosity.

When they reached the road, Nate lifted her up onto one of his family's farm wagons. Verity clung to her seat and stared straight ahead with a stony face, unwilling to give the onlookers anything more to gossip about. "I can't bear this," she said from between clenched teeth. "I won't tolerate it!"

Nate shook the reins and clucked to the horse. "You shouldn't have to," he growled.

Beulah was standing on the front porch of the Boone house. She watched with worried eyes as they mounted the front steps. "What happened, Mr. Nathaniel?"

"Someone tried to get into Mrs. Boone's grave," he said quietly. "But they gave up before they got too far. Would you bring Miss Boone some strong tea?"

Beulah looked at Verity's face and nodded.

Verity sank to a seat in the parlor. Nate sat down and put his arm around her. "We'll put a stop to this, Verity; I promise you. We'll get that wall moved . . . whatever it takes."

The front door opened and slammed shut, footsteps ringing sharply on the wooden floor of the hallway. Verity turned, expecting to see her father, and flinched sharply at the sight of Hadley Jones. He walked into the parlor as if he had every right to be there.

"I just heard," he said, breathlessly. "Miss Boone, are you all right?"

Verity stared with dismay at the young man, who surveyed her with an obvious and very personal concern. He was pale himself, his ginger locks disheveled, as if he'd run all the way from town on foot. He sported a bruise on his right cheek below his eye, which made him look more like a saloon brawler than a physician.

Nate sat stiffly beside her, his arm suddenly removed

from her shoulder. He said nothing, and she didn't dare look at him.

"I'm as well as can be expected, thank you," Verity said finally, finding her voice.

"Do you need anything?" His eyes flicked to Nate and then back to her. "Something to calm you?"

Her fingers curled on the sofa cushion, gripping it fiercely. "No, I don't need to be calmer. Someone just tried to dig up my mother's grave. Why would I want to be calm about it?"

Jones swallowed visibly and brushed perspiration from his forehead with the back of his hand. He *had* run up here to see her; she knew it. But with her intended husband sitting beside her, he could offer her no comfort except in a professional capacity. He could not hold her hand or put his arm around her. Verity was grateful for Nate's presence. She didn't know if she would have had the strength to refuse Jones if she'd been alone.

"What happened to your face?" Nate asked suddenly.

Jones appeared embarrassed. "Robbins."

Nate raised his eyebrows and said nothing.

Verity felt a surge of indignation. "Are you saying Dr. Robbins *hit* you?" A master who hit his apprentice was despicable enough; for a medical man to do so was unthinkable.

Jones waved a hand as if to erase the matter. "He

won't remember it tomorrow. I'm more worried about you — and your father, of course. How is he?"

"Shaken," said Verity. "And angry."

"He has a right to be," Jones replied. "She was the woman he loved."

Then there was silence again.

Verity closed her eyes, wishing these two young men were not together with her at this moment. It did not lessen her turmoil to know she found Hadley Jones as attractive as ever. There was something seductive about his transparent feelings for her — feelings he scarcely tried to hide even in front of Nate. He was like a bright, flickering flame, and she was a brainless moth, wanting to fly closer and burn herself.

Yet if she had wanted to go to him, she didn't think there was a limb on her body that would have obeyed her. She could not move from Nate's side; his presence anchored her in place.

As the silence deepened, Verity realized she could end this awkward tableau. Hadley Jones had not been summoned as a physician; this was a social call. He'd come here to express his concern for her, and she had the power to welcome or dismiss him.

She rose from her seat. "Thank you for coming. It was good of you to stop by."

She saw by the resignation on his face that he

understood her plainly. He dropped his eyes and bowed formally. "Miss Boone. I won't bid you good day, because I know it cannot be one. Please remember I am at your service if you or your father need anything." He straightened and gave Nate a curt nod. "McClure."

"Jones," Nate acknowledged, his voice flat.

Hadley Jones left as quickly as he had come, without looking at Verity again.

TWENTY-ONE

ERITY PACED the room. She glanced at Nate, almost daring him to make a derogatory comment about Hadley Jones or suggest that her behavior had encouraged him, even for a moment.

But Nate just watched her worriedly. If it bothered him that the doctor's apprentice was interested in her, he'd decided not to show it. *Good*, thought Verity. Hadley Jones's affections—unrequited or not—were the least of her concerns.

"Why do people think my father found that treasure?"

Nate shrugged. "Because he stopped looking for it?"

Verity clenched her fists in frustration. "Maybe he gave up. Maybe it doesn't exist. Maybe he decided there were better ways to spend his time!"

"You don't have to convince *me*, Verity. I'm on your side."

But she needed to think aloud, to reason it out. "If he *did* find it, why would he bury it again?" she demanded. "Uncle John searched for that treasure too. Why do they think it's in my mother's grave and not Asenath's?"

"Because John selfishly spent his half of the gold, while Ransloe buried his share in remorse."

Verity and Nate both turned around to stare at Clara Thomas, who entered the parlor with Beulah at her heels. Her matter-of-fact manner of speaking startled them into silence for a second, but then Verity blurted out, "That can't be true!"

"Of course not," Aunt Clara chided. She turned to Beulah, who set the tray with tea on the serving table. "Fetch sugar and cream for Verity."

"I prefer my tea plain," Verity said.

"You'll take it sweetened and with cream, for the shock," Aunt Clara corrected her. Verity blinked, taken aback.

"I heard stories like this when I was a child, Mrs. Thomas," Nate said. "But I can't believe grown men could be so foolish—would desecrate a grave!"

"The world is full of people who believe what they want to be true. And this isn't the first time treasure hunters have tried to get into that grave. The story's kept alive by the ignorant and the superstitious." Aunt Clara took the sugar bowl and creamer from Beulah and began to prepare the tea as if Verity couldn't do it herself. "The Pooles probably tell it to every wanderer who passes through town."

Beulah remained impassive, although Nate looked uncomfortable and Verity bit her lip in embarrassment. It was as if Beulah Poole were invisible—or so unimportant that Aunt Clara did not care what was said in front of her. Beulah spared Clara Thomas one sour glance and departed from the room as silently as she'd entered.

Verity sipped the oversweet tea and continued to pace around the room, holding the cup. "People think my father and your husband found this treasure and split it between them?"

"My family lives with obvious means and wealth, therefore John must have acquired a fortune through some illicit venture of his youth." Her aunt's tone was crisp and disdainful. "Your father lives an austere life and has grieved for years over his wife. Therefore, he must have buried his share of the treasure in her coffin, in penance for his ill-gotten gains."

"Are you saying they truly did find something of value?" Nate asked.

Aunt Clara sat down and folded her hands, keeping an eye on Verity. "No, of course not. John inherited his parents' property, and we've worked hard for what we have. And Ransloe, despite the way he keeps his house, makes a fine living on this land. There will be a substantial dowry for Verity—as I'm sure you know, Nathaniel."

Nate recoiled as if Clara Thomas had slapped him, and cast a look at Verity. She waved a hand, signaling him not to take offense, and found herself slopping tea over the edge of the cup. Feeling a little befuddled, she took another long sip. "I can't believe my father tolerates that kind of talk."

"One cannot squelch an idea at will," Aunt Clara said, "nor silence rumors whispered behind one's back. You should sit down, Verity."

She ignored the suggestion. "Do you think it was those men who grabbed Piper in the woods?"

"They or someone like them."

"Verity," Nate murmured.

"But Uncle John did search for that treasure," Verity went on. "And—he got my father to help him. That's what the diaries said—"

Her aunt's brow furrowed. "What diaries?"

"Verity!" Nate exclaimed.

She looked down and discovered she'd been dribbling tea down the front of her dress. How had she done that? When she turned back toward Nate, the room lurched, and she staggered. Nate leaped to his feet and strode toward her. Verity gaped at him in alarm, grabbing the back of a chair.

"I *told* you to sit down, Verity," Aunt Clara said disapprovingly.

"What have you done?" Nate growled over his

shoulder, gripping Verity by both arms. It took a moment for her to realize he'd already removed the cup from her hands. She blinked, trying to clear the heaviness in her head.

"A good, strong dose of laudanum," her aunt said. "For the shock. She needs to lie down and rest."

"She told Jones she didn't want anything."

"It was a mistake for him to ask her opinion."

Verity suddenly felt very ill. "Nate?"

His arm around her waist held her upright. "I'd better take her upstairs."

"To her bedchamber?" Aunt Clara was beside them now, taking a firm grip on Verity's upper arm. "I think *not*, Nathaniel! Beulah and I will take her."

Verity couldn't follow everything that happened next. She had a vague impression that sharp words were exchanged.

" . . . wouldn't *dare* drug my wife against her wishes . . ."

" . . . *not* your wife yet! Patience, boy! You'll get what you want soon enough . . ."

Beulah and Aunt Clara supported Verity up the stairs to her room, each step a monumental effort. The last thing she remembered was pitching face first onto her bed while the world spun and lurched between darkness and light, shadows careening against her wall like wraiths.

•   •   •

She was running in the Shades of Death again, her legs

stumbling with leaden clumsiness, vines slithering after her like snakes. Behind her, pursuers whooped and howled, leaping effortlessly over stumps and rocks, their faces lit with savagery. They would scalp her — they would run her through with bayonets —

The ground fell away, and she tumbled down and down until she lay at the bottom of a hole so deep, she could never hope to climb out. Above her, a shadow parted the writhing vines. "Hadley, help me!" she shrieked.

The figure, dark and formless, loomed over her, eyes glowing like embers.

"The Devil can get you out of here," whispered a voice in her ear. She flinched and looked around. That was Carrie's voice; Verity was certain of it.

"Make a bargain with the Devil," Carrie whispered again.

She thrashed, trying to push herself off the ground as the dark shape suddenly swarmed down at her like a cloud of bees. "No! No!" she cried, putting up her hands to ward it off. Someone grabbed her hands and pinned them to her sides.

"It really is a shame." Hattie leaned over her with cold, hard eyes — indigo blue, just like her brother's. "She was worth a lot of money."

"Hattie?" Verity whimpered, struggling to sit upright. She was in her own bed, thank heavens, but she couldn't make her arms and legs work.

"I suppose we'll have to cage her grave," Hattie said with a cruel smile. "We can't count on her to stay in it otherwise."

"I'm not dead—why do you think I'm dead?"

Long, silver hair brushed against her face, tickling and sticking like cobwebs. Hattie was gone, and Asenath hovered over her now, her breath cold and putrid. "Hush now, Verity. It'll be over soon." She drew the sheet over Verity's face.

"No!" She tried to sit up. "I'm not dead!"

The girl smiled sweetly, forcing her back onto the bed with impossible strength and raising the sheet once more. "Of course not. None of us *really* is . . ."

And then Verity found herself in the cemetery again, where she stared with shock at her mother's grave. This time the freshly dug holes were on the *inside* of the cage, and the dirt kept shifting, pushed up and away from the dark cavity. Slim, pale fingers emerged, wriggling, seeking purchase.

"Mother?" Verity choked.

A voice whispered back. "I was never supposed to die."

Asenath held the cage door open, inviting Verity in. Her corn-silk hair blew in the wind; her feet were bare beneath the white dress she'd worn in the photograph. In a voice as raspy as iron hinges, Asenath said, "You should never have come back to Catawissa."

"I should never have let you come back to Catawissa," Ransloe Boone muttered.

Verity lifted her head to stare in surprise across the kitchen table and then regretted the sudden movement. She felt as if someone had tightened a leather belt around her head. "Why do you say that?" she asked.

She and her father sat at the table together, late in the evening. Two lamps, left burning by Beulah when she retired for the night, provided the only illumination in the house. A plate of cold meat had been placed in the larder for them, as well as some freshly baked bread. Neither of them had much appetite.

She'd slept the entire day, waking to a dark room and nearly panicking because she couldn't sit up. After a fierce struggle, she'd broken free of the bed sheets, which had been pulled tightly across her and tucked beneath the mattress. When she'd trusted her trembling legs to carry her, she'd gone downstairs, meeting her father as he came in.

"I've never been able to live down my youth," Ransloe Boone said. "And your mother's memory is besmirched because of it."

"Did you ever find anything?" Verity asked bluntly, picking her bread apart without eating it. "Why did you even want it?"

"I was a fool, and God punished me for coveting it."

He hunched his shoulders, meeting his daughter's eyes for only a second before dropping his gaze again. "No, we never found anything, but I was wasting my time by the river looking for it when your mother took sick. I only got back here in time to send you out of the house and sit by her side while she slipped away."

"Do you think if you'd been here, she wouldn't have gotten ill?"

He stared at the table. "Doesn't matter. I should have been here. And now, fifteen years later, they're *still* disturbing her because of me."

"You should have told me," Verity chastised him gently.

"I didn't want you to know. The last thing in the world I wanted was for you to see your mother's grave opened by thieves."

"Father—"

"You were happy in Worcester, living with a good family. Maryett would have found you a husband in the city. You needn't have come back here and learned about this shame."

"Is that why you sent me away?"

He looked up again, and this time he didn't flinch. "Maryett convinced me it was the right thing to do. She said you'd have a family to grow up with if she took you back to Worcester." He shrugged uneasily. "I thought you'd be happier with brothers and sisters. I let you go, and I didn't visit much because I didn't want to confuse you. It was hard . . . watching you with Maryett and the other children. You hardly knew who I was."

Verity blinked back tears. His last visit to Worcester had been right before he went to war. He knew he might die, and he wanted to see his daughter one last time. Of course, he hadn't told her so. She hadn't even known he was called up into the army until after he was gone.

She reached across the table and grasped his hand. "I'm here now, Father, and I won't leave you again. I wouldn't want to be anywhere else."

TWENTY-TWO

N THE morning Verity woke with an unpleasant thickness in her mouth and a lingering headache, but she was thinking clearly. When she saw her mother's final diary open on her dressing table, she walked over and looked down on it without surprise.

November tenth through November fourteenth. The very same page as before. But who had left it open this time? Aunt Clara? Hattie and Carrie? Or Asenath?

Nate's sisters hadn't really been at the house last night, and Asenath was dead.

When she went downstairs, Beulah looked her over shrewdly. "Do you want breakfast, Miss Verity?"

"Tea," she replied. "With only *tea* in it."

"It wasn't me that did it."

"I didn't think it was." Verity sat down at the kitchen

table and watched the housekeeper for a few long, silent moments. "Do your people believe in ghosts, Beulah?"

"My people?" grunted Beulah, putting the pot on to boil without even looking back. "You mean the French or the Dutch?"

Verity looked down, embarrassed by her question and considering how she might rephrase it.

Beulah brought her a cup. Then she set a plate of sliced bread down, as well as a crock of butter. Suddenly Verity realized how hungry she was and reached for them with both hands.

"The Mohawk people believe in spirits." Beulah crossed her arms and watched Verity devour a slice of buttered bread. "Spirits of the earth and spirits of our ancestors. If you look closely enough, you see their signs and know the path to follow."

The water came to a boil, and Beulah filled the teapot and carried it over to Verity's cup. "None of my people would have sent anyone to your mother's grave," she said. Verity winced, remembering her aunt's callous accusation. "We don't desecrate the ground of our ancestors — and besides, that gold is cursed by betrayal and blood. We don't want it."

Later, Verity sat on the front stoop, holding Nate's hand and assuring him that she was, essentially, unharmed. She didn't tell him about the sinister dreams that had left her shaken and filled with foreboding.

"I don't care if she *is* the daughter of an apothecary," Nate grumbled, watching Verity's kitten attack the laces on his work boots. "That was uncalled for."

Privately Verity agreed, but aloud she said, "Some people always think they know what's best for you."

"The grave's repaired. Even your flowers have been re-planted." Nate shook his foot playfully, trying to dislodge Lucky from his shoe, but when he looked up, his face was grim. "I don't think your plan to rebuild the cemetery wall is going to be enough. We should have the casket disin-terred and moved inside the church grounds—publicly, so everyone can see for themselves there's nothing there that shouldn't be."

"Do you think so?" His use of the word *we* irritated her. They weren't married yet; it wasn't his mother, nor his decision. "Shall we open the casket, too, and let any-one who wants feel around inside, just to make sure?"

He flinched, but her point had hit home.

"The only way to put down a lie is to discover the truth," Verity said. "It's a shame no one's found that wretched treasure. You don't think my uncle really does have it, do you? He seems well off for money, but I never see him do a lick of work."

"He prefers other ways of making money." Nate

grimaced. "He gambles, Verity. Quite a bit—in town, in Wilkes-Barre, in Philadelphia, anywhere there's dice and cards. I'm sorry to have to tell you."

She sighed. "I'm not surprised, really. He doesn't seem . . ."

"Sensible." Nate looked out across Verity's front yard, toward the Thomas lands. "His wife's the one who manages the property and all the men working on it. If it weren't for her, that farm would probably be in ruins. And it's a fine piece of land."

A sharp pain shot through Verity's heart. She was tired of hearing how much Nate admired property. "It's a wonder no one suggested you marry Liza Thomas," she said tartly.

"Don't laugh," Nate replied, reaching down to scratch the kitten behind the ears. "That probably would have been my mother's next plan." And then he did laugh, but she did not.

Truth trumped lies.

Verity believed this without question. The gold was not in her mother's grave, so if it existed, it must be somewhere else. She was not equipped to find it, but there were other lies for her to expose—such as the idea that her mother had died of a sickness born of some curse on the Clayton family.

Rebecca Clayton had been the first person to die of this illness, which eventually took three more Claytons and, three months later, Asenath and Sarah Ann. And Rebecca's body had been stolen from its grave. Why? Had the strangeness of her death attracted the interest of someone who wanted to know the cause?

Verity would have liked to know the cause herself.

And then she realized she knew somebody who might be able to discover that very thing . . . if she dared ask him.

Calling on him in this manner was not a nice thing to do. But the need to know burned inside her. If Hadley Jones could provide her with a plausible explanation for the deaths, Verity could eliminate half the legend behind the caged graves.

She sat alone on a straight-backed chair in Dr. Robbins's waiting room, relieved that the senior physician was absent from the house. Knowing how he'd treated his apprentice, she had no desire to meet him again.

It was Hadley Jones she heard in the examining room — him and another man — and the consultation didn't seem to be going well. Although she couldn't make out the words, the patient spoke in a harsh and accusing voice, while Jones's calmer tones suggested an intent to reason with him.

The door opened abruptly, exposing her to their final

exchange. "If you don't do as I've instructed you, you'll end up with blood poisoning — or, at best, I'll have to take more of it off!" Jones said.

"All the same to you," growled the patient, a man in his early twenties with a thin, sickly build and unclean reddish-blond hair. "What's one more limb lopped off, here or there?"

Verity lowered her head as the men emerged but watched them from the corner of her eye. The patient shuffled into the anteroom, and his gaze raked over her with hostility. Hadley Jones reached inside his coat pocket. "Mr. Harwood," he said. "About your payment."

"Are you joking?" The patient turned on his heel angrily.

But Jones was taking cash out of his pocket. "Your change," he said, holding out a wad of folded bills.

Harwood accepted it with his left hand, and Verity, watching through her lashes, saw that his right arm was amputated just below the elbow, the exposed stump raw and swollen. She cast her gaze at the floor again, unable to shake off the impression that the doctor had just paid the patient.

Harwood made his departure, and when Verity raised her eyes, Hadley Jones nodded with a polite but reserved smile. "Miss Boone, how can I help you?"

Verity rose, clutching an embroidered bag in her

hand. "I was hoping you could diagnose an illness for me. Not my own," she added hastily.

"Your father?" When he took a step toward her, she saw that the bruise on his cheek had turned purple.

"No — it's no one you know."

He surveyed her with inquisitive eyes, then gestured toward the open door of the examining room. "Shall we — ?"

"*Here* would be fine." Verity indicated his desk in the waiting room, and he moved her chair, placing it opposite his own. He kept a respectful distance, and she knew she'd made her message clear.

Once they were seated, Verity opened her bag and pulled out her mother's notebooks. Slips of paper marked the pertinent pages. Jones sat in silence as she found the passages she wanted. "Severe pains in the stomach and gut . . . a slow heartbeat . . . watering from the eyes, nose, and mouth . . . stupor and death. Do you have any idea what illness could cause these symptoms?"

She looked up to find him gazing at her with bewilderment. "Whose illness are we talking about?" he asked.

"My deceased aunt — Asenath Thomas."

Jones frowned and ran a hand through his ginger curls. "You're asking me to diagnose the illness of someone who died twenty years ago?"

"Fifteen years."

"Well, *that* makes all the difference." He smiled wryly and held out his hand. "May I?" She handed the diary across the desk, and he read the entries. "It says she recovered."

"But three months later she died after suffering the same symptoms. And so did my mother." When he glanced up at her, she added, "Other people died of the same thing that August—four members of the Clayton family."

Jones flipped to the pages Verity had marked with paper slips and read through them. Verity opened her mother's last diary to the final page and laid it on the desk too. He leaned over to look, and his expression became grim as he saw the final, scrawled words. "Miss Boone, why are you pursuing this?"

"I want to know why my mother died."

"What good can come of knowing the name of the sickness?" Jones raised his eyes to hers. "I foresee nothing but heartache in this for you—even if I can identify the illness for you."

"I need to know the truth," Verity countered.

"You're not thinking this has anything to do with what happened at the cemetery?"

"I do think so. I'll pay you for your time."

He smiled sadly. "I don't want your money."

"Nevertheless, I will pay you."

Jones sat back in his chair and looked across the desk at her. She faced him, keenly aware of his concern, his interest—yet determined to keep this conversation professional. After a moment, he broke their gaze and cast his eyes over the two open notebooks. "You've marked the pages you want me to look at," he said, "but I'll have to read more. You might've missed things you didn't realize were symptoms. Are you comfortable with that? I promise I won't pry into your personal, private matters."

"I was two years old," she said. "My personal matters were not that private."

He grinned. "I'll do what I can to lay the matter to rest for you, Miss Boone. Please realize the chance is slim, but if I can help you, I will."

Hadley Jones pushed back his chair, and Verity stood up. He rose to his feet and offered his hand across the desk. With some hesitation, she took it. His fingers closed around hers, warm and strong. She could not deny she was affected by his touch, but she said the only thing she could. "Thank you."

"Anything — for you."

TWENTY-THREE

ERITY HAD treated Clara Thomas coolly since the day of the laudanum-laced tea, and when her aunt invited her to help decorate graves in the cemetery for the Fourth of July, she almost declined. But anything happening at the cemetery was of interest to her, and if she wanted changes made, it would behoove her to stay involved.

Finding Mrs. Eggars there did not make for a promising start to the day. The hatchet-faced woman was adorning her own family graves with flowers and flags when Verity arrived with her aunt and cousin. "She never lifts a hand to do anyone else's," Liza grumbled under her breath. While Aunt Clara and Liza carried their heavy baskets of red, white, and blue bunting into the graveyard proper, Verity veered left outside the cemetery gate and walked around the wall to her mother's grave.

One thing could be said about the cages: it was easy to attach the bunting. Flanked by ivy and forget-me-nots and draped in swoops of colorful fabric, the two iron structures looked almost beautiful. After adjusting the bunting on Asenath's cage, Verity moved on to the other gravestones sharing this sad banishment outside the cemetery wall.

"What are you doing?"

Verity deliberately pulled up two more handfuls of weeds obscuring the old, worn headstone before acknowledging Mrs. Eggars's pointed question. "I'm decorating the graves for the Fourth of July," she said.

Mrs. Eggars waved her hand impatiently. "Not *those* graves, you silly girl! If you want to do your mother's, I suppose I can't stop you, but you absolutely *cannot* drape the Stars and Stripes over the other ones!"

"You're right you can't stop me," Verity said, climbing to her feet and approaching the cemetery wall.

"*He* was a deserter!" Mrs. Eggars jabbed her index finger toward the worn, illegible stone.

Verity resisted an urge to slap that finger down. "He paid for his crime with his life. There's no reason to shame him after death."

"The Claytons are all heathens!"

"Yet I see them in church every Sunday." Not Eli Clayton—but Verity had seen Idella and Cissy, with her out-of-wedlock child. They sat in the back, shunned by most of the other congregants. "There are plenty of Claytons buried inside the cemetery."

"And they've caused no end of trouble!"

Before Verity could ask Mrs. Eggars what kind of trouble dead Claytons caused, Aunt Clara broke into the conversation. "Susanna Eggars, you had your way when you kept those two women out of the churchyard. Can't you be satisfied and let my niece decorate the graves however she chooses?"

"I don't remember you objecting at the time, Clara," Mrs. Eggars snapped. "Had your eye on the prize as always, didn't you?"

Verity glared at Mrs. Eggars. "What did my mother ever do to you," she demanded, "that made you go out of your way to shame her?"

"I had nothing against Sarah Ann until she started consorting with witches."

"Mrs. Eggars's sister nearly died of childbed fever," Aunt Clara explained to Verity. "And midwives are always convenient scapegoats."

"That little Clayton witch left one of her heathen spells in my sister's birthing chamber, and Belinda sickened," Mrs. Eggars exclaimed. "Thank heavens I found it and removed it in time! Mrs. Harper wasn't as lucky — her baby died of whooping cough before he was eight weeks old. And Gladys Morrow got a sty in her eye after Asenath mumbled some curse at her in the street."

Verity gaped in disbelief. Aunt Clara clucked her tongue with annoyance, but Mrs. Eggars appeared to be quite serious. Spit flew from her lips as she continued her rant, pointing a bony finger at Asenath's grave. "Finally, the Lord saw fit to smite her down, and if He took your mother too, I can only assume she'd gone to the Devil as well!"

"Mrs. Eggars," Verity said through clenched teeth, "I suggest you keep your slanderous statements to yourself. As for these graves, I'll decorate them as I see fit. If you don't like it, you can take it up with my intended, Nathaniel McClure."

Hearing Verity wield the name of the most powerful family in town, the woman took a step backward. Verity wasn't entirely sure she was proud of herself for resorting to it.

"Come take your meal with us this afternoon," her aunt said when the decorating was finished.

"No, thank you, Aunt Clara."

"I insist."

Verity had to return to the Thomas house to retrieve her sewing basket, which she'd used when they'd assembled the bunting that morning, but she had every intention of refusing to stay for the meal—until set upon by

Piper and the twins. She found it impossible to disappoint the boys, and after all, she reminded herself, Aunt Clara had defended her mother against Mrs. Eggars.

After lunch, when she rose to leave, her aunt cornered her with a stack of papers, wanting her to choose a pattern for her bridal quilt. As Aunt Clara thumbed through the selections with her, explaining the history and significance of each, Verity wondered if she was trying to make amends for the laudanum. Polly Gaines would have advised Verity to let bygones be bygones, and so she listened patiently to her aunt and even volunteered an idea of her own. "I have some clothing of my mother's that is too worn to be of use, but the fabric would make a nice quilt."

"Very fitting," Aunt Clara said. "It would be good to think Sarah Ann had a hand in your bridal quilt."

Verity had narrowed her choices down to two when Liza pushed Stephen and Samuel through the kitchen door, calling out, "The doctor's here to see the boys."

"Ah," said Aunt Clara, "it's about time."

Verity glanced up and met Hadley Jones's eyes as he entered the kitchen. "What seems to be the problem today, Mrs. Thomas?" he asked, tearing his gaze away from Verity. "Teeth, you said?"

"Samuel has a rotted one, and Stephen—possibly two. I expect you'll have to pull them."

The boys shrieked in unison, each one fleeing in a different direction. Aunt Clara caught one by the collar and thrust him into Verity's hands. "Hold Sam for the doctor," she commanded. Then she followed Liza on the trail of the other twin.

Startled, Verity hung on to her cousin while Jones rolled up his sleeves. "Open up, Samuel," he said.

The child shook his head and clamped his lips together. Jones regarded the boy for a moment, then pinched his nose shut. Verity made an outraged noise, but Jones grinned at her. "It'll take only a few seconds."

Samuel's mouth popped open as he gasped for air, and the apprentice grabbed his open jaw with both hands. "Bite me and I'll bite you back," he warned.

The child rolled his eyes toward Verity for help, but she shrugged. "I suggest you do as you're told."

Jones took a long look into Samuel's mouth, pulling the boy's lips apart and tilting his head back. "I know what you're going to ask," he said quietly. "But I don't have an answer for you yet."

Samuel stared at him, puzzled, but Verity knew he was talking to her. "You must have some thoughts on the matter."

"I do," he admitted. "But I'm not certain. Well, there's no way I could be certain, this long after the fact." He sighed and released the child's mouth. "The tooth *is* rotted, but it's a milk tooth and loose enough to fall out on its own. I'm surprised Mrs. Thomas hasn't tied a string to a door and taken it out with a good slam."

Samuel flinched.

"Just wiggle it around," Jones advised the boy. He reached into his pocket and produced a piece of toffee. "Chew on this for a bit and see if you can get it out yourself."

He swatted the boy away in dismissal, and Samuel vanished like a shot through the outside kitchen door. Then Jones met Verity's eyes. "I wish you'd drop the matter."

"I'm determined to know why they died."

"I want to talk to Eli Clayton, and then I might be able to tell you something." He reached out a hand and touched her arm. "Any answer I give you is going to make you unhappy; you realize that, don't you?"

The back door opened and Nate strode in, carrying a bushel of peaches.

For just a moment they all three froze — and then Hadley Jones belatedly removed his hand from Verity's arm.

Nate shoved the basket onto the kitchen table, scattering quilt patterns and spilling fruit. "Here are the peaches your aunt wanted." He turned on his heel and was out the door again in a second.

"Nate!" cried Verity.

She bolted from the kitchen and ran to catch up with his long, angry strides. "Nate! Don't you dare walk away from me like this!"

He turned back so suddenly, she collided with him.

"There's something between you and Jones, isn't there?" Nate demanded.

Verity stared up at him, horrified to realize she couldn't say there was *nothing* between them—because that would be a lie. "He's a friend," she finally said.

"Jones isn't chasing after you because he's feeling friendly." Nate glared at her. "He's *everywhere* you are. Did you—did you go into the Shades to meet him the day you got hurt?"

Verity gasped in outrage. "No! How dare you suggest such a thing?" She stamped her foot. "Is that what you think of me? Is that the kind of girl you think I am?"

Nate seemed to realize the dishonorable nature of his accusation, because his expression changed immediately. "No," he said quickly. "No, I'm sorry, Verity. I shouldn't have said that."

"Indeed you shouldn't have," she snapped back. She twitched her skirts around him, prepared to march home in righteous fury, but Nate moved to block her path.

"I'm sorry," he repeated in a penitent voice. "Please forgive me. I don't think before I speak. It's a terrible fault of mine, and I apologize."

Verity put her hands on her hips and glared up at him. It was true: Nate was certainly more eloquent in writing than he ever was in person.

He took her gently by the shoulders. "Verity, you can't tell me you're unaware of that man's interest in you."

Here her anger faltered. Nate was right. She'd led Hadley Jones on; she'd encouraged him by not spurning him from the very beginning. "I asked him for help," she admitted. "That's why we were talking alone together when you came in."

Nate's hands tightened on her shoulders. "Are you ill?"

She looked up into his eyes. "I gave him my mother's diaries, Nate, and I asked him to find out what illness killed her."

He backed away, dropping his hands from her shoulders and spreading them wide. "Why?"

"Because truth is the only way I can defeat the lies."

She watched him react to this. She saw him narrow his eyes and stare at her in exasperation, as if he wanted to shake her and insist that she give up her crusade. She saw him clench his fists and look at the Thomas house as if he wanted to go back in and punch someone in the face. And then she saw him deliberately decide to do neither of those things.

He unclenched his hands. "Let me walk you home." Putting an arm around her shoulders, he prodded her forward on the path, away from the Thomas house. Verity looked back once. A white curtain fell across one of the front windows, as if someone had just pulled it closed because there was nothing more to see.

TWENTY-FOUR

ATE DIDN'T say another word about Verity and Hadley Jones, and it bothered her. She was aware that Nate had a right to complain. After his initial outburst, however, he dropped the subject.

Did he trust her that much?

Or did he not want to risk their engagement?

Verity felt the little thread of doubt she'd carried inside her weaving itself into something more substantial. How badly did Nate want the Boone lands?

When she looked up into his stormy eyes, prompted one of his stunning smiles, or melted under his kiss, she felt ashamed of herself for suspecting his motives. He was a good, solid young man. He would be a reliable husband, a loving father, and a responsible member of the community.

Only when she was alone did she allow herself to ponder less admirable reasons for his devotion. Nate had been pushed in her direction by his mother, who proudly claimed her son always did as he was told. He'd courted Verity and won her heart in his letters, and even if their first meetings had not gone as planned, he'd successfully made up for his blunders afterward.

As Hattie had said, Verity was worth a lot of money.

But—Verity pressed her hands to her head in confusion—Hattie had *not* said that. Verity had dreamed the whole disturbing episode. Only Aunt Clara had been insensitive enough to repeatedly point out the monetary value of the marriage. Why, then, did Verity continue to doubt the McClures?

Could Verity even imagine calling off the wedding and welcoming the courtship of Hadley Jones? She visualized herself telling Nate she didn't want to marry him— and was struck by pain that frightened her with its intensity. What was wrong with her? It was as if she wanted to keep the bird in hand while letting the bird in the bush show off his plumage.

What kind of wanton girl was she?

Catawissa took pride in observing Independence Day. American patriots had fought for independence in this valley, and a terrible number had perished at the disastrous Battle of Wyoming. The townsfolk had no intention of allowing their sacrifice to pass without notice.

This year's celebration included picnics on the town

common, fair booths, charity auctions, dances, and fire-works. Verity baked her acclaimed jam tarts and did not receive a single complaint from Beulah about untidiness.

Nate won all the tarts in the auction, bidding an un-precedented three dollars.

Verity found him resting in the shade after he'd ex-hausted himself in foot races and wrestling contests. "You silly goose!" she exclaimed. "I would have made jam tarts for you any time you liked!"

Nate gazed at her lazily from under the wide brim of his hat. "I wasn't going to let anyone else have them." Verity stiffened. She'd seen Hadley Jones at the auction and was thankful that he hadn't bid on her items. But Nate grabbed a handful of her skirt and yanked her to the ground beside him in a heap. "It's for *orphans*," he said with an ornery grin. "Come here and reward me."

Verity snatched the hat off his head and swatted him with it. "I'll reward you in a manner you won't soon forget!"

"Is that a promise?" he called as she rolled away and scrambled to her feet.

The common was crowded with all the inhabitants of town and some two dozen outlying farms. The Pooles, Verity noticed, tended to congregate together. The men, mostly farm or mill workers, took their food down to the waterfront to eat. The women wandered the common in isolated groups, and the booths run by Pooles seemed to be patronized only by other Pooles. Even their children didn't mingle with their counterparts from town.

There were exceptions, of course. Nate's nephews were playing tag with some Poole boys, and Verity spotted Mrs. McClure buying several jars of a purplish concoction she suspected was cabbage beet relish from a woman who must be Daniel Poole's mother. Daniel himself and his sweetheart, Daisy Brant, sat under a shade tree with Ransloe Boone, eating fried chicken. The mixed-race Indians of the township didn't all have the same surname, Verity had learned. There were Brants and Montours and Kerrs among them, but the townspeople insisted on referring to them all collectively as Pooles.

"I don't know why the Pooles insist on coming every year," Verity overheard a woman say to a friend. "It takes a lot of nerve for them to celebrate *our* independence."

"It's like a regiment of British regulars turning up," the second woman agreed.

Verity turned to face them, holding some embroidered pillows she was considering buying for the front parlor. "The Pooles and their kin served our country in the last war," she pointed out.

"Only when paid to," muttered the first woman.

"No, Miss Boone is right," her companion said with false brightness. "The Pooles are better than some." The woman's name was Harper, Verity recalled, recognizing her from church. According to Mrs. Eggars, Mrs. Harper's infant child had died of whooping cough after being delivered by Verity's mother and Asenath.

"The Pooles didn't hide in the hills from the conscription officers," Mrs. Harper went on, "clutching hexes and spells and cursing the men who gave their lives for this nation. That would be *your* kin, am I right, Miss Boone?"

Verity assumed she meant Eli Clayton. Instead of pointing out that the Claytons were no kin of hers, even if one of them had married her uncle, Verity set down the embroidered pillows and walked away before her tongue got the better of her. Arguing with those who'd renounced the use of reason, according to Thomas Paine, was like administering medicine to the dead.

The afternoon culminated in dancing on a makeshift wooden floor. Nate took Verity's first dance and many of those that followed, but he also danced with his mother and each of his sisters. Verity danced with the husbands of Carrie and Annie and sat out once with Hattie's husband, William, who gripped his cane and watched the dancers sadly. It took a bit of trouble, but she even coaxed Ransloe Boone onto the floor. He led his daughter in a waltz with surprising grace and confidence. Her father could indeed dance.

As he swept her across the boards, Verity looked up at him in amazement. "Do you play the fiddle, Father?"

"Where did you hear that?" he grumbled.

"Well, do you?"

They made half a turn around the floor before he admitted, "I did."

"I'd like to hear it," Verity declared.

Ransloe Boone looked down at her face and smiled. "For you, I'd take it up again."

When the sky darkened, the fireworks began. Verity was not surprised to discover Nate was in charge of the display. He and some of the other young men set up their rockets in Water Street, and the crowd gathered on the common to watch. Flowery fireballs ignited in brilliant blues, vibrant greens, and blinding white over their heads.

In between the displays, Verity surveyed the crowd. Her father had gone home already. The Thomas boys were present and underfoot, and so were Nate's nephews and nieces. She noticed Hadley Jones, standing on the front porch of Dr. Robbins's house, watching the men light fireworks with a disapproving expression.

And then, in the light from the pyrotechnics, her eyes fell upon a man standing apart from the crowd, between Dyers General Goods and the Catawissa Land and Building Company. At first Verity didn't know why he'd attracted her attention. When a spectacular shower of white sparks lit the sky, she saw that the left side of his face was drawn down and misshapen.

This fellow had one side of his face all puckered. That's how

Piper had described the man who'd grabbed him in the woods.

Verity realized she was probably looking at the man who'd dug up her mother's grave.

And in that moment she also realized he was looking right at her.

She took a step backward, into the crowd, and moved sideways around a group of people before peering across the common again. The man still stood there, although now he appeared to be watching the fireworks.

Verity's first thought was to tell Nate, but she'd have to walk out to the street in front of the entire crowd to get his attention. The suspect would see her point him out; he might flee. She turned toward the doctor's house, just down the street from where the man stood, but Hadley Jones was no longer on the porch. In fact, she couldn't see anybody familiar in the mass of faces, all of them shadowed one second, then lit up in strange colors the next.

Verity moved toward the general store, threading her way through the crowd and looking for someone who would believe her and help her. She kept an eye on the figure standing in the shadows, turning her head away only for brief moments, hoping to spot John Thomas, Daniel Poole, Nate's brothers-in-law, or even the sheriff. She scanned scores of unfamiliar faces, and when at last she stood in front of the store, the man was gone.

Had he joined the crowd? Or retreated into the narrow alley between the buildings? She peered into the dark passageway. At that moment a barrage of fireworks lit the sky, illuminating an empty alley. No one was there.

Emboldened by the firelight and the merrymaking only a few yards away, Verity ventured into the alley, thinking to make her way down to the end and see where the fellow might have gone from there. She'd crossed half the distance when the light faded and darkness fell around her again. She paused as her eyes tried to adjust . . . and a hand touched hers.

She cried out and skittered backward. Somebody was there, between her and the crowd. His dark shape blotted out the light from the town square.

"Lost, pretty lady?"

"No." She tried to move toward the open street, but he blocked her, crowding her toward the alley wall. She could smell his sweat as he towered over her.

Something brushed at her curls, and she shuddered, trying to back away. The brick wall of the dry goods store connected painfully with the back of her head.

"I think you enjoyed the fireworks." He laughed shortly. "You like shiny things? Fiery lights? Gold coins?"

"Move out of my way." She meant to be forceful, but her command sounded weak to her own ears.

"Where's the gold?" A hand groped at her. She flung it

off, shrieking out loud. Her cries were lost in a cacophony of whistles, blasts, and explosions.

"She doesn't know anything. She's only lived here a month."

This was a new voice, a softer one, from the end of the alley. Verity turned her head, trying to see the speaker. A dim figure stood at the far end of the passageway. "You've got the wrong girl. Let her go."

The other, the one who was pressing her into the brick wall, growled with displeasure. "This one's under protection, is she? *Don't bother the Boone girl.* Is that what *he* told you?"

Verity flattened her body against the wall and held very still, listening. "*I'm* telling you now. Let's get out of here." The voice was familiar, but she couldn't place it.

The man in front of her laughed. "Another time, pretty lady." When the next round of rockets shot into the sky, the dark, looming body retreated. And Verity bolted.

Stumbling into the street, her throat dry with panic and her heart pounding, Verity discovered that the world had not noticed her absence. Nate crouched in the middle of the street, arranging the next sequence of fireworks; people clapped and laughed and milled around. What had felt like a long ordeal had lasted mere seconds. Trembling, she walked briskly away from the alley and collided with Hadley Jones.

"Oh!" She grabbed hold of him and clung desperately.

"Miss Boone!" he exclaimed in surprise. "What's the matter?"

"A man—he—" She shuddered, and Jones, looking alarmed, pulled her toward the doctor's house. "In the alley! He—"

"What happened in the alley?" He had her by the elbow now, directing her onto the porch and in the front door, to a parlor dimly lit by gas lamps. "Are you all right? Did he hurt you?"

"His face was burned." Verity cupped her hand over her left cheek. "And he was asking me questions about gold coins . . ."

Jones led her to a large cushioned armchair and gently urged her to sit down. "A lot of men are in their cups tonight," he said. "They've been drinking since noon, and there's already been a brawl at the tavern."

Verity glanced around the doctor's parlor and found it to be the sort of cluttered, unfashionable room one might expect from two men living alone. A half-eaten piece of chicken lay on a plate on an end table, and someone had left a waistcoat draped over the back of a settee. Casting her eyes down, she folded her hands in her lap and tried to control their trembling. "He frightened me. He wasn't drunk. He was asking about the Revolutionary War treasure."

"Then he *was* drunk," Jones assured her. "You can wait

here until McClure is finished trying to blow off the hand he offered you in marriage."

Verity raised her head to stare at Hadley Jones in horror, but he was already waving his arms as if trying to erase his words. "Sorry. I'm sorry. But after two years in the war, I'm not fond of explosions of any type, nor of patching up what's left of men afterward. I'll never enjoy fireworks again." He cast a worried look at the curtained windows, lit up in bright colors. "I need to talk to you anyway."

He crossed the room to a secretary's desk and lowered the front panel. Verity turned to watch him, opening her mouth to say what she suspected about the man with the scarred face. Then she saw Jones remove her mother's notebooks from the desk and stopped with the words unspoken.

"I'll ask you again," he said, turning to face her, "to drop the matter and tell me you don't need to know."

Verity shook her head.

With a sigh, he sat down in a chair opposite her, opened the diaries, and began to thumb through the pages. "The key to the mystery was the salivation." He glanced up. Verity was staring at him without understanding. "It was one of the more startling symptoms." Jones read aloud from the notebook. "*She waters from the eyes, nose, and mouth. Chokes if we lay her down.* That's Asenath. And then here—" He turned to the other notebook. "In your mother's final hours, she wrote: *Watering like dog.* I take that to mean she was drooling, just like her sister-in-law."

"I didn't understand what she meant," Verity whispered. "I thought she was delirious."

"I don't think so." Jones met her eyes. "You see, excessive salivation is not usually a symptom of gastric illness or infectious diseases."

"Then what . . . ?"

"It's most often a sign of poisoning."

TWENTY-FIVE

OISONING?" VERITY gasped. "You think they were poisoned?"

"Accidentally, yes." Jones eyed her grimly. "Just as you nearly were, in the Shades." Verity shook her head in disbelief. "In each case, the onset was sudden—gastric distress, followed by salivation, diminished heart rate, and stupor. The victims all recovered—or died—within a day or so."

Verity put one hand over her mouth.

"She was suffering from nausea during her pregnancy, and so was your aunt," Jones went on. "The diary says Mrs. Cahill brought cabbage juice, which is supposed to calm the stomach. Later, there's mention of someone else visiting with 'a remedy.' It looks like half the town brought these women homemade concoctions that were supposed to ease their trouble. And I suspect one of them contained an unintended ingredient." He sighed. "It's why I always insist on gathering my own herbs. People make mistakes."

Verity lowered her hand. "A mistake?"

"Sometimes people mistake water hemlock for parsnips, but I think the simplest answer is the same thing that almost got you. Mountain laurel would have caused those symptoms — and so would rhododendron, which grows all over this area."

"Are you saying someone mistook mountain laurel for something else?" Verity hadn't known the flowers were poisonous, but she thought the people who grew up here must know it.

Jones shook his head. "Probably not. I've never heard of anyone except small children — and very nearly you — eating nectar from mountain laurel. But in a very dry summer, bees sometimes make honey from mountain laurel and rhododendron, if there's nothing else available."

Verity stared at him incredulously. "Honey?"

"It can be very dangerous. In the first century B.C., an entire Roman legion was poisoned by honey made from rhododendron," Jones told her. "It led to a rather famous Roman defeat. Careful beekeepers know the signs to watch out for, but the Claytons aren't careful people. You remember your mother thought Rebecca Clayton had been stung by bees? Well, August was honey-gathering season."

"You think Rebecca ate poisoned honey?"

"Or baked it into something. I spoke to Eli Clayton just yesterday. He doesn't remember if Rebecca was baking the day she fell ill, but he admits she used to gather wild honey, and she had a real sweet tooth." Jones shook his head regretfully. "From what I read in your mother's diary, I suspect Rebecca baked honey cakes, which were served the day of her funeral—poisoning the rest of the family, including your aunt Asenath."

Verity shuddered. Her parents had been offered those cakes, but Eli Clayton had behaved so unpleasantly, they'd left without eating any. Tears stung her eyes, and she blinked furiously, trying to hold them back.

Jones stood up, plucked a handkerchief from his coat, and offered it to her. She buried her face in it gratefully, and he laid a hand on her shoulder.

"They didn't all die from it," she said.

"The two adults who died were already in poor health, and the third victim was a baby. Other family members were similarly afflicted but recovered, as did Asenath. Of course," Jones went on, "Eli Clayton has his own explanation for what happened. Would you believe he laughed at mine—preferring to believe in curses?"

Verity raised her face from the handkerchief. "But my mother died three months later!"

"You can put honey up in jars and save it." His voice was kind but logical. "You can take it out three months later and bake with it . . . or give it away. It's the most reasonable explanation I can think of for a second episode of poisoning so soon after the first."

She stood up, clutching the arm of the chair for support. "Verity," he murmured, and she stepped into his arms.

He wasn't as tall as Nate. His shoulder was the perfect height to cry on, and she did. For several long minutes, he simply held her while she sobbed out her grief over something so foolish that did so much harm.

"It was an accident." His breath rustled her hair. "I thought about lying to you — telling you it was some rare illness . . ."

"No. I'm glad you didn't. I don't like lies." Verity didn't lie to herself about what would happen when she lifted her head from his shoulder and tipped it back to look at him.

Hadley Jones kissed her.

She didn't think; she made a conscious effort *not to think*. His arms tightened around her waist, pressing her body against his. She'd felt his strength before, and she succumbed to his power willingly, just as she had in the Shades. He was bold and forceful, not gentle or playful like . . .

Verity put a hand on his chest and held him back, blinking at him in confusion. Sky-blue eyes met hers. "Do you love him?" Hadley Jones demanded.

Of all the things he could have asked, he drove unerringly at her greatest doubt.

"I don't know," she whispered.

He nodded. "I can live with that." He tightened his grip and kissed her again. Her backside hit the arm of the settee, and she braced herself with one hand, lest they tumble onto it together.

Heavy footfalls sounded above. "Jones!" The bellowing voice reverberated through the ceiling, followed by footsteps on the front staircase. "What's all that shouting in the street?"

"It's Independence Day!" Hadley Jones barked. "*You drunken bungler . . .*" The last was muttered under his breath as he turned back to Verity, but she'd already withdrawn from him, the spell broken. Her eyes were riveted on the stairs in the front hall as a large, menacing figure appeared.

"No!" snapped Dr. Robbins. "Someone's been hurt, you fool boy!"

The fireworks had stopped. Verity pushed Jones aside in sudden terror. "Nate!"

The front door burst open as though kicked. Two men dragged a limp body into the house, their injured companion's arms thrown across their shoulders.

He was unconscious, his feet dragging on the ground. Blood stained his shirt and matted his dark hair. His face was so lacerated and swollen, he was barely recognizable. But Verity knew him at once.

It was John Thomas.

"Get him to the examining room!" Dr. Robbins ordered, pointing the way through the house. Hadley Jones dashed from the parlor in their wake.

Verity snatched up her mother's diaries, then hesitated, uncertain whether she should follow after her uncle or get out of the doctors' way. Guilt for having nearly been caught in the parlor with Hadley Jones—for what they'd been doing—made up her mind and drove her out of the house.

The women and children who'd been watching the fireworks were now heading home as fast as their feet and carriages could carry them. An angry mob of men milled in the street outside the doctor's house. Shouted questions overlapped attempted answers.

"His boys found him . . ."

" . . . anyone know how long he's been there . . . ?"

" . . . unconscious behind Dyers . . ."

"Was he robbed . . . ?"

Verity listened to the tangled accounts with growing horror. Darting forward, she grabbed a nearby man by the arm. "Where's the sheriff? I know who's responsible!"

When she'd had her scare in the alley, had her uncle been lying unconscious a few feet away? Had he been abandoned there, bleeding and alone, while she was in the house with Hadley Jones?

The man whose arm she held stared at her blankly for a moment, then his eyes grew wide in recognition. "You're Miss Boone! Why, Nathaniel's looking for you!" Catching her wrist with one hand, he dragged her down the street. "Where's Nathaniel?" he hollered. "Tell him I've found his girl!"

"Listen to me!" Verity cried. "I can describe the man who hurt my uncle!"

Manhandled and thrust through the crowd, Verity found herself passed along, her protests unregarded, until she landed in a familiar embrace.

"Verity! Where have you been?"

"Nate! No one will listen to me! I know who did this!"

"I'll listen to you." Nate and Verity turned as one at the sound of the voice. Not nearly as tall as Nate, the bristly, gray-haired sheriff exuded an air of aggression. He glowered at Verity, his eyebrows crunched into an arrow between his eyes. "Who assaulted Mr. Thomas?"

Verity described the incident with Piper in the woods and her own encounter with the scarred man in the alley. She told the sheriff what she'd seen of him by the light of the fireworks and how a second man in the shadows had called him away.

"Verity!" Nate exclaimed, his face clouded with outrage and worry.

The sheriff squinted at her as if he didn't believe her. "What did you do, Miss Boone, after being frightened so badly? Why didn't you raise an alarm?"

She dared not look at Nate. "I went into the doctor's house."

Nate's hand tightened on her arm, and she winced. But the sheriff was not satisfied. "Dr. Robbins was not concerned about thugs grabbing young ladies off the street?"

Verity clasped her mother's diaries to her chest. "Dr. Jones said it was probably someone who'd had too much to drink at the tavern."

Nate let go of her arm. Verity turned toward him, but the sheriff commanded her attention. "What did the second man in the alley say, exactly? About the wrong girl?"

She shook her head. "I don't remember . . ."

"John Thomas has a daughter. Where is she?"

Verity gasped, horrified. She hadn't given a single thought to who the *right* girl was.

"Liza Thomas went home with her mother hours ago, as far as I know," Nate said.

The sheriff nodded grimly. "Nathaniel, can I ask you to look in at the Thomas house, make sure everyone there is all right?"

"Absolutely, sir."

"And take this bunch with you." The sheriff pointed to the boys huddled in the street near Dr. Robbins's front steps. Johnny Thomas held a twin under each arm, and

Piper squatted at his feet, freckled face screwed up in a fruitless attempt to ward off tears.

"Boys!" Verity opened her arms, and the three younger children launched themselves toward her. She wrapped herself about them, holding their shivering bodies close against her own. "We're going to take you home," she told them, glancing up at Nate.

Avoiding her eyes, he muttered that he was going to fetch his horse and wagon and strode off.

Johnny stepped forward. "I'm not going home. I'll stay with my father."

Verity nodded at him over Piper's head. "Go inside and don't let anybody remove you until you see Dr. Jones. Tell him I said you could stay and sit by your father."

The boy nodded back at her solemnly like a young gentleman — and then burst into tears. When Verity reached out to him, Johnny took a shuddering breath, straightened his back, and marched into the doctor's office.

TWENTY-SIX

AMPS IN nearly every window lit up the Thomas house like a beacon. Verity didn't think that was a good sign, and Nate swore softly under his breath. When the boys made a move to scramble out of the wagon, he grabbed the nearest one and held him back. "Wait here!" He climbed down and started up the front walkway without another word.

Nate hadn't spoken to Verity at all during the ride from town. She knew he was furious, and with Hadley Jones's kisses burning on her lips, she figured he had even more right to be than he knew.

The front door banged open and Clara Thomas emerged. Verity was shocked to see her aunt haul a shotgun onto her shoulder and cock it with a resounding snap. "Who's that?" Aunt Clara hollered.

"It's Nathaniel, Mrs. Thomas! I've got your boys with me!"

Verity watched Nate and Aunt Clara meet halfway along the path and exchange a volley of quick words. Then movement in the doorway caught her eye, and Liza stepped onto the front porch. The surge of relief Verity felt, seeing her cousin unharmed, surprised her.

Nate looked back and beckoned with his hand. Verity shooed the boys before her. "Two men tried to force their way into the house," Nate said to her quietly as the children ran past him toward their sister.

Verity turned to her aunt. "Was anyone hurt?"

"I hope so." Aunt Clara coolly uncocked the shotgun. "If not, it wasn't for lack of trying. Where's Johnny?"

"I left him at the doctor's," Verity said. "He wanted to stay by his father's side."

Aunt Clara nodded approvingly. "About time that boy grew a backbone."

"Mrs. Thomas, I'm going to take Verity home, and then I'll fetch my brothers-in-law and come back." Nate looked out into the darkness worriedly. "We won't leave you here alone tonight."

They were back in the wagon and halfway between the two houses when Verity could stand it no longer. "Are you going to say nothing to me at all?"

"Do you really think this is the time to talk about it?" It sounded as if his teeth were clenched.

"No," she admitted, but to her surprise, Nate wrenched the horse to a stop and pivoted in his seat to face her.

"Do you want to break off our engagement?"

She gasped. "No!"

"A man threatened you tonight, and you ran to *Jones!* I was right there on the street launching fireworks—don't tell me you couldn't find me!"

"I didn't run to him! He found me and took me inside, and then . . ." She raised the notebooks from her lap.

"Oh, the diaries! I should have known!"

Verity glared at Nate. "He told me why my mother died. Don't you care?"

Nate shook his head angrily. "Not as much as I care about Jones using the matter as an excuse to be alone with you."

She slammed the notebooks down on her lap, furious.

Nate wasn't finished. "What feelings *do* you have for your good friend Jones?"

Verity looked up at him defiantly. "I don't know."

"That doesn't comfort me much." Nate picked up the reins, then flung them down again. "I think you'd better decide," he growled. "I'll leave it to you. If you want to be released from our agreement, then tell me."

"You're leaving it up to me? If you doubt me, why

don't you call it off yourself? Is it because my land is too important to you?"

"Is *that* what you think?" He laughed outright, without much humor. "If I wanted to marry a girl for her fine acreage, there's plenty in this township who'd be a lot less trouble to court than you, Verity Boone!"

"Then why don't you go pick one of them?"

"Because I love *you*, you senseless girl!" He moved so suddenly, she flinched. But he just slid across the seat until she was pressed against the side of the wagon. "I love you 'to the depth and breadth and height my soul can reach,'" he said, his voice pitched low and urgent. "Freely, purely, with a passion — 'with the breath, smiles, tears of all my life' —"

She stared at him in surprise. "I thought you said you didn't understand that poem."

"I understand it now," Nate replied. "I daresay I understand it better than you do."

Looking up at him, Verity thought he was probably right.

Slowly, Nate eased back to his place, picked up the reins once more, and urged the horse onward. Verity hunched her shoulders and clasped her hands in her lap, prepared to finish the ride in the same unhappy silence with which they'd begun it.

He stopped the wagon in front of the Boone house and didn't offer to help her down. After a moment she climbed out by herself. She didn't know what to say to him. There was only one thing he wanted to hear from her, and she couldn't speak the words. She folded her arms over the diaries, clasping them to her breast.

"If you don't know what you want," he said, "do me the favor of cutting me off. I don't want to marry a girl who doesn't love me back."

In spite of his anger, Nate did not leave Verity unprotected. By the time she'd woken her father and told him what had happened, Annie's husband was knocking on the front door. Nate had dropped him off to help Ransloe Boone protect his household before driving with Carrie's husband back to the Thomas home.

Beulah fired up the stove. A massive manhunt had been organized; the citizens of Catawissa were beating the fields and woods and swamplands, looking for the men who'd assaulted John Thomas and tried to force their way into his house.

While Verity and Beulah worked side by side to fuel the searchers with bread and meat, news of the evening's events trickled in bit by bit. Clara Thomas might have filled one offender's backside with buckshot, but he was still able-bodied enough to flee before she could deliver more.

The assault on the house had come mere minutes after

the last farm worker had left the Thomas property for the day. Some people assumed that the Pooles were in collusion with the villains, and others concluded that the house had been under close observation for some time.

It had taken seventeen stitches to repair John Thomas's face, but common opinion reckoned that a little less handsomeness wouldn't hurt him. He'd also been hit pretty hard in the head, which might account for how little he remembered of the attack and why he couldn't tell them a single thing about the men who'd done it.

Piper and the twins were unable to provide an adequate description of the men who'd frightened them in the woods three weeks ago. After furious debate, they agreed that one was "very ugly" and the other was "not *as* ugly."

No one got any sleep that night, and by afternoon of the next day Beulah suggested that Verity go upstairs and lie down. Too weary and heartsick to argue, she climbed the stairs and undressed. As she took down her hair, she eyed her mother's trunk.

So now she knew. Her mother had been suffering from nothing more serious than pregnancy. Someone had brought her a special treat or homemade remedy for nausea. And her mother, kind soul that she was, had shared it with poor Asenath, a girl too ignorant to be sure she even *was* pregnant and who tried to ward off evil with little bags of herbs and flowers. In fact, Verity realized, the poison might even have come from Asenath herself. She might have mistaken one of her charm ingredients for something that belonged in a soup.

Hadley Jones was right. It had been a tragic accident.

Verity lay back on her bed. Thinking about *him* made her miserable. Remembering her inexcusable behavior, she was embarrassed; she'd been raised better than that. And what was she going to do about Nate? She lifted her hand to examine, for perhaps the five thousandth time, the ring on her finger.

Last night Nate had fed Barrett Browning's poem to her like medicine on a spoon — not reciting it by rote, but quoting from it forcefully, ardently.

He knew what that poem meant, and she didn't.

She didn't know if she was in love with either one of them. Attracted to both of them in different ways, yes — but how, at seventeen, was she supposed to recognize love? Wasn't it supposed to be obvious? Shouldn't she feel it in every breath and heartbeat?

Her last coherent thought, before she drifted into sleep, was that she wished her mother were alive to explain it to her.

Darkness had fallen by the time she awoke. Propping herself up, she stared into the early-evening gloom. Across the room her mother's diaries lay stacked on her dressing table. She'd half expected to find them open again — but no, it was her own memory guiding her this time, not some spirit she didn't believe in anyway.

Rising from the bed, she selected the notebook she wanted and riffled through the pages until she located August and the death of Rebecca Clayton.

It was just as she remembered.

Except for the day of Rebecca's death, Asenath did not visit her family home. She lay in bed at the Thomas house for days, refusing to get up—all because she'd seen six black crows and believed more people were going to die.

How, then, could she have eaten the honey cakes that poisoned the rest of her family?

TWENTY-SEVEN

HE MANHUNT proved fruitless. John Thomas's assailants were nowhere to be found. Popular opinion divided on whether they'd vanished into the Shades or merely hopped a train out of town.

A deputation of Catawissa men went so far as to search the Poole land. "They wouldn't take our word that we didn't have them," Beulah remarked bitterly. Verity looked away, embarrassed and ashamed. It wasn't her place to apologize for other people's unjust actions, but she felt as if she ought to.

Three days passed without a visit or any word from Nate, and Verity experienced a deeper sense of loss each day he did not come. There was no sign of Mrs. McClure, either, who'd been planning to show Verity all the fabric swatches she'd ordered from Philadelphia. Verity understood this to mean that wedding plans had come to a halt.

She still wore Nate's ring. On the day after the Fourth of July, she had taken it off and placed it inside one of her mother's wooden boxes for safekeeping. An hour later she ran back to get it, sobbing. She didn't want to give up Nate . . . but she couldn't stop thinking about Hadley Jones, either.

Nate only wanted three words from her, but she wouldn't say them unless she was certain they were true.

On the fourth day of Verity's misery, Hattie came calling. Verity received her warily, wondering if she had brought a message from her brother, but it seemed to be an ordinary social call.

They talked about the events of the Fourth. Hattie asked about John Thomas's injuries, and Verity was able to report that her uncle's recovery seemed certain, although he had no memory of the event.

She'd almost begun to relax when Hattie placed her teacup on the serving table and said, "I know you and Nate have had a spat."

Verity swallowed hard, feeling her tea go down her throat like a lump of unchewed bread.

Hattie waved her hand. "He didn't ask me to come. But I thought . . . well, I always had two older sisters to advise me on matters like this, and you don't have anyone. Is it too forward of me to offer myself for the position?"

Verity surveyed the young woman opposite. She had

indeed longed for a confidante, but she couldn't possibly confess her muddled feelings for Hadley Jones to Nate's sister.

Decisively, Hattie rose and moved to sit next to Verity. "You realize it's customary for a bride-to-be to feel nervous, don't you?" she asked. "And irritable . . . and thinking she's made a mistake."

"Oh!" Verity gasped, startled to hear her own thoughts expressed out loud. "Hattie, I'm so *very* fond of him, but he's angry with me right now, and I hardly blame him. I don't know what to do."

"Nate suffers from the misconception that he's always right. He just needs a firm hand, and you mustn't let nerves frighten you away." Hattie clucked regretfully. "When William went away to war, I cried every single day, afraid he would never come back to me. And when he did come back — why, I cried even harder, because then I had to redeem my promise and marry him!"

Verity couldn't suppress her smile at that.

Hattie smiled back. "And Carrie! Oh, my! Carrie and Timothy had a row so terrible a few weeks before their wedding, we thought they might call the whole thing off!" She leaned closer and said in her loud whisper, "Nobody knows what they fought about, but everybody knows how they made amends. Little Timmy was born only seven months after the wedding."

Verity inhaled so sharply, she sucked down a mouth-ful of tea. Surely Hattie wasn't suggesting . . .

The older girl's eyes twinkled as she patted her cough-ing hostess on the back. "All's well that ends well. And men are such simple things, really. So easy to please."

Hattie was wrong. Men were perplexing and complicated.

A letter arrived that afternoon. Beulah handed it to Verity with a raised eyebrow. The handwriting on the envelope was unfamiliar, but Verity knew immediately whose it was. With a guilty glance at the housekeeper, she took it upstairs to read.

> Dear Miss Boone,
>
> First of all, I owe you an apology for my conduct the other night. No gentleman would have taken advantage of your emotional state, nor any proper physician, either. I'm afraid I've made a poor showing at both occupations.
>
> I know that my second statement will make me out to be a cad of the lowest sort. After repeatedly making my interest known to you, even though your affections were otherwise engaged, I must tell you now that I can offer you no future. For a time I hoped to make my home and my living here in Catawissa, and I would have been proud to do so with a woman like you at my side. How-ever, circumstances have changed, and I find myself in a

position of uncertainty. I have no doubt you will make
a happy life with Mr. McClure and remember me with
derision for this abrupt change of face. I can only say
that I will, in turn, remember you as the one bright mo-
ment in a difficult time.

Sincerely and regretfully,
Hadley Jones

So now he didn't want her. She'd made a fool of herself and compromised her values over someone of fickle temperament. She ought to have expected this, because what good man, after all, would have pursued another man's intended bride?

Verity took the letter downstairs and, while Beulah was occupied outside, burned it in the stove. Somehow, as she watched it disintegrate to ash, she couldn't muster any anger toward Hadley Jones.

Instead, she felt a strange, nagging worry for him.

The next morning Nate drove by the house in his family's carriage. Verity leaped to her feet, dumping Lucky out of her lap, and burst out through the front door. He was already past the house by the time she got outside, and tears of disappointment welled in her eyes.

But he'd seen her, apparently, and even as he reached the point where she thought he wasn't going to stop, he did. When the carriage came to a halt, she walked down the steps and across the grass to meet him.

He still looked angry, she thought, trying to read his face as he came toward her. She knew what she *ought to* say to him, but when she was close enough to speak, she found herself unable to. She grabbed his coat with both hands and pressed her tearful face against the front of his shirt. After a moment, Nate put his arms around her. With her cheek against his chest, she could hear his heart beating almost as fast as hers, the familiar feel and scent of him a comfort to her.

Just tell him what he wants to hear, she told herself.

But she couldn't. There was something shameful about saying it now, right after Hadley Jones had rejected her —as if she loved him because he was the only choice left.

Nate deserved better than that.

When Verity didn't speak, Nate loosened his hold on her and stepped back. She let go of him reluctantly, wiping her tears with the back of her hand.

"There's been a telegram from Tamaqua," he said, without addressing the unspoken rift between them. "They think they have our men."

That was good news, even if she was more worried about the ruins of her engagement than about capturing the men who had assaulted her uncle.

"I'm taking Mr. Thomas on the train to see if he can

identify them," Nate went on. "He's not recovered enough to go by himself."

"But Uncle John says he never saw them."

Nate lowered his voice. "Nobody believes that, Verity. This is somehow related to his gambling. He's in trouble with these fellows, and he doesn't want to admit it. But I'm taking Piper and the twins as well. They saw both men, in daylight. Perhaps your uncle will come to his senses when he sees these men in custody."

Verity wrapped both arms around herself nervously. "I hope it's the right men."

He nodded. "I do too. But just in case, don't go anywhere alone."

"I promise," she said. She wished it were as easy to promise him everything he wanted. She was abruptly struck by the desire to tell him everything she felt, all her contradictory worries, tangled emotions, and lingering doubts. Perhaps the only way to understand her feelings for him was to express them out loud.

But Nate was already walking away, headed back to the carriage. He glanced back at her, and she was certain his eyes passed over the ring on her hand.

"We'll talk when I get back," he said gruffly.

Verity stood there, rooted to the ground, and watched him leave without kissing her goodbye, without even looking back a second time.

Nate didn't want her anymore either.

TWENTY-EIGHT

ERITY SPENT the day in tears. She'd gone from two suitors to none, and still she was befuddled in her mind and heart. One moment she trembled from head to toe at the thought of Nate McClure asking her to return his ring; the next she considered marching into town to confront Hadley Jones and demand an explanation.

When she answered the door to Liza in the late afternoon, she was in no mood to be polite. "What do you want?" she asked abruptly, glancing briefly at Johnny, who stood sullenly behind his sister.

Liza lifted her head like an animal scenting something interesting on the wind. Clearly she had noticed Verity's swollen eyes and blotchy skin. "Reverend White sent a note telling us to take down the bunting in the cemetery.

He said we've left it too long already, and it'll get ruined in the rain tonight."

Verity looked at the sky. It didn't look like rain to her.

Liza put her hands on her hips. "Mother told Johnny and me to do it, but you helped put them up, so you ought to do your fair share taking them down."

"Asking nicely was all you needed to do, Liza. Let me get a basket, and I'll go with you." Spending the afternoon in the graveyard suited Verity's mood perfectly.

The White house was shut up tightly, Verity noted, with curtains all drawn and windows closed in spite of the hot day. She assumed, rather sourly, that Mrs. White didn't want to accidentally catch sight of them and feel obligated to assist.

Liza went first to their grandparents' graves, carefully folding up each decorative drape. Johnny looked as unhappy as boys usually did when asked to do girls' work. He wandered aimlessly through the grounds, ripping bunting from the headstones and throwing it over his shoulder. Verity attended to the caged graves, and then, because she knew nobody else would, she took time with the Clayton graves—first outside the cemetery and then inside.

"You needn't bother." Liza had come up behind her while she was pulling weeds from around Rebecca Clayton's headstone. "Nobody cares."

"I care." Verity yanked handfuls of clover out and flung them aside. "Even if there's no longer a body buried here, the memorial stone can still look nice."

After a moment of silence, Liza said, "But there *is* a body in there."

Verity shook her head. "It was stolen."

Liza crossed her arms. "No, it wasn't. They put it back when they were through with it."

"You can't tell me grave robbers *returned* her body," Verity exclaimed.

"Hey!" Johnny yelled from halfway across the cemetery. "If you aren't working, neither am I!"

Liza threw him an angry look, then turned back to Verity. "What are you talking about? What grave robbers? It was Eli Clayton who did it; everybody knows that."

"Did what, Liza? What happened at this grave?" She was so tired of secrets and lies and misbegotten legends!

"Why do you think your father put a cage over your mother's grave?"

Verity rose to her feet and faced her cousin. "Why don't you just tell me?"

Johnny stuck his head between them. "What're you two arguing about?"

"You really don't know, do you?" Liza looked triumphant.

"About what?" Johnny asked.

"She doesn't know why there's a cage over her mother's grave!"

"To keep people from chopping her up." Johnny looked back and forth between Verity and Liza.

Verity winced at his words. "That's right," she agreed. "Medical students."

"Who told you that?" Liza demanded. "That's nonsense!"

"Then what *did* happen? For pity's sake, won't one of you just tell me?"

Liza pointed a finger at the place where Rebecca lay. "*She* died. Then other people in her family got sick. A whole bunch of them. They thought it was the family curse—a blood curse, because Silas Clayton betrayed his comrades and his country, and every one of his descendants is destined to pay the price. They thought Rebecca had come back from the grave to kill her kin, just like Caleb got out of his coffin and tried to kill his wife. So Eli Clayton dug her up and cut her body into pieces."

Verity stepped backward. She felt lightheaded, as if all her blood had rushed toward her feet.

"That's what the mountain people do if they think someone's not *completely* dead," Liza went on. "Her own father chopped off her arms and her legs and her head. Then he cut out her heart and burned it."

Johnny licked his lips nervously. "Stop it, Liza."

"He fed the ashes to the people who were sick, and

those people recovered." Liza's eyes were alight with malice. "The other ones who died—he chopped them up *before* they went into the ground, just in case. That's why the cages are there. Our family built them so the Claytons would think Sarah Ann and Asenath couldn't get out— but mostly so the Claytons couldn't get *in*. Grandmother told me. That's the truth."

Verity's limbs had gone numb with cold, even in the heat of July. She staggered and tripped on her skirts, falling to the ground in a heap. Liza smiled in satisfaction and returned to the bunting, while Johnny stood there, looking back and forth between his cousin and sister.

This was a terrible, *backward* place—full of ignorant, violent people. Why had she ever come here? She wanted to go home—to Worcester—to a civilized place where things like this didn't happen.

She might as well go back to Worcester. Nate had loved her, but she'd spoiled it with her doubts. And Hadley Jones had never wanted anything but a dalliance. She ought to pack her things and take the first morning train . . . back to Aunt Maryett, who was the closest thing to a mother she'd ever known.

Verity lifted her head. She could just make out, on the other side of the cemetery wall, her mother's headstone:

SARAH ANN

Wife of Ransloe Boone

Her father had lived alone with his grief, guarding his wife's grave, for fifteen years. No matter how humiliated and brokenhearted she was, Verity couldn't abandon him.

"Cousin Verity, are you all right?" Johnny leaned over her. He pulled a handkerchief, expertly starched and ironed by his mother, out of his pocket and offered it to her. "I don't know why Liza has to be so cruel. That is, I guess I do know. She likes your fellow. But he never even looked at her."

Gratefully, Verity pressed the boy's handkerchief to her face.

"Mother puts such thoughts in her head, but you're so pretty," Johnny said. "If I were Nathaniel, I wouldn't look twice at Liza, especially if you were my—I mean—"

She needed to stop her twelve-year-old cousin before he ended up pledging *his* love to her. "Johnny—" She broke off and stared past him, over his shoulder. "Who's that? Do you know that man?"

A young man with long, straggly locks of reddish-blond hair was talking to Liza on the other side of the cemetery. He awkwardly tried to drape a wreath of flowers over a grave, and she approached him to lend a hand.

Because the young man had only one hand of his own.

"No," said Johnny. "I've never seen him before."

Verity scrambled to her feet, recognizing the patient she'd overheard arguing with Hadley Jones last week.

Even before the thinking part of her brain had caught up with her instinct, she was sprinting across the cemetery. "Liza, *run!*" she yelled.

Liza looked back with annoyance and did the exact opposite, stepping within reach of the one-armed young man — the one whose voice, Verity now realized, had spoken from the shadows in the alley on the night of the Fourth of July.

When he saw Verity running toward them, he tossed the flowers aside and grabbed Liza around the throat with his one hand. Liza staggered, her hands clawing uselessly at the one clenched around her neck. Then, recovering her wits, she started beating at his face.

Seeing Liza fight back, Verity diverted her path, her eye on a fallen tree branch, thick and sturdy. She scooped it up and kept running. This fellow had only one hand and could barely hold on to Liza. How could he harm Verity?

Hefting the branch over one shoulder, she ran straight at him. He jerked back and yanked Liza under his fore-shortened arm, wrapping it tightly around her throat. Then his hand snaked into his coat pocket.

Verity skidded to a halt, a revolver leveled directly at her head.

"Drop it, Miss Boone," he said, staring her down. His eyes were a surprising light blue.

Behind her, Johnny yelped in alarm. Glancing over

her shoulder, Verity saw him struggling with a large figure who'd appeared from the woods behind the cemetery.
She didn't need a good look to recognize this new arrival.

Across the street, Reverend White's house remained
closed up tight. The Whites were not home and, Verity
realized, had probably not sent any letter to the Thomas
house.

Nate and her uncle were gone to Tamaqua, summoned
by telegram.

Realizing just how gullible they all had been, Verity
cast the tree branch to the ground in defeat.

TWENTY-NINE

NCE THEY reached the woods behind the cemetery, the scar-faced man released Verity and Johnny with a shove. Johnny stumbled to his knees, but Verity steadied herself against a tree. She turned to face her assailant, rubbing her wrist where he'd gripped her.

Tall and broad-shouldered, he was just as formidable here as he'd been in the alley on the Fourth of July. Even more so: the darkness that night had concealed the vicious sneer on his face and the leering way his eyes wandered over her figure. Verity shuddered, and he laughed as though reading her mind.

"We've got an extra one, Harwood," he said. "You weren't expecting *her*, were you?"

"Oh, I had a feeling Miss Boone would involve herself

eventually." The younger man pushed Liza toward her brother and cousin. "Tie this little hellcat's hands." He felt gingerly at his face where Liza had scratched him.

Verity looked around for anybody or anything that could help them. There was nothing, of course, nothing but trees and rocks and the long incline down to the Shades of Death.

The man with the scars drew a length of twine and a pocketknife from inside his coat. With casual cruelty he wrapped the twine around Liza's wrists, twisting it tight enough to make her wince. He tied it off and cut it, then bound Johnny and Verity the same way.

"You going back for the woman?" Harwood asked.

"I'll need one of her children as a shield against her damned buckshot."

"Take the boy. He's a sniveler."

Johnny made an attempt to scramble away, but the scarred man grabbed him by the collar and hauled him back. "Can you handle both girls?"

Harwood threw his lank hair out of his eyes with a toss of his head and eyed his companion angrily. Verity saw he didn't appreciate having his weakness pointed out to their captives. "Tie the Thomas girl to my belt," he ordered.

The other man took a section of his remaining twine and tethered an unhappy Liza to the one-armed man.

"We're going to take a walk, Miss Boone," Harwood

said in a mockingly pleasant voice. "Your cousin is coming with me, and you'll walk in front of us. If you move more than ten feet away from me, I'll shoot her. Then I'll cut her corpse loose and come after you. Do you understand me?"

Johnny bawled, and Liza trembled from head to foot, but Verity eyed him steadily. "I won't cause you any trouble," she said with a calmness that surprised her. "You don't need to frighten the children."

The man with the scar pushed Johnny ahead of him and started back through the woods. Harwood waved the gun at Verity. She looked into his eyes, suppressed a shudder, and then picked her way downhill between rocks and fallen tree limbs.

There was something strangely familiar about this man. She'd seen him briefly at Dr. Robbins's office, and on the Fourth of July she'd heard his voice. But now that they'd come face-to-face, Verity felt as if she knew him from somewhere else as well.

With their hands tied, Verity and Liza were unable to steady themselves against tree trunks or boulders as the ground grew steeper. Their captor tucked the gun into his belt so that he, at least, had his one hand free, but his infirmity left him off balance, especially with Liza tethered to his body. When she lost her footing and fell on her bottom, she nearly took him down with her. Verity turned around, hoping he would fall, but the young man grabbed a sturdy tree branch, bracing himself and stopping Liza's slide. Verity trudged back uphill to help Liza. The girls linked hands, and Verity pulled her cousin to her feet.

When Liza was steady, Harwood ordered Verity to back away, reaching for his gun. She stepped back obediently and felt him watching her as she preceded him down the hill.

Eventually they reached the lowlands by the river, where the ground was wet and slippery. Harwood called out, "Over there — that cabin."

There was a cabin perched precariously on rocky ground near the edge of the bog, although *shed* might have been a more accurate term. It didn't seem large enough for anyone to make it a home, but when they entered, Verity could see that people had been living in it. There were two bedrolls on the floor, a couple of haversacks, and the smell of a recent fire in the tiny stove. Drying animal skins hung from nails on the wall, and fishing poles stood in a corner. A long table made of roughly hewn wood, heavily pockmarked and bloodstained, filled most of the space. Angrily, Verity thought the Catawissa search parties had been frustratingly incompetent if Harwood and his ugly companion had been hiding here all along.

The young man released Liza's tether and made them sit on the floor, in separate corners. Then he set the gun down on the table, turned his back to them, and began to untie the knotted sleeve over his stump. Verity kept her head down in an attitude of submission, watching through her lashes. Harwood was sweating from the effort of the walk, and when he eased back the sleeve from the stump, she could see he was in great discomfort. The amputated limb had been raw and swollen when she'd seen him in the doctor's office last week. Now it was inflamed even worse, with red lines radiating up from the stump.

Harwood cursed under his breath and rolled the sleeve back down, looking over his shoulder at his captives. Liza was staring at the floor, lost in her own misery, and when he turned his gaze on Verity, she had already cast her eyes down innocently as well.

But her mind was churning restlessly. If she wasn't mistaken, this man was ill, weakened by blood poisoning. If they were alone with him long enough, perhaps he would make a mistake.

The other man had gone for Aunt Clara. She supposed they were after the Revolutionary War treasure but hadn't gotten any satisfaction out of beating her uncle. Now they'd sent him on a wild goose chase while they kidnapped other members of his family. Nate was gone — too far away to help her — and Verity felt a pang remembering how she'd promised him she'd be careful. Instead, she'd left the house without telling anyone. Her father would be at work in the fields until dusk, and Beulah would assume she'd gone visiting.

She glanced up at the mysterious Mr. Harwood, who was now lighting a pipe with his one shaking hand. He'd probably been the person in the graveyard the night she'd walked down from her house. He'd been smoking a pipe and contemplating the deserter's grave, wondering where Silas Clayton had hidden his stolen treasure. She wondered if she dared ask him questions — *What are you going to do to us? If there is no gold or we can't tell you where to find it, will you let us go?* — but she decided there was no point. She feared she knew what answers he would give.

They'd been sitting on the floor of the cabin for half an hour when Liza began to sob quietly. Harwood, who'd been leaning against the opposite wall, smoking his pipe and looking pale, sighed. He laid down the pipe and bent over to remove a war-issue canteen from one of the bedrolls. "Do you want water?" he asked roughly.

Liza shook her head. She cast him a frightened look, then cut her eyes desperately at Verity. "I have to . . . I have to . . ."

"She has to go outside," Verity translated.

"Girls," he muttered, as if it were a uniquely female problem. He dropped the canteen and hauled Liza to her feet by her bound hands. Pushing her toward the door, he retrieved his weapon off the table.

"Same deal as before, Miss Thomas," he said. "You can go outside and around the corner of this cabin, no farther than ten feet. I'll count to sixty. If you're not back by the time I finish, I'll shoot Miss Boone in the head and come find you."

Liza looked at Verity with wild, frightened eyes and dashed from the cabin.

Harwood watched her go, then turned around and grinned at Verity. "Do you trust her, Miss Boone?"

Verity did *not* trust her, though she would never have told him so. However, thoughts of Liza and possible betrayal were erased by the sight of the young man's grin, which sent a cold shiver through her body.

Harwood leaned out the door to check on Liza's progress. Frightening young women apparently revived him, for he seemed in good humor. Barking a short laugh, he stepped back into the cabin and called out loudly, "Fifty-eight, fifty-nine . . ."

"I'm coming!" Liza screamed from outside. "Don't shoot her!" The girl burst into the cabin with her skirt tangled and her petticoats hanging out, her face red and streaked with tears. When she saw her tormentor laughing and his hostage unharmed, Liza flung herself across the room. She nearly fell upon Verity, looping her arms over her cousin's head, her wrists still bound. They were in danger and dependent on each other for survival. Even so, Verity was surprised by this show of affection.

Liza pressed her lips against Verity's ear and whispered, "This is Hawk Poole's hunting cabin. He might find us. If he hunts today, he might find us!"

That was it. Now everything made sense, and Verity felt she was sinking, as if the very ground beneath her had turned into quicksand. She could not tell Liza she was wrong—that no rescue would come from Hawk Poole—because Harwood yelled at them to separate. Liza released her, scuttling backward to her former place.

Verity closed her eyes and leaned her head against the wall of the cabin. How stupid she'd been. How utterly naïve and stupid.

Hearing voices outside, Verity reluctantly opened her eyes. Harwood took his gun and went to the door, opened it wide, and looked out. Liza stirred, a hopeful expression crossing her face.

Johnny stumbled in first, looking worse for wear with a swollen lip and a ripped shirt. He ducked past Harwood and scrambled over to his sister.

Next, Clara Thomas entered the cabin with a straight back and a raised chin, even though her hands, too, were bound. She surveyed the situation calmly, her eyes passing over Liza and Verity in their corners and turning to appraise Harwood.

"Mama!" Liza gasped, with a choked sob.

"Welcome, Mrs. Thomas," Harwood said with mock courtesy. "I'm sorry we can't offer you a chair."

She turned on him coldly just as the scarred man stepped into the doorway. "You two are the sorriest excuses for criminals I've ever seen."

"And yet here we are, with two of your children plus

your niece," returned the young man. "Your husband is out of town, I understand, but I think it's better for us to converse without him. The man needs a keeper, and I suspect you're it. I should have come to you in the first place."

"Just get on with it," growled the larger man. "Enough talk. I'm tired of this swamp and this miserable town. Where the hell's the gold?"

"There is no gold, you fools," Aunt Clara said in her unemotional voice.

Harwood laughed. "We've seen the gold coins, Mrs. Thomas. Your husband produces one every time he has a gambling debt he can't pay off by other means."

Verity watched carefully. Her aunt's eyes did not waver for a second.

"There were only ten coins," Aunt Clara said finally. "John and his brother-in-law found them years ago. Ransloe wanted no part of them after his wife died, so John kept them, and we used them as we needed them. They're all gone now — used up and spent. We have no more."

The men looked at each other. The one with the scarred face moved away from the door to stand at her back, and Harwood took a step toward her as well, so that she was hemmed in by the two of them. "We don't believe you, Mrs. Thomas," the younger man said quietly. "Ten coins don't make a payroll for a regiment of soldiers, not even a hundred years ago."

"The man who originally stole them spent them or lost them—"

Harwood overrode her. "If you found some, you know where the rest are. You have them in your house, or else they're hidden in this valley somewhere."

Aunt Clara shook her head, but Johnny shot Liza a significant look. Verity watched as Liza glared her brother down. They all knew something, every one of them except her, and in that moment she hated them all.

"There are no more," Aunt Clara repeated.

"Mrs. Thomas," Harwood said sadly, "I didn't want to hurt your children, and now you're forcing me to do so."

His accomplice grabbed Johnny by a fistful of hair and dragged him to his feet. The boy flung his bound hands over his face and wailed in terror, nearly drowning out the sound of the cabin door being thrust open with a resounding bang.

"What the hell are you doing?"

Johnny whirled, his face lighting with hope. "Doctor!" he cried. "Help us!"

Verity threw her weight against the wall of the cabin and used this support to stand without the help of her bound hands, now numb and useless. "Don't waste your breath, Johnny," she said, staring across the cabin at Hadley Jones, whose eyes widened at the sight of her. "He's with *them*—and he always has been."

THIRTY

ADLEY JONES didn't deny his guilt, and the sudden peal of laughter from Harwood confirmed it.

Verity wrenched her gaze away from Jones and nodded toward the laughing man. "They're cousins or some other kin," she said, sick at heart. The color of Harwood's eyes and the shape of his grin had perturbed her, but she hadn't been forced to acknowledge his resemblance to Hadley Jones until Liza told her whose cabin they were in.

"Half brothers, actually," Harwood declared. "*Worthless* half brother is probably what Hadley calls me — the kind you'd leave to fester in an army tent after cutting off his arm."

"Shut up, Geoffrey," Jones muttered. "Are you all right, Mrs. Thomas?" He pushed past the scarred man to examine her bound hands.

Aunt Clara answered him coldly. "As well as can be expected while in the hands of common criminals."

"I'm sorry." Jones spoke with quiet regret, moving to Johnny to take a quick look at the boy's split lip. Then he bent to examine Liza's bound hands. "You've tied her too tightly," he complained over his shoulder. "I'm going to cut her loose."

Harwood lifted the revolver again and cocked the hammer. "No, Hadley, you won't."

Hadley Jones stood upright and glared at his brother, but instead of cutting Liza's bonds, he turned to Verity. "Let me see," he said, reaching for her.

Verity recoiled, but there was no place for her to go. "Don't touch me!"

He grabbed her by the arms and forced her into the corner. Then he bent his head and tried to loosen the twine around her wrists. "Can't you trust me a little longer?" he murmured in a barely audible voice.

"Let him examine you," Harwood called out, laughing. "My little brother's sweet on you, Miss Boone. Even hit Barrow here with a shovel to stop him digging up your mother's grave."

The scar-faced man growled. "And if it turns out that's where the gold is hid after all, I'll do more than blacken his eye!"

Verity gasped, remembering Hadley Jones's bruised face on the day after the grave desecration. With a surge of fury, she shoved the man she'd once considered a friend —possibly more than a friend—away from her.

Jones caught his balance and turned on Barrow. "The gold's not in the graves," he said slowly, as if speaking to a stupid child. "How would John Thomas get it out when he needed it?" He turned back to Aunt Clara. "I didn't bring them here, Mrs. Thomas. They followed your husband's trail of gambling debts and the rumors that he paid his way with gold. I don't control them, and they don't answer to me."

Hadley Jones stabbed a finger at the scarred man. "Jasper Barrow killed an officer and escaped from army prison; he's got a price on his head." He jerked his head toward Harwood. "My *esteemed brother* is a deserter and a convicted felon. Neither one of them has anything to lose. I've tried to prevent them from doing any harm here, but now"—he looked around at the bound hostages and drew an anxious breath—"I can't protect you."

"That's right; he can't." Harwood sneered. "Never much love lost between us, and I *owe* him."

Verity shuddered. Harwood didn't seem sane—or maybe he was crazed by the sickness in his blood. She couldn't guess what had happened between the brothers, but she knew that Hadley Jones had lied for Harwood, tending to his arm, giving him money, hiding him in Hawk Poole's cabin, and probably helping him elude the searchers. Jones's silence had allowed these two men to conduct their treasure hunting with increasing violence; he'd placed Verity and her uncle's whole family in danger.

Verity began to shake, frightened now as she should have been from the moment Harwood pulled a gun on her in the graveyard. She'd been misled by his resemblance to someone she cared about; she'd been fooled by his infirmity and ill health. Verity had thought Harwood was bluffing, but now she realized he'd shoot any one of them without a second thought — his brother included.

"Just tell them!" she burst out. Clara Thomas shot her a withering glare that might have quelled her own children but made no impact on her niece. "We all know you've been lying, Aunt Clara. Just tell them where they can find the gold, and they'll let us go."

The scarred man, Barrow, leaned close to Aunt Clara and whispered in her ear with the intimacy of a lover but loud enough for Verity to hear every word. "I hear Jones has a knack for amputations. If you like, we can shoot your son in the foot and watch him operate."

Aunt Clara jerked her head away and shoved Barrow defiantly with her shoulder. "Enough," she snapped. She turned and pinned Johnny with eyes like nails. "You know where to take them, don't you? Your father showed you what to do."

The boy's eyes were wide and frightened. "But Mama, I—"

"Do what you're told," his mother snapped. "You've been instructed on this. Be obedient."

Liza whimpered, and Verity eyed her cousin with suspicion. It sounded as if Aunt Clara was finally cooperating, but Liza showed no sign of relief. If anything, she looked terrified.

The men didn't seem to realize.

"That's better, Mrs. Thomas," Harwood said with his cold smile.

"My son will take you to the hiding place," Aunt Clara replied. "It's among the caves along the river."

"He'll take Barrow," Harwood corrected. "You three women will remain here with me until they return—*with the gold.*"

Aunt Clara raised an eyebrow as if to question this, but Barrow grabbed the boy by the arm and thrust him toward the door. "It's you and me again, Johnny-boy."

"Ma—?" Johnny cast one panicked look back at his mother before disappearing out the door.

Verity was certain the Thomases were up to something. Her aunt had not directed the boy to hand over the gold; she'd made it clear he was to *do as he'd been told.* They had a plan for a situation like this, and Johnny was supposed to carry it out. Liza's pale, worried face suggested that Barrow and Harwood would not be happy with the results.

Hadley Jones let out his breath and eyed his brother warily. "Put the gun down, Geoffrey. They're doing what you ask. There's no reason for anyone to get hurt here."

"You're such a *good* doctor, worried about your patients." Harwood uncocked the gun and lowered it. Then he leaned his shoulder against the wall of the cabin and closed his eyes, as if fighting off a wave of dizziness.

Every other person in the cabin froze. Verity's heart pounded as she watched the occupants of the room, each one weighing the moment carefully, and for an instant she spared a thought for someone who was far away and whom she might never see again.

Hadley Jones shifted his weight, and his brother's eyes snapped open. Harwood jerked his head up and lifted the gun suspiciously.

"You should have gone with them," Aunt Clara said.

"I'm not equipped to climb the cliffs along the river, Mrs. Thomas," the young man snapped.

"Pity, then," she replied. "You'll never see a lick of that gold. My Johnny will hand it over to your friend, and he'll take off with it. You'll never see him again."

"No, he—" Harwood broke off in midsentence and looked at his brother.

Hadley Jones shrugged indifferently. "She's right."

Harwood cursed and launched himself toward the door, flinging it open and sticking his head out, and his brother hit him from behind.

Jones's left fist slammed Harwood face first into the doorjamb, while his right hand reached for the gun. Harwood howled with anger and pain and—with a slight advantage in height—kept the gun just out of reach. His thumb cocked the hammer again, and he swung the weapon back toward the room. Verity gasped and flinched.

Deliberately, Jones grabbed the stump of his brother's arm and squeezed. Harwood screamed and dropped like a stone, weapon and all. Jones kicked Harwood as he went down, and Verity threw her bound hands up and over her face. She heard the body hit the floor, heard a second scream, choked off—and then silence.

Shuddering and trembling, Verity didn't attempt to move. Her captor lay on the floor, unconscious and still, and her rescuer whipped a scalpel out of his inside coat pocket. Hadley Jones flicked the knife through Aunt Clara's bonds first, then bent to release Liza's hands.

"Don't worry about your son, Mrs. Thomas," he said. "I'll go after him in a moment. Just let me get the three of you free."

Liza gasped as her hands came loose, and Jones rubbed vigorously at her wrists to restore circulation. He looked up, darting his eyes at Verity and Aunt Clara.

"I'm not here alone," he said. "Hawk's out on the hillside, watching the cabin. Get yourselves out of here—head in any direction, and he'll see you. He'll come for you and escort you to safety."

Then he approached Verity, his eyes sad and weary.

She was still shocked by his vicious attack on his brother. It had been necessary, and it had probably saved their lives, but she could hardly stand to look him in the face.

"I'm sorry, Verity," he murmured as he sawed his knife through the twine around her wrists. The twine fell free, and her hands dropped heavily to her sides.

He reached for them, but Verity wrenched away from him, hauled back one numb hand, and slapped him soundly across the face.

Blinking a little and taking a sharp breath, he stepped backward. His face was pale against his red hair, but his expression was resigned. "I'll go after Johnny now," he said dully. "Where's Geoff's gun?"

"I have it," Aunt Clara said, picking it up off the floor.

Clasping it in both hands, she turned around and fired it directly at Hadley Jones.

THIRTY-ONE

ERITY'S SCREAM was lost in the sound of gunfire. Jones's body hit hers, and they both went down heavily in a room suddenly thick with smoke.

"Mama!" Liza cried. "He was going to help Johnny!"

"Johnny doesn't need anyone's help. He knows what to do when he gets to the caves."

Their voices sounded far away to Verity's ringing ears. She struggled to sit upright, but Hadley Jones was lying on top of her, and when she tried to move him, she froze in horror.

There was blood everywhere.

"Hadley." Her voice shook. "Hadley."

A wave of emotion overcame her. *Nate . . . oh, Nate . . .* Nate was far away — safe and sound — but he couldn't help her.

She forced herself to look at Hadley Jones and the

gaping wound in his chest. If there was ever a moment she would have liked to faint, it was now.

Liza turned her head and gagged. "Oh, Lord. Oh, Lord."

Verity's hands shook. She was uncertain where to touch him, but she knew she had to stop the bleeding. "Bring me something! Bring me—bring me—one of those bedrolls." She tried to sit up again, easing him back. His head fell limply into her lap, his face pale and still. "Get something!" She looked up—to find herself staring into the barrel of a revolver.

"Be still, Verity," Aunt Clara instructed her.

"Mama?" Liza asked in confusion. She was holding one of the filthy bedrolls in her arms.

Verity had thought, a moment before, that her aunt had fired the gun by accident.

But Verity had been wrong.

"For a while I thought you'd throw Nathaniel over for this man," Aunt Clara said, her mouth turned down as if she were disappointed by a small setback. "But you didn't. Then I decided it might be better to let you marry Nathaniel so he could get the Boone land, and I could deal with *you* afterward. But this is too good an opportunity to miss. No one will be able to say what happened here today."

Hadley Jones stirred, the first sign he was still alive. Verity gasped and tightened her arms around him. Aunt

Clara was eyeing him dubiously, as if considering whether to take another shot at him.

But the gun was still pointed at Verity.

"Mama," Liza whimpered again.

"Hush, you foolish child. I told you I'd get Nathaniel for you. Did you think it could be done without a little spilled blood?" She spared her daughter a derisive glance. "I told you — life's a battle."

She'd said that once before, to her niece, and now Verity recognized it for the threat it was.

"Is that how you got your husband, Aunt Clara?" Verity said, her voice shaking. "By spilling blood? You poisoned them, didn't you? You gave Asenath and my mother the poisoned honey that killed Rebecca Clayton. You were there when Rebecca died; you knew what killed her, and you kept some for yourself."

Liza whimpered, but her mother made a noise of exasperation.

"The honey didn't kill Asenath — just made her sick. The second time, I brewed the mountain laurel directly into tea, as strong as I could make it."

"You poisoned my mother," gasped Verity.

"I had no grudge against Sarah Ann," Clara Thomas said. "I truly regretted her passing. I had no idea she'd turn up that day, wanting to try my remedy for nausea along with Asenath. There was nothing I could do."

Asenath pins her hopes on Miss Piper's remedies, Sarah Ann had written. How had Verity not recognized her aunt's maiden name? She'd given it to her second son, after all . . .

"You never did a thing for yourself," Aunt Clara berated Liza. "You never spoke to Nathaniel or did any of the things I told you would catch his attention."

"Mama!" the girl wailed.

"You can't expect what you want to be handed to you. You have to *take* it! Put that down, stupid girl!" She snatched the bedroll from Liza's arms and flung it to the floor. Then she forced the gun into her daughter's hands.

Verity watched in horror as the woman wrapped Liza's reluctant fingers around the weapon. The girl's eyes grew round as saucers. "Now," said Aunt Clara gruffly, "do it. You'll never appreciate him if you don't pay the price yourself."

The price was murder. Clara Piper Thomas had murdered two women—two pregnant women—to marry the man she wanted. And she'd gotten away with it. She'd raised his five children for almost fourteen years, without penalty or remorse.

Plain, gawky Liza must have hated golden-haired Verity at first sight—perhaps months before the first sight, when Fanny McClure had initially suggested to Ransloe Boone that their children might marry. Liza's hands trembled, and her eyes wandered from her cousin down to Hadley Jones and his blood-soaked shirt. She swayed on her feet.

"For pity's sake!" Aunt Clara reached over as though to squeeze the trigger herself, but Liza shoved her away with an elbow.

"I'll do it, Mother!"

And when Aunt Clara stepped back, smiling in approval, Liza turned around, hunched her shoulders, and fired the weapon into the dirt floor — once — twice — three times.

"You fool!" Aunt Clara lunged for the weapon.

Verity let Hadley Jones fall to the floor and launched herself up, reaching for the surgeon's knife on the table. Her aunt snatched it before she could touch it and swung it at her viciously.

Recoiling, Verity ducked under the table. "Liza, help me!" she shrieked.

But Liza's rebellion stopped at emptying the revolver. After firing twice more, she threw the gun across the room, flattened herself against the wall of the cabin, and threw both hands over her face.

The smoke in the room was now even thicker. Aunt Clara bent and felt under the table with her free hand. Verity dodged her and burst out from under the table. Her shoe caught in her skirt, and she staggered, unable to stand upright. Aunt Clara got her hand on a hank of Verity's hair and wrenched her backward.

The back of Verity's head struck the table, and for a moment everything dimmed around her. She fought the darkness desperately, knowing that to lose consciousness now meant death. Flailing, trying to rise, she found one arm immobile, pinned beneath her aunt's knee. Clara Thomas leaned over Verity, her corkscrew curls swinging around her chiseled, plain face. Her stony eyes surveyed the helpless girl as if she were merely a nuisance farm animal that needed slaughtering. Tightening her grip on Verity's hair, Aunt Clara forced her head back, exposing her throat. Then she raised the scalpel.

Verity caught her aunt's wrist with her one free hand, which was slick with blood — her own or Hadley's. That hand was slipping, sliding inexorably up Aunt Clara's arm as the woman bore down with unrelenting force.

A third hand suddenly appeared in Verity's field of vision, a large, sinewy hand with long fingers that wrapped around Aunt Clara's wrist, jerked her arm upward, and slammed her clenched fist against the edge of the table. Aunt Clara gasped, her fingers flying open, the scalpel falling to the floor by Verity's head. Then she disappeared entirely, hauled backward and tossed aside.

The man leaned over Verity. It was the second time she'd seen his face looking down at her in this swamp, dark skinned with high cheekbones, an angry expression, and a scar running across his eye and down his cheek.

This time, Verity could have kissed him.

•   •   •

No more than two minutes had passed since Clara Thomas had fired the first shot. It seemed impossible that it had all happened so fast, yet Hawk Poole assured Verity it had been no longer than that. He'd been watching from the woods, with instructions to help the captives if Hadley Jones could free them, but he'd abandoned his post at the sound of gunfire.

Aunt Clara had fled the cabin.

"Let her go," Hawk Poole said, sparing a brief glance at the unconscious Harwood and then turning to the more gravely injured brother.

"But she shot Dr. Jones!" Verity protested. "And she killed others — my mother, my aunt!"

Liza gasped and sobbed to hear it said a second time. No matter what Aunt Clara had advised Liza about Nate, Verity was sure the girl hadn't known about her mother's murderous past.

"Let her go," Hawk Poole repeated. But he nodded toward Liza, murmuring, "What about her?"

"She saved my life," Verity replied.

Liza met Verity's eyes tearfully for just a moment, then sank to the floor and covered her face with her hands.

Hawk Poole peeled Hadley Jones's shirt, stiff with blood, away from the wound, probing with gentle fingers. "Hadley," Verity said, brushing ginger curls away from the young man's pale face. "Hadley, do you hear me?"

"Don't try to wake him, Miss Boone," Hawk Poole said, stuffing a handkerchief into the wound. "He's better off unconscious. If he wakes and starts moving around, he'll bleed more, and he can't afford it." The man rose to his feet. "The bullet is lodged in his shoulder. It needs to come out, or he'll die of infection, even if the bleeding stops. We need to get him to the doctor."

Dr. Robbins of the shaking hands. Verity shuddered at the thought. "How can we move him?" Even Hawk Poole's gentle examination had caused a fresh welling of bright-red blood. They couldn't possibly carry him up that hill without injuring him further.

"Leave that to me." Hawk Poole strode to the door and whistled shrilly. Two boys appeared at once, as if they'd been waiting for his signal. One was a year or two younger than Verity. The other couldn't have been more than twelve. Hawk Poole stepped outside to speak to them softly, pointing into the swamp and apparently giving instructions. Then he returned to the cabin with the older boy, while the younger one ran off.

The boy's eyes widened at the sight of the wounded man. "We'll need a sling to carry him, Uncle Hawk."

Verity promptly picked up one of the bedrolls. "Will this do?"

She and the boy unrolled the cotton ticking and eased it under the unconscious man, while Hawk Poole bound Harwood's feet and one hand with fishing line.

"What about my brother?" Liza stood up, still snuffling and wiping tears from her eyes. "My brother is out there with that other man!"

"I sent my son Joseph after him, Miss Thomas."

Verity looked up in alarm. "Alone? That man is dangerous!"

Hawk Poole spared her a brief, humorless smile. "Not alone. Joseph's got three older brothers. Barrow will never see them coming." He stood up and surveyed the trussed-up Harwood. "That'll hold him. Now let's see to our friend."

When the two men lifted the makeshift sling, Hadley Jones groaned and struggled. Verity caught his hand and, clasping it tightly, walked alongside as the Pooles carried him out of the cabin. "Be still," she urged him, leaning close to speak in his ear. "You're safe. We're taking you for help."

To her surprise, his eyes flew open and his hand crushed hers. "Tell Robbins to wash his damned equipment," his voice rasped.

"I will!" exclaimed Verity. "I promise!"

They didn't carry him up the hill. Hawk Poole and his nephew took him down through the Shades, through thigh-deep water, lifting the sling up as high as they could carry it. Verity slogged along beside them, her skirts soaked in the green, slimy water, hanging on to Hadley Jones's hand.

She raised her head at the sound of a voice hailing

them. Ahead, two men paddled a fishing boat through the swamp waters. One threw down his paddle and jumped over the side to splash his way toward them. It was Daniel Poole. "Miss Boone!" he called. "Thank heavens! Your father is worried sick, and Nathaniel's got half the town searching for you." Then Daniel got a good look at Verity and the occupant of the sling and staggered to a halt. "What happened?" he gasped.

"I need that boat," Hawk Poole said, his breath short. "And I need you to get a message to town. Tell them we've got Miss Boone and Miss Thomas. Robbins should ready his surgery, and there's a man at the cabin needing a jail cell."

Daniel nodded, but his eyes were on Verity's hand, clasped tightly to the injured man's.

Let him think what he will, she thought fiercely. Hadley Jones had been wounded trying to help her. Clara Thomas had shot him merely to eliminate a witness, before she'd tried to murder her own niece. Verity felt no shame in holding his hand now.

"Go!" ordered Hawk Poole. Daniel bolted. A few splashes and he was out of the water, through the trees, and running uphill.

Verity glanced over her shoulder. Several yards behind, Liza trudged along dejectedly, her head bowed and her eyes downcast.

"Clara Thomas is still out there," Verity reminded Hawk Poole. "Do you have anyone looking for her?"

He refused to meet her eyes. "What happens to one crazy white woman in the Shades of Death is none of our business."

She would never leave the swamp. That was what he was saying. It might be because of her own design, by accident, or by the action of other, nameless persons, but Clara Thomas would never be seen again.

THIRTY-TWO

AWK POOLE navigated the fishing boat through the swamp until they reached the Susquehanna River, and then they made swift progress toward town. It took long enough, in Verity's opinion, but she was still surprised that Daniel arrived in Catawissa before them. He must have, though, because half the town had gathered on the dock to meet the boat.

Hadley Jones was lifted out, and before Verity had even climbed onto the dock, he'd been whisked out of sight.

Verity's appearance caused a wave of shock; outcries and gasps greeted her, and grown men jumped back at the sight of her. Covered in blood and blackened with soot from the gunfire, she was sure she looked as if she'd just clawed her way out of her own grave.

"Liza!" John Thomas ran down the dock, passing Verity without even a glance. Liza burst into sobs and held out her arms. Verity turned away. She did not want to witness what would surely be a painful reunion. Besides, her eyes were frantically scanning the crowd for the face she most wanted to see.

She found him in the same moment he saw her. He blanched and shoved people out of his way, panic in his eyes.

"Nate." She mouthed his name, her voice failing her. She took a step toward him, but someone caught her by the arm and whirled her around.

"Verity!" Ransloe Boone's fingers dug into her arms, and then he began to run his hands over her, his eyes wild. "Where are you hurt? Verity!"

"I'm not hurt," she tried to tell him. "It's not mine. Father, I'm not hurt."

But he wasn't listening. He was crying, clasping her face in his hands and then turning her around, trying to find the source of all that blood.

Nate grabbed him by the shoulder. "She's not hurt, Ransloe! She's trying to tell you it's not her blood." Nate's worried eyes met hers. "Is it?" Verity shook her head, speechless, and he sucked in his breath, looking her up and down. "It couldn't be," he murmured. "Or she wouldn't be standing here." And then his eyes tracked through the crowd. She could see him drawing his own conclusions about how she'd come to be covered in Hadley Jones's blood.

"I need to see Dr. Robbins," Verity said. She desperately needed to talk to Nate, too, but that would have to wait. His eyes were pained, but he nodded and took her hand.

Nate dragged her off the docks, past the paper mill and the train station, shouldering people aside. Verity hung on to his hand, straight across the town common where she'd once picnicked and danced. Ransloe Boone followed, not willing to let his daughter out of his sight. People parted at the sight of them, clearing a path to Dr. Robbins's house, around the back to his waiting room and into his surgery, where the doctor was arguing with Hawk Poole.

"The bullet has to come out," Hawk Poole insisted.

"Don't tell me my job," Dr. Robbins blustered. "It's better to close him up. He's lost too much blood, and digging for the bullet won't do him any good!"

"He'll die of sepsis if you don't remove it."

"Sepsis?" Dr. Robbins glared at his hired man. "You think you learned something about doctoring while driving my carriage?"

"No, I learned it on the battlefield—fighting in *your* place." Hawk Poole narrowed his eyes at the doctor.

"You don't want to do it because your hands aren't steady enough to get it out. Take a shot of whisky before you operate, then. Everybody knows you need it."

"You're dismissed," Dr. Robbins growled.

"I quit," Hawk Poole shot back.

Verity glanced at Hadley Jones, pale and still on the examining table, and decided enough time had been wasted. "Dr. Jones said to wash your equipment first!" she announced in a loud voice.

The doctor turned his head, and his eyes grew wide with alarm at Verity's appearance. Then he seemed to come to the same realization as Nate: if it were her own blood, she wouldn't be standing. He looked over at his apprentice. "He said *what?*"

"Actually, he said to wash your *damned* equipment." When Dr. Robbins looked back at Verity in surprise, she added, "He thought you could do it, doctor. He was relying on you."

Dr. Robbins wiped a hand over his face and looked again at the injured man. He cared for his apprentice, Verity realized. He was shaken and distraught. "Damn fool youngster," he muttered. "As if soap and water would make a difference."

"That's what he thinks, though," Verity insisted quietly. "He told me they had neither on the battlefield and lost hundreds of men because of it."

The doctor approached the table. His hands trembled as he examined the gaping hole in the young man's chest. "I don't know . . ."

Nate cursed under his breath and let go of Verity's hand. "Wash your surgical equipment and take the bullet out," he said roughly, stepping up to the table and looking Dr. Robbins in the eye. "If you need whisky to get you through it, I'll fetch some myself. Do what you have to do to save him." Nate flicked his gaze back at Verity, then away.

For her. Save him for her sake. That was what was in his mind, she knew.

Dr. Robbins's shoulders sagged. "I can't do this kind of work without assistance," he said quietly. "Someone with younger eyes and a steady hand." He looked at Nate. "Can you do it?"

Nate turned nearly green at the thought. He looked at Hawk Poole, who indicated his damaged eye.

"I can do it," Verity said.

There was a moment of astonished silence, and then Dr. Robbins burst out, "You're just a girl!"

"He was shot because of me." *By my aunt, who murdered my mother.* Verity swallowed hard and looked at her father, dreading the moment when he would learn how and why his wife and unborn child had died. She turned back to the glowering doctor. "My hands are steady, and I'm not afraid of blood. I've already seen his wound — look at my dress!" She rolled up her sleeves and said to Hawk Poole, "Bring some water. I need to wash too."

"Yes, Miss Boone."

Dr. Robbins looked helplessly from face to face, ending up with Nate.

"If Verity says she can do it, she can do it," Nate told him.

Dr. Robbins started shouting orders, clearing the room of spectators, throwing open drawers, and selecting his tools. Verity steadied herself, drawing long breaths while gazing at the doctor's array of frightening implements.

Her father refused to leave. One look at his face and Dr. Robbins didn't dare try to throw him out. Ransloe Boone crossed his arms and stood stoically by the door.

Nate had a quiet word with him before departing, and from her father's surprised expression and the way his head snapped around to look at her, Verity could guess what had been said. Then Nate met Verity's eyes and nodded briefly in farewell. The pain in his expression made Verity's chest ache. She wanted to stop him and explain —but Hawk Poole presented her with a bucket of soapy water, and she let Nate go without a word. Hadley Jones's need was greater.

It wasn't a pleasant procedure, but Verity faced it. If it needed to be done, then she was strong enough to do it. Robbins performed the better part of the doctoring, but when his hand trembled or his eyes weren't up to the challenge, Verity followed his instructions. Ransloe Boone stood behind her, his own eyes averted, but whenever Verity faltered or felt sickened, her father sensed it. He reached out and gripped her shoulder tightly, and she drew upon his strength to get through the worst moments.

At one point she felt his hand on the back of her head, smoothing down her hair. "Is he the one you want, Verity?" Ransloe Boone's voice was quiet, calm. "If you want this man, I'll stand by you."

She glanced back, grateful he would make such an offer, especially since she'd come to realize he loved Nate like a son. "Thank you," she whispered, "but now's not the time to talk about it."

No, it wasn't a matter to discuss over the surgery table, with Hadley Jones unconscious and helpless and Dr. Robbins listening curiously. This was not the time to expose her feelings, even if she did finally and undeniably know her own heart.

Verity was startled to see how dark it was when she left the doctor's rooms and climbed aboard her father's wagon. Staring up at the starry sky, she marveled at how completely she'd lost track of time.

She asked her father to take her straight to the McClure house, but he refused. "It's after midnight," he said. "You're so tired, you can barely stand up. And covered in blood like that, you'd scare Fanny and her daughters to death. I'm taking you home. They're all asleep — *he's* asleep — and I'm taking you home."

Nate surely wasn't asleep, but she didn't have the heart to argue with her father. Ransloe Boone knew everything now; the sheriff had talked to him while Dr. Robbins and Verity cleaned their patient up after surgery. He knew what his sister-in-law had done, and the burden of that knowledge seemed to have aged him ten years.

The horse headed home of his own accord, hardly needing any encouragement. They rode in silence, lost in exhaustion and grief. When Hawk Poole stepped out of the woods into the center of the road, neither one of them reacted with surprise. Verity's father just slowed the wagon down, and Hawk Poole grabbed onto the side and clambered aboard while it was still moving.

"What word?" Ransloe Boone asked.

"No sign of Mrs. Thomas. We think—"

"What about Johnny?" Verity interrupted. "Is he all right?"

Here Hawk Poole was able to report good news. When Johnny left the cabin that afternoon, under orders from his mother to *do what he'd been told*, he led Jasper Barrow to the cliffs along the Susquehanna River and pointed out a crevasse in which he claimed the gold was concealed. He even offered to fetch it out, then squirmed into the narrow crack in the hillside and disappeared.

It hadn't taken Barrow long to realize that the boy had outwitted him. Blustering, threatening, and cursing, he'd hollered into the crevasse all the dire things that would happen to Johnny's mother and sister if he didn't come out. Although he could hear the boy crying, he couldn't reach him. "When my boys arrived," Hawk Poole said, "Barrow had wedged himself into the crevasse, trying to squeeze his way in. They pulled him out by the feet."

The Pooles had not been able to coax the boy out of the cliffs. Eventually they had to send for John Thomas, who called Johnny out. Then, with his weeping son in his arms, Verity's uncle had looked at the sheriff and the Pooles in defeat. His wife, who'd confessed to a double murder, was missing and most likely dead. His children had been kidnapped, threatened, and terrorized. "I'm sorry" was all he said before he climbed up the cliff face himself, disappeared into a completely different cavern, and returned with a tattered and worn leather satchel.

"It was real, then," breathed Verity. She looked at her father.

Ransloe Boone stared at the road ahead, his face lined with grief and regret. "If it was up to me," he said, "I would have sunk it in the swamp fifteen years ago."

"You lied to me," Verity whispered sadly.

"I was trying to protect you. Not that it did any good," her father added bitterly. "We found that cursed gold the day our wives died. We were celebrating down by the river the very hour they took sick — while they were . . ." *Being poisoned by Clara Piper,* Verity thought. Her father couldn't bring himself to say the words. "I was punished," he whispered.

"As treasure, it wasn't much to speak of," Hawk Poole said quietly. "I don't know how much was originally stashed up there" — Verity's father shrugged, as if he didn't care to say — "but there's not much left. The sheriff isn't very happy. That gold belonged to the United States government, even if it was a hundred years old. The sheriff thinks they'll take a dim view of a man who spent it on his own pleasure."

Verity found it hard to muster sympathy for her uncle, but she felt a pang of grief for her cousins. They'd lost their mother and might see their father go to jail.

Hawk Poole swung his legs over the side of the wagon, as if to jump off. Verity stuck her hand out to him. "Mr. Poole," she said loudly. A smile crossed his face, and he clasped her hand, shaking it firmly. "Thank you," she said. "Thank you for my life. Twice."

Holding on to his hand, she leaned over and kissed his cheek, right beside his scar.

Hawk Poole laughed. He leaped off the side of the wagon and disappeared into the woods.

THIRTY-THREE

ERITY NEEDED two basins of warm water to wash all the blood off her body. Beulah
heated the water, took away the dirty basins, and never
said a word about the tears that ran down Verity's face.

The blood had soaked through her dress and dried.
Peeling the fabric away from her skin stung. It was an
oddly intimate thing, to have clothing and undergarments
stuck to one's body with someone else's blood.

Afterward, she climbed into bed, certain she would
fall asleep instantly. Instead, every time she closed her
eyes, visions of the day's events appeared on the canvas
of darkness. She lay there an hour or more, sleepless, her
thoughts a blur of painful memories.

Then she sat up and swung her feet over the side of
the bed. Out of habit she glanced at the dressing table, but

her mother's diaries were stacked the way she'd left them. There was no reason for them to be left open any longer; she'd finally understood the message they contained. Nevertheless, Verity crossed the room in her bare feet, opened the door, and leaned out.

The hallway was dark, her father's and Beulah's doors closed. Verity stepped into the hallway and then approached the stairs. She didn't stop to light a candle but passed the dark parlor and dining room without mishap, her way lit by a dim glow coming from the kitchen.

Two candles flickered on the table, providing a circle of light in the otherwise shadowy room. Beulah stood at the stove in a white nightdress, stirring a pot. Lucky wove in and out between Beulah's bare feet, mewing plaintively and rubbing his head against her ankles. As Verity watched, the old woman bent and poured a bit of warm milk into a saucer on the floor, then turned and faced Verity without surprise. "I suppose you'll be wanting some?" she asked.

"You knew all along," said Verity.

"Fetch your own cup." Beulah poured milk into a cup sitting on the table. "This one's mine."

"You were in my room," Verity went on. "While I was sleeping and whenever I was out. You kept opening the diaries—no, just that one diary—and leaving it open to the same page." Verity had the entry memorized by now:

"You left that photograph out for me, too. The one of my uncle and Asenath."

When Verity made no move to get her own cup, Beulah took one off the drying rack, poured the rest of the milk into it, and held it out.

Verity accepted the offering but glared at the old woman. "You *knew*. And you said nothing!"

"I suspected, but I had no proof." Beulah's unbraided hair hung down to her bony rump; she swung it out of the way before sitting at the kitchen table. "I didn't know that diary still existed until you mentioned it."

The warm milk was a welcome comfort in spite of her anger. Verity sat down and sipped at it, staring at Beulah, who suddenly seemed very interested in the contents of her own cup.

"Why didn't you say anything?" Verity demanded. "Why didn't you just tell me?"

"I'm a Poole. She was Clara Thomas. If poison was suspected at the time, who do you think they would have blamed? Folk considered her a good woman—though there were always some who died who ought to have lived. People who'd crossed Miss Clara in one way or another, if anybody cared to notice." Beulah sniffed with disgust. "I thought you'd be smart enough to reason it out for yourself. The woman who married your uncle so soon after his wife died, coming to the house with a remedy the day those two took ill?"

"I might have," Verity snapped, "if I'd known her name was Clara Piper before she was married!"

"How could you not know that?" Beulah asked in astonishment.

Verity threw both hands over her face. How utterly maddening to find out that Beulah had known all along! Yet if Beulah had aired her suspicions earlier, would Verity have believed her — or dismissed her as an ignorant old Indian woman? Verity, to her chagrin, knew she'd made some highhanded assumptions about almost everyone she'd met in Catawissa. And most of the time she'd been wrong.

"I waited up for you, the night that woman took you to Cissy Clayton's lying-in," Beulah said, "to make sure she brought you home. That girl of hers had always mooned after Mr. Nathaniel. I didn't put it past her to do you some harm."

Verity almost hadn't come home. Her heart thudded as she remembered the horse knocking her down. The cracking sound right before must have been her aunt's whip, she realized. Eli Clayton had never meant her any harm; he'd *saved* her life, grabbing the horse's bridle and stopping the carriage from running her over.

Verity uncovered her face and looked at Beulah. "The medicine she gave me that night — it disappeared."

Beulah Poole nodded.

"And you stayed in the room with me, the time she gave me the laudanum." Verity remembered someone with long white hair leaning over her and thinking it was Asenath.

Beulah sniffed again. "That wasn't laudanum. You were seeing things and raving. I don't know what she gave you, but I had to pin you to the bed with sheets to keep you from hurting yourself."

Verity clasped her hands around the warm cup. "Did Liza tell me the truth — the real reason for the cages?"

"I don't know what Miss Liza told you."

"Eli Clayton." Verity swallowed hard. "What he did to his daughter —"

Beulah nodded. "That's the truth. After your mother and Miss Asenath died, there was great fear here that he might violate their graves. Mr. Boone and Mr. Thomas were talking about standing guard with shotguns every night, for as long as it took. But then old Mrs. Thomas, your grandmother, said they should have metal cages made. Those cages caused some scandal in the town. That's the reason Mrs. Gaines was able to persuade your father to give you up. She didn't want you to grow up under that shame."

Verity set down her cup. If she'd come to Beulah at the beginning, looking for the truth, could she have avoided all that had happened? Or were confessions like this only possible late at night, after the worst day of one's life?

"I was against sending you away," Beulah continued. "Not that anybody asked my opinion. The poor man had lost his wife; they shouldn't have taken his daughter away from him too." She sipped from her cup again and added, almost as an afterthought, "Having you back is the best thing that ever happened to him."

Verity blinked rapidly. "I thought you didn't like me."

"Why wouldn't I like you? I helped your mother birth you, didn't I?"

Tears blurred her vision. "You said I needed spanking half a dozen times a day," she whispered.

"You still do," Beulah snapped. She plunked her empty cup down on the table. "So what are you planning to do about *him*?"

Verity didn't need to ask who she meant.

THIRTY-FOUR

HEY FOUND Nate in the orchard the next morning, as Verity guessed they would. She wasn't surprised he would turn to something that gave him comfort. It grieved her to imagine how he must have felt last night when she devoted herself to the care of another man, and she didn't know if he would forgive her. Ransloe Boone didn't drive the wagon away after she climbed down but instead sat there silently.

Verity knew what Nate thought when he realized that her father was going to wait for her; she could see it in his face.

Nate dropped his eyes as she approached, and she sensed that he was gathering his composure. When she was close enough, he looked up and spoke first. "How is he?"

How like him to ask about Hadley Jones before

anything else and to sincerely care about the answer. "Better this morning," Verity replied. "Dr. Robbins sent word."

Heartbeat stronger, Robbins had written. *Not much color, but he's awake and asking for you.* Then, at the bottom of the note, he'd added: *Miss Boone, if you were a boy, I'd sign you on as apprentice.*

"He'll make it," Nate said. "I'm sure of it."

"I don't know what will become of him if he does." Verity knew that the sheriff was anxious to have a long conversation with Hadley Jones.

"He was trying to protect his brother as long as possible," Nate said. "And when he wasn't able to any longer, he made his stand. People understand that. You might find he's even respected a little more for it. We take care of our own. People will try to keep those little Thomas boys from learning what their mother did. My mother's already gone down to the house to see about those children, and I expect . . ."

Verity flinched at the mention of Clara Thomas, and Nate broke off what he was saying. "I'm sorry!" he blurted out instead. "You were right all along, and I kept telling you to leave it alone. I was wrong and stubborn and jealous. If I had listened to you in the first place—"

Verity shook her head sadly. "You couldn't have prevented it. Even I never dreamed the truth could be something like this—that she would do such a thing."

Or that she would plan to do it again.

I decided it might be better to let you marry Nathaniel so he could get the Boone land, and I could deal with you afterward. Without the opportunity to deal with Verity on the spot, Clara Thomas might never have been found out. Beulah's watchful eyes would have failed someday, and Verity would have succumbed to a cup of tea or a honey cake.

All for the young man who stood before her.

Gazing up into his stormy eyes, Verity marveled that, once again, his presence left her nearly speechless. She didn't even know where to begin telling him everything she wanted him to know.

He took a step back, his gaze dropping to her hand. "I know what you've come here to say. There's no need. I won't stand in your way."

Verity looked down. The ring. Perhaps that was a good place to start. She began to twist it loose from her finger.

Nate took another step back. "Give that to my mother. I don't want it. I could never give it to anyone else." His voice was hoarse.

"I was hoping," she said, holding it up, "that you would offer it to me again. Properly this time," she added, "without letting your mother speak for you."

"I didn't—" Then he clamped his lips shut. He *had,* and they both knew it.

She felt a little teary, but she blinked to clear her eyes. "On your knees, too, I think."

Nate took the ring and closed it tightly in his palm. "I don't understand," he admitted. "Verity, I saw your face when he was hurt. I know you love him."

"He was shot before my eyes!" she cried. "I was horrified! I didn't want him to *die*, Nate, but I don't love him. Do you think I could have stood there and assisted at his surgery if I was in love with him?" A wave of emotion came over her, and she shuddered. "If it had been *you* on that table, I would have fainted. And I never faint."

Nate looked confused. "I don't understand," he repeated.

"Nate, you asked me days ago if I loved you, and I didn't answer. You were right: I read that poem, but I didn't know what it meant until now." She glanced at the trees around them, groping for the right words. "I thought love was—big and loud and sudden, like a thunderbolt." She looked back, meeting his eyes. "I didn't know it was deep and quiet and grew upon a woman slowly, until one day she realizes it's the very breath and smiles and tears of her life. Do you want to know the first thought in my head when Hadley Jones was shot? *Thank God that wasn't Nate.* It felt horribly selfish to think such a thing at the time, but there it was. *Thank God it wasn't you.*"

She reached for him, dissolving into tears, and he

gathered her into his arms. She pressed her face against his chest. This was love, then: the safe feeling of his arms around her. His hand holding hers tightly in the cemetery when her mother's grave had been disturbed, and him dragging her into the doctor's office when his rival needed saving. There were the letters they'd exchanged, the poem, and the kitten. And it was more than just the two of them. There was the relationship between Nate and her father, and the growing one between Verity and his sisters. She and Nate had even played together as children.

All she'd ever had with Hadley Jones was a flirtation —an exciting and flattering one that she'd been too vain to give up.

She didn't want to imagine a life without Nathaniel McClure in it.

Nate put a hand under her chin and lifted her face. She could see he was still befuddled, but her favorite smile in all the world was dawning as he realized this was going his way after all. "I don't know if I'll ever be able to reason out what's in your head," he said.

"You can have as long as you like to try," she said. "If you want to, that is." She hadn't forgotten that the ring was still enclosed in his fist.

He remembered then too, and promptly dropped to both knees, right in the middle of the orchard. "Verity Boone," he said, "will you let me spend the rest of my life trying to reason you out? Will you raise our children

—even though they're bound to be stubborn, ornery little cusses? Will you let me struggle through your favorite poetry—even though I'll probably never like it?"

"I can't stand Gulliver and those ridiculous Lilliputians," Verity said vehemently, "but I do love you, Nate."

"Will you marry me?"

"Yes, I will." Laughing, Verity held out her hand. He grinned, knowing this time what he was supposed to do, and slid the ring back onto her finger. "Thank heavens you finally asked."

He tugged her down on her knees beside him, and then he kissed her. Wrapping both arms around his neck, she reveled in the feel of his familiar body against hers and the absolute joy of knowing she never wanted any other lips but his on hers again.

Then her bottom hit the ground, and she protested halfheartedly, "Nate! My father . . ."

"He left," Nate said between kisses. "Some time ago."

Verity giggled as he lay down beside her on the grass of their orchard. When it came to love, she reflected, the poem might have left out one or two things.

The sky had been overcast in the early morning, but sunlight was breaking through the clouds in broad beams just as Ransloe Boone's wagon came to a stop in front of the Mount Zion Church. Congregants arriving by carriage, wagon, and on foot were assembling inside for the Sunday service, but Verity looked immediately toward the cemetery grounds, wanting to see what work had been done.

Her father jumped off and offered her a hand down, and she smiled, remembering her first day in Catawissa when he had met her at the train station. Perhaps he remembered too, because after she was safely on the ground, he made a point of extending his arm, his lips curved in amusement. As Aunt Maryett had promised, it hadn't taken Verity long to reteach him his manners. Together they passed by the front door of the church and strolled into the cemetery.

The wall that separated her mother's grave from the rest had come down the day before, dismantled in a single afternoon by a handful of townspeople. Nate had been one of them. He promised Verity that the new wall would be finished before their wedding in the fall. Several members of the congregation had already pledged to contribute labor and materials. Some were men who'd done business with her father for years; others were families whose children had been delivered by Sarah Ann.

Setting aside any question about why these people hadn't defended her mother fifteen years ago, Verity had thanked each one graciously. She knew from the diaries that Sarah Ann had demonstrated only kindness and charity in the face of ignorance and resentment, and Verity thought that Catawissa had long been suffering from the lack of her mother's example. She didn't know if she could fill those shoes, but she certainly planned to try.

When plans for the cemetery were being discussed and Reverend White lamented the impracticality of building the new wall around just the two women's graves, Verity was quick to respond, "Surely you weren't planning to exclude the Claytons?"

"Miss Boone," the minister said, sighing, "you don't know what kind of men they were."

"No, I don't," she admitted. "But I assume they've accounted for their lives in the hereafter. I don't think our cemetery is the place to pass judgment on them." She lifted her chin. "That's why, if Liza Thomas and her brothers want to put up a memorial stone for their mother, you'll hear no objection from me." She must have shamed him, for he dropped his eyes, and plans moved forward with no more complaints from Reverend White.

This morning's sunlight washed the cemetery grounds in unaccustomed cheer, and Verity noticed that someone had left flowers at both Asenath's and Sarah Ann's headstones. Ransloe Boone stopped in front of his wife's grave and removed his hat. Verity folded her gloved hands in front of her and sighed deeply.

Without that wall standing like an accusation, she thought, the two iron structures looked less like cages and more like decorative coverings for the graves. Perhaps, with additional flowers and ivy, she could improve their appearance further. They would, after all, be standing here a long time. Removing the cages would require disinterring the caskets, and she, her father, and Uncle John had decided to spare Sarah Ann and Asenath that indignity. Verity fancied that with a little effort, she might make "hooded graves" a new fashion.

Her father nodded in satisfaction at the openness of the cemetery grounds. "Your mother would be proud of you," he said, replacing his hat on his head.

Verity looked up at him. "Do you think so?"

Ransloe Boone regarded his daughter with a smile. He wore a newly tailored frock coat this morning, livened with a fashionably wide necktie looped in a bow. "You've been here less than two months, and you've already changed all our lives. Yes, I think Sarah Ann would have been very proud."

Verity slipped her hand back into the crook of his arm so that he could escort her inside for the service. "Father," she said, raising her eyebrows, "I'm only just beginning."

THE CHARACTERS in *The Caged Graves* are fictional. However, there really are two caged graves in an abandoned cemetery outside the town of Catawissa, Pennsylvania. One belongs to Sarah Ann, wife of Ransloe Boone, and the other belongs to Asenath, wife of John Thomas. The women died within days of each other. Local historians have been able to prove they were sisters-in-law (John was Sarah Ann's brother), but how they died and why the cages were erected over their graves remains a mystery.

Belief that the dead could rise from their graves and attack the living was not uncommon in North America in the nineteenth century, although the term "vampire" was not generally in use until after the publication of Bram Stoker's *Dracula* in 1897. The customary "cure" for the state of being undead was dismemberment of the corpse. I've based Rebecca Clayton's treatment at the hands of her father on the story of Mercy Brown of Exeter, Rhode Island.

Although it seems like common sense today, most people of the mid-nineteenth century had no concept of germs and did not realize the importance of cleanliness when treating wounds. Some researchers were advocating sterilization of medical equipment, but many physicians were resistant to the idea. I may have stretched credibility when Hadley Jones insists on clean equipment, but by 1867 a number of articles on the subject had appeared in medical journals, and a young, open-minded doctor might have read and believed them.

The Poole family is loosely based on the Pool Tribe of Bradford County, Pennsylvania, believed to be descendants of the Native Americans who assisted the British at the Battle of Wyoming in 1778. The British soldiers and their Indian allies really did burn their way through the Wyoming Valley, killing civilians and executing some of their prisoners of war. It is believed that at least two American prisoners escaped, fleeing into the Shades of Death swamp. If one of those men carried a small fortune in gold coins, nobody is telling.

I hope that residents of Columbia County, Pennsylvania, will forgive me for the numerous geographical liberties I have taken with my fictional version of Catawissa.

Finally, I couldn't have written this book alone, and I'd like to thank my agent, Sara Crowe, and my editor,

Dinah Stevenson, as well as my critique partners, Marcy Hatch and Krystalyn Drown, and beta readers Andrea Burdette, Gwen Dandridge, Katie Mills, Al and Kay Past, Sri Upadhyay, and Lori Walker. My entire family supported me in this project, but I want to especially thank my daughters, Gabrielle and Gina, for their outspoken opinions (!), my sister, Laurie, for a timely comment, my brother-in-law, Larry, for his expertise on nineteenth-century firearms, and my husband, Bob, for tracking down the location of the real caged graves.